Glynis Peters lives in the
she was shortlisted for the Festival of Romance New Talent Award. She is a *USA Today, Globe and Mail,* and *Toronto Star* bestseller.

When Glynis is not writing, she enjoys family time and making greetings cards. She also enjoys walking Harry the Cockapoo, and coffee breaks with friends.

Her debut novel, *The Secret Orphan,* was an international bestseller.

www.glynispetersauthor.com

x.com/GlynisAuthor1
facebook.com/glynispetersauthoraccount
instagram.com/glynispetersauthor
bookbub.com/authors/glynis-peters

Also by Glynis Peters

The Red Cross Orphans

The Red Cross Orphans

The Orphan's Letters

The Orphan's Homecoming

The Orphan's Last Goodbye

Standalones

The Secret Orphan

The Orphan Thief

The Forgotten Orphan

The Orphan's Secret Library

THE ORPHAN'S LAST GOODBYE

GLYNIS PETERS

ONE MORE CHAPTER

One More Chapter
a division of HarperCollins*Publishers* Ltd
1 London Bridge Street
London SE1 9GF
www.harpercollins.co.uk
HarperCollins*Publishers*
Macken House, 39/40 Mayor Street Upper,
Dublin 1, D01 C9W8, Ireland

This paperback edition 2025
25 26 27 28 29 LBC 5 4 3 2 1
First published in Great Britain in ebook format
by HarperCollins*Publishers* 2025

A catalogue record of this book is available from the British Library

ISBN: 978-0-00-878298-6

Printed and bound in the United States

To the readers who have followed Kitty's journey throughout the series, this final book is dedicated to you. Your patience is appreciated, and your support is incredible!

Chapter One

8th May 1947

'I am going back to Canada. It's time.'

Kitty McCarthy stared across the breakfast table at her husband in disbelief. Her heart raced, and she nervously twisted the corner of her napkin as his words hung heavy in the air. Each syllable felt like a weight upon her shoulders, threatening to crush her spirit. She felt the chill of his words seep into her heart, leaving her numb with shock.

She scoured Michael's face for a joking smile, but his usual twinkling eyes were downcast, and Kitty watched as he toyed with the crumbs on his plate. What he said was serious, not a teasing threat because she had burnt the toast that morning. He'd spoken and then looked away, avoiding her eye. He did not ask if *she* would like to live in Canada; he clearly said 'I'. He planned to return to his country of birth. Fear clutched at Kitty's throat, and she swallowed it down.

'What do you mean? You're leaving?' Kitty asked.

'I have to go…' Michael replied. 'It's all a mess. My life used to be action-packed with rescues and dangerous missions. But my head injury took it all away. The adventurer in me is not satisfied. Being a general practitioner in England – the war—'

Kitty took an impatient breath and released it with a slight slap of her hand onto the table.

'The war, the war. All I hear from you is constantly blaming the war. It's over, we must move forward – not forget, but live for those who cannot…' Kitty's voice snapped with annoyance.

Michael sighed.

'I'm struggling with the humble life you want for us: the nurse and the doctor living in a quaint house in the north of England. The war brought out something inside me – a daredevil – which won't go away. The war, it made me—'

Kitty cut in. She had heard it all before, and it irritated and hurt her that she was not enough for him anymore.

'It brought out the need to rescue, yes, I understand that. I did it too, remember? But it will never be something we do again in such an horrendous way. Mentally, we can't Michael. We can help rescue someone whose mind is in a dark place, the men and women who need help to adjust, but when we do, we must set aside our own demons. And we mustn't add their fears to our own.'

Michael went to speak, but Kitty shook her head, her voice urgent and determined. Her husband had opened a door, and Kitty would not let this discussion slip away. She was going to walk through that door with the confidence her fear had triggered.

'Acceptance is a word which sometimes sticks in our throats, but we have to accept that war did more than kill people; it is because of them that we have to strive forward. If you're running away, then go. We must…'

Kitty trailed off as she watched Michael give a slow shake of his head.

'Michael, we *must* find a way to understand who we are now. We are the couple who ran onto French shores and worked around exploding bombs, and in Britain we crawled in and out of collapsing buildings, but it is over. We have learned how to live in a tidy house with a quaint garden for two years, and we can carry on if we accept this and not live in the past. At twenty-seven, I want the settled life we have. I am not sure I want dangerous adventures, and I'm concerned about you.'

Michael sat, his face expressionless.

For want of something to distract her from crying, Kitty snatched a pile of clean clothes from the linen basket and began folding them into neat piles, her hands trembling with emotion. Her mouth felt dry, but she couldn't drink due to the lump in her throat as she held back the tears. How dare he say something life-changing and then go quiet on her like a sulking child? His recovery from the head injury was a thing of the past, but there were nights when a terrifying memory of their time during the rescue missions on Normandy beaches triggered him, and she would hold him, soothing him back to a settled sleep.

Kitty had always considered their marriage, right up until this moment, a strong one. They laughed together and faced daunting tasks as a couple, and Michael had never even hinted at wanting to leave the practice or his adopted country. She thought he was content with living in a village with a Canadian name – Quebec – and the north of England was where he wished to settle for his retirement. Kitty realised she must not know her husband as well as she thought, and it hurt. The sense of betrayal was like a knife in her heart, twisting with each passing moment. The pile of linen was attacked again, and she refolded each item. The scream inside her was only just kept at bay. It bubbled and brewed, threatening to create an argument she did not want to be a part of.

Michael remained silent. Trying to avoid her eye, he walked past her to the kitchen window, leaned on the windowsill and stared at their garden.

Kitty loved their garden; it was a place where she always found peace after a busy day supporting the clinic or local orphans. She had turned most of the area into fruit and vegetable patches, retaining one section to grow flowers, such as snowdrops, daffodils and primroses in the springtime, followed by clematis, forget-me-nots and wallflowers leading into the summer. After that, many roses and peonies would show off their beauty and fill the air with their fragrance.

'Take a break. Book some time off, and see Smithy and Trixie. Spending a few days in Yorkshire and enjoying an ale with your best friend is just the rest you need, dear. You work too hard,' she said gently, breaking the silence between them. 'Or go and see a friend in Canada, but then come home. Just upping sticks without discussion is a bit much for me to understand.'

Michael did not reply; instead, he continued to avoid her eyes and walked past her into the garden. His soap-scrubbed hands scraped back his hair as he paced. Kitty could see he was troubled, but her Canadian hero was stubborn. She knew him well enough to leave him alone for an hour and then try to talk to him again later in the day.

Kitty and Michael skirted around one another for two days, avoiding the conversation that would end their awkwardness. Kitty cried herself to sleep, and Michael offered her no comfort.

Their marriage was in crisis. Kitty knew she had to do something. She approached her husband before he met his first patient of the day. He looked tired, and she heard him tut when they met in the hallway.

'Michael, I missed you at breakfast,' she said. She knew he'd eaten – she'd seen dishes he had washed on the draining board. 'When you have finished the clinic, please come and find me. We need to talk. This situation is unhealthy for both of us.'

Michael nodded and walked into his surgery, closing the door without a word. The silence that followed fell heavy on Kitty's shoulders. In previous conversations he had always blamed the war for making him unsettled – a constant cycle of blame. Kitty resigned herself to listen, but now felt she had to speak out. She had to take control of the situation, but his silence as he walked away was a stark reminder of the growing distance between them.

When she heard his clinic door open three hours later and his last patient call out 'goodbye', Kitty rushed from cleaning the front parlour, prepared a pot of tea for them and took it into the back room, which looked out over the garden. They called it the snug. Michael often said it was his favourite room and would sit reading there on days when they could not get out to walk. Having wiped the surfaces with rose water to make the room smell homely, Kitty hoped he might sit and rethink his startling decision to leave Britain.

Today was their anniversary, a pleasant spring day, just like the day they married, a year after Victory in Europe Day. She'd had other plans for today, and the gift of a navy and pale blue cravat in cotton sat in the drawer beside her bed. She had chosen cotton as the traditional symbol to celebrate two years of marriage and had planned to surprise Michael with it later in the day, after the village remembrance service.

But for the past few days she had agonised over one question that nagged at her. Had they been so caught up with the end of war that they had grabbed what they thought would make them happy – marriage?

'I've taken us tea through into the snug,' she said before he could find a way out of talking to her.

Michael said nothing; he walked into the room, and she watched as he went to the table, poured himself a cup from the teapot and stood by the window, cup in hand.

'Busy morning?' she asked, unsure why, because she had seen the steady flow of patients walk the front path and knew it had been.

She poured her tea and waited.

Michael nodded, but didn't turn around; he continued looking out of the window. Kitty wondered if he was waiting for her to broach the subject of him leaving, and then explain his plans for them. The atmosphere was heavy with silence as each waited for the other to say something. But Kitty was no longer prepared to hope life would go back to how it was. Getting him to finally explain himself was the only way forward.

Chapter Two

'Are you ready to talk?' Kitty asked, waiting for Michael to finish his tea, clear his head and speak, but he just stared out of the window. Only the clock in the hallway made a sound as it ticked away the day.

She heard his cup rattle slightly in its saucer, and Michael placed it on the windowsill. And turned to face her.

'I can't live like this anymore. The walls of Great Britain are suffocating me. I need open spaces again.'

Kitty gave a huff. 'You liked it well enough to live here for years. To train here – and get married. Two years ago today, by the way.'

'Happy Anniversary,' she added with a touch of sarcasm.

Michael walked over to the mantelpiece and picked up their wedding photograph. He looked at it and then looked at her.

'Our wedding is not a day I regret. What I do regret is not having control over this need to become Canadian again. My family's blood is pure, and I know that the day we have a child, it will be mixed, but for some reason, I need—' Michael's face flushed as he hesitated '—I need my children to be Canadian-born. As an orphan yourself, I hope you understand. I've been here a long time, and now it is time to return.'

His words hit her like a cold wave, her breath hitched in her throat, and with a steady hand Kitty took the photograph from him.

'All I see in this picture is two people in love, and not once have I thought that marrying a Canadian would weaken my British blood – my English bloodline. All I've wanted to do since you proposed is marry you and, if blessed, have children, then live out our lives together until the end. But I am obviously not enough for you.' Kitty sniffed back a sob. Now was not the time to cry.

'I … I can't,' Michael said, almost apologetically, and touched her arm. Kitty pulled away.

'You can't what? Stay?' she asked.

Michael nodded.

Kitty suddenly felt she was holding him back. Their marriage was not enough for him. It did not give him the adventure he yearned for, and she could not provide him with pure Canadian children.

'Maybe we must consider getting divorced so you can marry a true Canadian woman, if that is what it takes to make you happy,' Kitty snapped at him sarcastically. She wanted a reaction. The tension in her throat made it ache, and she moved her head from side to side to ease the discomfort. She had never had the need to consider divorce or separation; her words now were simply to snap him out of his mood.

'Divorce?' Michael asked, and Kitty heard a heavy sadness in his sigh. She watched him slump into the armchair and put his head in his hands. 'I've put your name down to travel with me – my wife,' he said, his feet tapping the floor agitatedly.

Confused by his reaction, Kitty thought for a moment before she responded.

'Michael, why would I want to travel with you now? You have made your point. I am not a true Canadian.' Her voice was tight with emotion.

Michael looked at her and shrugged, then lowered his head again.

'Do you have pain? Is something hurting? Are you worried about your head again, and that's why you want to return to Canada? To go back to the hospital?' Kitty asked gently, her chest aching with distress at his words and seeing him so upset.

'I bought your ticket and assumed you would come with me, you are my wife after all,' he said ignoring her question.

Anger bubbled. How dare Michael take her for granted, assume that she would give up her life in England and go with him, without any discussion or consideration for her thoughts on the matter.

'Assumed I would do my duty as your wife? Well, if it is for medical reasons, of course I'll drop everything. But anything else, it would have been courteous of you to have asked me what I think of the idea of leaving, and so soon!' Kitty replied.

Michael continued tapping his foot and wringing his hands.

Something didn't seem right. Michael was far too edgy, and she suspected he was holding something back. She paced around the room. Her breath was heavy in her chest, and her head swam with confusion.

'So, if it isn't medical, what is it? Another woman?' Kitty's voice nipped the air.

She watched Michael hesitate and then shake his head, but

her suspicion was heightened. He had a flush across his face. A guilty face.

'So, just like that, you want to leave here. Giving me no notice. For what? Is there a home out there for us? For me? I have to get permission to enter Canada. It takes time, or have you done that for me already?' She turned to face him as she fired the question.

'I can go on my own if you'd prefer,' Michael said, and Kitty heard a pinch of hope in his tone. It hit hard, and her stomach turned with the realisation. He didn't want her to go with him.

'If I'd prefer? Can you hear yourself? One minute you're telling me you're leaving, have bought me a ticket without discussion, and then if I'd prefer not to go, you would … go alone … and you almost sound happy at the prospect!' Kitty's voice was harsh. She disliked her anger, but Michael was winding her up by not telling her the truth.

'That's not what I am trying to say. I don't know what Canada would be like for you. You might hate it, but I need to go back,' Michael replied.

He had confused Kitty far too much for her to think clearly, and he had now stirred too many concerns into the situation. Kitty dissected what he had told her. Although it was drastic and a huge decision, time apart might be what they needed.

'I wonder if we have allowed the war to hold us together. Maybe we should try and live apart for a while,' she said, daring to say aloud thoughts that she had pondered since his announcement. Words that she had tried to ignore and failed. They were too painful to bear. And yet, a small thought nagged in the back of her mind the moment she heard them out loud. Maybe they had forged a marriage out of their shared fears during wartime missions. Had it lost its ability to hold them together in times of peace?

Michael raised his head and looked at her, his brow furrowed.

'But you wanted children,' he said.

Giving a laugh and shrugging her shoulders, Kitty looked at him in amazement, again confused by his words.

'I did. Sadly, it seems you married the wrong woman to give birth to any you might have. I can't believe you put my name down to travel with you, then tell me I am not good enough for you, not Canadian enough. I'm sorry, Michael, but this has made me nervous. What if I go and you decide I am still not Canadian enough to be the mother of your children? I'd rather be left here alone than travel to another country and then be abandoned out there.'

The room was once more heavy with silence. The atmosphere was tense, and Kitty waited for reassurance that he had not meant what he said, but Michael offered none.

'I said I am afraid of being abandoned out there,' she repeated, but still Michael kept quiet. He gave her no reassurance.

Kitty felt anger bubble deep in her belly, as her world began to collapse. She once thought she was his number one girl, but now she felt a shabby second best. Despair rose in her, and she could think of no fresh words with which to fight her corner. Confusion clouded her mind. She needed more time to think.

'Let's cancel the tickets and work this out. If you'd like me to be by your side in Canada, let's make a plan. But always remember, any children we have will be half English. If that is—'

'Stop going on about children!' Michael suddenly shouted, and Kitty, startled, stumbled backwards.

It was obvious to her that they were going round in circles

and getting nowhere. Michael was showing signs of stress again. She had ignored it during the winter, thinking everyone was in the same boat, but now, on reflection, maybe she should have taken more notice of his mood, considering his past.

January and February had been bleak and unforgiving months. The coal supplies in the north had been utterly depleted, leaving homes shrouded in an uncomfortable chill. Snowdrifts loomed like towering white giants around them, some over ten feet high. With the harsh winter disrupting electricity and telephone services, isolation settled heavily upon many. Amidst this chaos, a relentless flu epidemic swept through the region, adding to the burdens faced by them both.

Kitty had braved the icy winds and trudged through the snow-laden streets, checking on their less abled neighbours and took on other functions as the midwife to mothers in need. Meanwhile, Michael pushed through the villages, tending to flu victims and often losing himself in their plight when he returned at night. By mid-March, as the last remnants of snow gave way to slush-laden streets, both were left utterly exhausted. Experts later declared this winter one of the harshest in over eighty years.

To Kitty, Michael's unwavering commitment to his duty was both admirable and heartbreaking. Now she realised she had failed to see that it was restlessness that kept him going, and that caring for those men had brought back the past – a place where he felt valued and challenged. Kitty guessed her husband's selflessness was ultimately his undoing, and it had taken its toll on their marriage. She looked at him through damp lashes; all they had left were words and thoughts. Both had been selfish in their differing needs – Michael about Canada, and her in her pressing desire for a family. Time apart might make them appreciate one another more and reunite them through a love they once felt.

'Maybe I'll stay up the road with Stanley for a few days. Give ourselves time to think about what's best. You have rather sprung this on me, and it is a lot to take in,' Kitty said, still taken aback by his outburst. She kept her voice calm, much calmer than she felt inside. She waited for him to respond, but Michael stared down at his hands.

'You must feel as sad as I do that we are bickering like this. Let down maybe, but think about what you said, Michael, then put yourself in my shoes.'

'I won't change my mind,' Michael told her, his voice more determined than before. 'I can't. My heart belongs to Canada.'

Kitty felt another wave of shock rush over her. A childish retort came to her, and she released it before thinking.

'Silly me. I thought it belonged to me. Your wife. After hearing all you have said, then maybe divorce *is* the only solution.'

Chapter Three

Kitty telephoned her friend Stanley and briefly told him that she needed a roof over her head for a few days. She would explain everything when she arrived.

She packed a bag, pulled her bicycle out of the shed and made her way through the village lanes. She found no joy in their prettiness as she would normally do.

At one point, she stopped to reflect on the conversation with Michael. Had he meant he wanted a Canadian wife, or was he worried that people would learn she was British and not Canadian? Why would he suddenly make such an outlandish remark? Why had she not seen the signs of his longing for Canada?

As she continued her ride to Fell Hall, her anxiety and agitation grew with each turn of the pedals. Once she arrived at the entrance of the long gravel driveway, she dismounted and pushed the bike, hoping her distress would ease as she walked. She did not want to arrive in tears.

When she had stored her bike in a side barn, she walked to the kitchen. The smell of a hearty cooked meal told her that Daphne was hard at work doing what she did best. When Kitty had first arrived at Fell Hall after leaving the hospital, Daphne cared for her like a daughter, and now Kitty longed for a moment with her.

She pushed open the door and stepped inside the steaming kitchen.

'Do I smell mutton stew?' she asked as she watched Daphne forming suet dumpling balls on the flour-dusted table.

'Ee bairn, there you are. Stanley said you were coming to stay for a few days. He said Michael's going away for a course.' Daphne spoke as she continued cooking.

Kitty took a deep breath. Thank goodness for Stanley. He had given his cook a reason for Kitty's visit.

'He is, so I thought I would take a break myself, Daphne,' she answered as she pulled off her gloves, hoping her white lie would convince her friend.

'Aye, pet, I was told to make sure you rest and don't take on work. I hear you both had a busy time at the surgery,' Daphne replied and continued with her chores. 'When I've finished here, we'll chat. Take yourself to your room; it's aired and ready for you.'

Kitty smiled. 'You spoil me.'

'You're worth it, pet,' Daphne replied, offering a broad smile that made Kitty's heart enjoy a pain-free moment.

Upstairs, she opened the window and listened to children playing in the extensive grounds. Their laughter lifted her spirits, and a sense of coming home washed over her.

The stately home in Brancepeth was an officially registered private orphanage. She was proud to have been a founding member of staff after Stanley's wife, Jenny, died early in the war. Jenny temporarily housed war orphans and cared for them as if they were her own.

A gut punch of sadness hit Kitty as she listened to their squeals and giggles. She realised that now she would never hear her children, the ones she had dreamed of having with Michael; their voices would never be heard. He had ordered her to stop talking about them, in a way that made it clear he no longer wanted a family with her.

Kitty closed the window and drew the curtains, shutting her distress away from the outside world. Climbing onto the bed, she curled into a ball, unable to cry yet feeling as if she had shed a waterfall. Her mind was battered and bruised, and her heart filled with the pain of love lost. Michael had stripped her of her place in his world, and it would take a lifetime for her to understand his sudden change of mind.

Life in Canada might be exciting, Kitty McCarthy, she told herself.

But only if you are with a man who loves you.

Why did you say the word 'divorce'? Has your marriage become so weak that you use words as ammunition?

Questions. So many questions. Michael didn't argue with the idea of divorce. And at one point he seemed keen on going alone.

He paid no notice to you saying you were frightened. And he talked about 'pure Canadian' children.

Talk to Stanley. Sleep. I'm sure you have your answer, but you have to dig deeper to find it.

A tap on the bedroom door roused Kitty from a sleep she had not realised she needed until she stretched out on the bed. Her head felt clearer, and her body rested.

'Come in,' she called out.

'I'd rather you came downstairs for dignity's sake, ma'am,' a male voice replied, and Kitty smiled. She responded with a giggle.

'Thank you, sir. I'll be right down.'

Stanley had not lost his sense of humour; no matter how many times bad luck was thrown his way, he battled to make others smile, even on days when he knew he could not.

Rinsing her face in the guest room basin and changing into a fresh set of clothes, she recalled their first meeting. He was a beaten and broken young RAF war hero facing life with a prosthetic leg, and she was a novice nurse with the Red Cross.

They had experienced much together: his learning to walk again and Kitty nursing him; his wife Jenny's death due to cancer, which had deprived her of having children; Kitty moving in to help, the setting up of the orphanage, their escape from a bomb attack at Roker Beach … those were just a few of their shared memories.

Stanley also played a significant part in her life when Michael was injured. He had ensured both of them were fully supported, recognising Kitty had also suffered the shock of her then fiancé's injuries. Stanley was at her side when Michael was taken for treatment in Canada. He also told Michael about the care she had given him when he was unaware of life around him, and that he need not be afraid of Kitty still wanting him in her life after his return from the Canadian hospital. Stanley did everything he could to distract Kitty during those bleak times.

For Kitty, Stanley had every quality she would wish for in an older brother, and she loved him deeply. He was dependable and reliable, and she knew he might have answers to her problems she had not considered. Walking down the sweeping stairs with her hand on the wooden banister, she composed a few words in her head: a statement to Stanley about her situation, a request for advice about seeking a divorce – and the costs of one. The word 'divorce' made her stomach clench.

The shame and gossip would be hard to deal with, but she had experienced more traumatic things in her life than other people's opinions. Nothing seemed real. All she had done was delve into why Michael wanted to rekindle his life in Canada – and question her security if she travelled thousands of miles to start a fresh life with him, leaving behind all she knew.

More questions overwhelmed Kitty with each step she took. What if they moved there, and he didn't settle? Or she didn't settle? What if she wanted to stay, and he returned to England, or met someone else?

Her mind became overloaded with worries. Her head ached and she wanted to curl back under the covers and block out the world, but the questions kept coming.

Where would she go if she were alone? What if it did all work out but then something happened to Michael? How would she feed a family? What would she do for work if she couldn't nurse out there?

Each question lay on her shoulders heavier than the last. Yet no matter how hard she tried to stem the flow, she could not control them.

Kitty stopped walking and closed her eyes, trying to shut out her concerns, but nothing could. It was as if she were analysing her whole life ahead of her before it happened.

She breathed through the onslaught of self-doubt, fear and

the nagging feeling that Michael had set her up. She was the reactive one, and her words had made it easier for him to walk away as the victim. Could she cope with being the villain? Then came the buried thought, the suppressed idea that without Michael's traumatic nightmares and moods, her life might be less stressful.

Stop it, Kitty! It is your duty as a wife to stand by him. Stop thinking and take action!

'There she is...' Stanley said when she entered the room. He stood with his arms wide open, a large grin on his face.

Kitty did not hesitate to let him envelop her in a comforting hug, but it broke her reserve. All week, she had been stoic, holding her emotions together and concentrating on reasons and plans, but now, in Stanley's arms, she allowed the tears she had held back to flow profusely. Eventually, her sobs subsided and she pulled away, composing herself. She reached into a pocket for a handkerchief, blew her nose, dried her eyes and gave him an apologetic smile.

Stanley nodded towards a large, comfortable chair. 'Sit down and tell me about it – I assume you and Michael have fallen out?' he asked, tilting his head in question. Kitty saw a frown of concern flitter across his face. It was on the tip of her tongue to say it was nothing but a spat, but the whole point of her asking to stay was to seek advice.

She gave a short nod.

'It's difficult to explain. We've not fallen out, but he is leaving. We'll have to divorce.'

Kitty hurried her words, glancing at Stanley to gauge his reaction.

He sat quietly, and it unnerved her. The silence in the room irritated her. When she was surrounded by silence, her thoughts built up a wall of sadness, and she could not think straight.

'Stanley?'

Stanley shook his head and then frowned.

'Divorce is a tad strong. Michael's leaving, you say – can I ask why?'

Inside her chest, Kitty felt a knot of anxiety, and she rubbed her palms together.

'I'm not a Canadian, and he wants to return to his roots. He wants pure Canadian children,' she said, and her whole being felt as flat as her voice sounded. 'But then he told me to stop talking about children, so I don't think he wants any.'

'He said that? Or did he say he wanted to return to Canada, and you have—'

Kitty rose to her feet and took a deep breath to calm herself.

'I have jumped to conclusions, run here to you and decided to divorce the man I love because I…'

Kitty heard her voice rising, along with her anger towards Michael. This was not the moment to explode and release her genuine emotions; Stanley was not at fault. She could not tell him she doubted her love for Michael. She was not sure she did, but it nagged in the back of her mind. They were friends who had fallen into post-war exuberance and married as a celebration of war's end.

'If I can stay a few days and think about what he said, it will help me calm down, and maybe we can talk about the situation better. He said a few things that worried me. I am not sure if he is having an affair.' Stanley gave a snorting laugh, and Kitty glared at him.

'I told him I couldn't go to Canada with him because I was frightened of being left alone – if he left me… I think there's something else going on with him. He wants more excitement in his life. I want to settle, have a family and a home we've built together, but he wants adventure … and from the way he shouted at me "no children", I am not enough for him.'

Stanley sat for a moment, waiting for her to compose herself.

'I think you're in shock and reacting – it's understandable. I also think it will work out. Michael may be homesick, so when you get home, suggest a visit to his hometown for a month or so and see how you both feel about the situation.'

Kitty ran her fingers through her hair, much like Michael did when he could not cope.

'I don't know. I don't know what to do,' she whispered.

'Listen, let's eat and relax by the radio this evening, and tomorrow we'll walk by the beach and blow the cobwebs away. Then you must go back to him and persuade him to hear your reasons for the outburst. Compose yourself first. Some time out by the sea, how does that sound?'

Having been born by the sea, Kitty knew a brisk walk in a salty breeze often soothed the soul.

'It sounds perfect. Thank you, Stanley.' She hoped the outcome would not lead to more dramatic outbursts from either her or Michael.

Chapter Four

The following morning was cool, but Kitty was ready and waiting for Stanley on the driveway when he pulled his car around to the front of the house.

'Morning!' she called out over the engine's hum. The Bentley he had first shown her still looked loved and cared for; it was Stanley's pride and joy. After it was adapted to suit his prosthesis, he accepted that he would no longer fly and instead put his efforts into learning to drive again. He looked at home behind the wheel.

'Morning. Ready to blow away those blues?' Stanley asked as he rewrapped his scarf around his neck.

Kitty nodded and climbed into the passenger seat.

'Ever thought of learning to drive, Kitty?' Stanley asked partway into their journey.

His question threw her, and Kitty pondered it for a moment.

'Do you know, it has never entered my mind. I walk, cycle or travel by train and bus,' she replied. 'Besides, I don't think I would trust myself to drive in a straight line.'

Stanley laughed. 'Don't doubt yourself. It's something to consider later down the line,' he said.

Once they arrived at Roker Beach, Kitty took a moment to inhale the salty air and listen to the seagulls' cries. She and Stanley were the only ones walking there, and as the waves crashed against the rocks, they paused to take in the sight.

'It was bleak here in February,' Stanley said, 'but Jack, Daphne and the older children came down to collect driftwood. To their surprise, sea coal had also washed in when the tide turned, and they gathered several sackfuls for the locals and ourselves. It wasn't safe for me to go far,' he added, tapping his prosthetic leg. 'I was frustrated to see the children doing what I couldn't, but they were willing workers.'

'It must have been dreadful. Keeping two of us warm was hard enough.' Kitty sighed at the memory, and then shook it off, recalling another day at Roker Beach.

'Do you remember the cider you brought to the picnic the day the German plane flew over?' she asked Stanley, trying to change the subject.

'Strong stuff, that Chipper's sauce,' he replied, laughing. 'We suffered many a headache thanks to our RAF cook. I swear if we had used it as fuel for our planes, we could have travelled further and higher.'

Kitty giggled, then stopped, her happier memories getting the better of her, as it felt disrespectful to the local people. 'It was a dreadful time for the residents that day. Their homes were bombed, and lives were lost. The children we took in that evening still write to me, some still mourn, others don't remember their parents. It is sad. I do write back, reassuring them, that's all I can do,' she said.

Stanley offered her the crook of his arm and a smile.

'I'm not surprised. You always invested your heart in each child who stepped over the threshold.'

Kitty linked her arm through his as they gazed out at sea.

'Michael blames the war for so much that he can no longer focus on what life has given him. I think he still wants the buzz of action again. We were luckier than most, and he … well, he survived the most dreadful injuries and has a bright future ahead of him. Why does he want to give it all up – me, give me up?' she asked, her heart weary of asking herself the same questions.

When Stanley couldn't give her answers, Kitty decided it was time to gain them from other women. Friends like Wenna and Trixie. Married friends who might understand her struggle and concerns. She pulled her coat collar higher around her neck.

'I wonder if I should visit Wenna, Pots and Meryn,' she said. 'Prepare for starting a new life in Cornwall if it all goes wrong and Michael disappears to Canada.'

Stanley stopped walking, placed his hands gently on her shoulders and turned her to face him.

'You can still be together, Kitty. Go with him,' he said softly.

With a slight shake of her head, Kitty glanced sideways across the vast expanse of water – a sea that would separate her from everything she knew and take her to a land where she would constantly worry about her husband's desires and restless mind.

'There's no point. I'm not what he wants with him in his homeland. I'm afraid I'll be a burden. Part of me thinks he regrets putting my name down to travel,' she said over the noise of the wind and gulls.

Stanley tutted.

'He put your name down to travel because you're his wife, and he still recognises that. I hate to say it, Kitty, but do you think you're using his words about being Canadian to avoid leaving?'

Kitty stepped away and shot him a glare. Stanley, of all the people she would have thought were on her side, was suggesting she was the one ruining the marriage.

'I don't think that, no. Are we finished here? I'm getting cold,' she replied, aware that she was being rude.

Her feelings were hurt, and she no longer wanted to discuss her relationship with Stanley if he believed she was afraid of living abroad. He didn't understand her fear. How could he? Stanley's upbringing was different. For orphans, life could be a lonely one even when surrounded by people. Fear of another loss was a significant issue they had to learn to face; losing friends and – if they had any – remaining family members took away an already fragile life-balancing foundation. She and Michael understood that fear, but getting married had meant they were the starting point of building a living family tree. Without her husband, her tree would fail to grow, and she would be alone again, and Kitty wasn't sure she was strong enough to find another love to help her rebuild. Her fears were hard to put into words, and when she did, they came out sharp and dismissive, so it was best that she kept them to herself. She could not lose her friends; they, and her uncle, might be all she had left.

'Don't be angry with me, Kitty. Please, I am trying to help you see beyond your pain. You feel rejected and, I am guessing, more than a little frightened. We both know Michael struggles with communication. He failed to tell you he was back in England a few years back, when he recovered, but you worked through it,' Stanley said, his voice soft and caring. But Kitty's mind was in turmoil. She could only hear his criticism of her for mentioning divorce and his support of Michael. She felt defeated and drained.

'I'm sorry I sound like a grouch, but it has been such a shock for me. A few days away from home might not be the answer. You're right, Stanley. Communication is important, and I've run away. I'll go home later and speak with Michael again,' she said, raising her voice to convince him she was more upbeat than she felt.

'That's the girl. Keep your chin up and fight the demons,' Stanley said, walking towards the car as the sky clouded over. Kitty followed him deep in thought. No matter what happened, she knew she and Michael needed to fight through their toughest challenge together to reach victory or a peaceful agreement.

Chapter Five

'I'm sorry to have been an overnight guest, Daphne. I feel bad for adding to your workload. I'm happy to take the bedding home and wash it.'

Daphne shooed her towards the door.

'It was lovely to see you, and if your husband is home early, go and enjoy his company,' she instructed, and Kitty did not say a word. She hugged her friend and rushed outside.

She felt too emotional to see the children, fearing that an embarrassing moment of tears in front of them would not be pleasant for anyone.

As she turned the handle of her back door, she found it locked. A rare event. She rummaged in her bag for the key and stepped inside. The house was quiet. A glass sat on the draining board, but there were no rinsed dishes beside it, and Michael was not one to wipe and put away the crockery.

'Michael?' she called out in an upbeat manner, hoping to show her happiness at being home again.

Her voice echoed into the hallway. She crossed the kitchen and approached the door to his surgery. After tapping lightly, she waited for an invitation to enter. No response. She turned the handle and stepped inside. The room was tidy but cold, making her shiver. Glancing at his desk for clues about a possible call-out, she picked up some scraps of paper. One thing caught her attention: a train timetable with a morning departure to Liverpool and one for London. She scanned the paperwork for a date, a clue as to whether she could get to the cities in time and try to reason with Michael before he attempted to leave the country for good.

'Michael?' she called out again, her voice ringing hollowly down the hall. Still, there was no reply.

Kitty ran from room to room, calling out his name. She checked the garden and the sheds, but he was nowhere to be seen. She ran back to his office and looked at the timetable again, then she saw his appointment diary, and opened it in the hope of finding clues. On the days leading up to the previous day, he had made short, local visits, but yesterday was empty. He had planned to leave, not rushed away on impulse like she had, and the idea he could do that to her was too painful to bear. Her breath came fast, and panic set in, making her heart race. Trying to ignore the truth, Kitty rushed upstairs to their bedroom, hoping he was resting. She pushed open the door, and the truth hit her hard as she entered. His brush and shaving items – her wedding gift to him – were absent from his dresser. She yanked open the wardrobe door and noticed that his good suit still hung in place, but the rest of his clothing was missing. Drawer after drawer revealed that he had packed everything he owned. Checking the small valise at the bottom of the wardrobe, Kitty discovered all his legal papers and his passport were gone too.

'Michael!' Kitty yelled at the top of her voice, then sank onto the mattress of their large bed. A place that once knew endless days and nights of happiness was now a stark reminder that she was alone.

Stay in control. Think. Look for a letter – he must have left you a letter!

Scrambling from the bed, Kitty searched each room and surface for a note from Michael, but she found nothing.

'What am I to do now?' she whispered to herself as she stood staring at the closed surgery door.

Perhaps Michael had telephoned Fell Hall while she was cycling home.

She pushed open the door, went to the telephone, dialled the number and waited for the operator to put her through.

'Kitty?' Stanley's voice called down the line, and Kitty waited a moment for the click as the operator disconnected her line.

'Stanley, did Michael ring you?' she asked, her words rushed with the urgency of the situation.

'No. Is everything all right?' Stanley's voice was heavy with concern.

'He's gone. Taken everything – passport, everything.' Kitty replied. She reached for a chair when her legs threatened to give way.

A silence fell between them.

'Stanley?' Kitty whispered, 'what do I do now?'

Still, Stanley said nothing, and then she heard him cough.

'I'm coming over; this is not for discussion on the telephone. I will be there in thirty minutes.'

The line went dead before Kitty had an opportunity to reply.

Dear Stanley, you are always there for me, no matter what.

Kitty's heart sank as she considered her future. Her position as a surgery support nurse and district nurse was tied to Michael's practice, as was the house they lived in. With him gone, she faced the prospect of becoming homeless. Although she knew Stanley would always provide her with a roof over her head, it would be too close to all she had lost.

As she wandered around the house, she affectionately touched their ornaments, and when she glanced at the mantel in the sitting room, where the wedding photograph of her and Michael stood, she let out a sad sigh.

You were too hasty with your words. You have sent him away – ended your marriage.

'Hello? Kitty?' Stanley's voice interrupted her thoughts.

'In the snug,' she called back, quickly dabbing away her tears and composing herself.

Stanley entered the room and stood looking at her, his expression one of concern.

'He's not left a note, but he has definitely gone. I saw timetables for a journey to Liverpool and one for London. So I am guessing he is sailing to Canada from Liverpool, but not sure about London,' Kitty said, doing her best to remain calm, 'My paperwork is on his desk – the travel documents he arranged – they go from Durham to London – but look, it is crossed out and no longer valid. There's nothing for Canada.'

Stanley looked over at a chair, and Kitty nodded for him to sit, and he did so.

'Maybe, and hear me out, maybe, he took you coming to mine as a sign you had let him go…' Stanley held up his hand to prevent her from interrupting. 'If he is set on returning to Canada, then nothing is going to stop him. Not even you. We both know his mind is not as it was before the mission, but we also know what a stubborn man he can be at times. I suggest you wait to hear from him. I suspect he will write to you when he is settled, and time apart from you may make him realise what a fool he has been, and he will come home.'

'But there will be no home to come to. The medical board will want their rent and a working GP. I can't live here without Michael – not in a sentimental way, but financially. I don't know what he was thinking. Why didn't he come to yours and speak to me – or you – and let us know he was leaving?'

Kitty slapped her hands on her knees in frustration and jumped to her feet.

'What do I do with all of this?' she said, sweeping her arm around the room.

'We could store it on the upper floor of Fell Hall. You can live there until you are organised for whatever happens next.'

Pacing the room, Kitty smiled at him.

'That's kind of you, Stanley. Thank you, it will be a big help.'

'You will need to ring the medical board and find out if Michael has been in touch, and persuade them to allow you to live here if you still work the district – I'll cover the rent until you're back on your feet.'

'That's so kind but this is Michael's mess, and he needs to pay for my welfare until we're no longer married. We have a few pounds in our National Savings account. I will withdraw some money to tide me over,' Kitty said.

'I'll help in any way I can. You're not alone, Kitty.'

Sinking back onto the sofa, Kitty let out a loud sigh.

'It feels like it without Michael. I am not ungrateful, Stanley, but without Michael…'

Stanley nodded. 'I will take you into town and vouch for you if asked. I will try to find outgoing passenger lists for you; at least you will know where he is headed.' He rose to his feet. 'Are you staying here, or coming back with me?'

With a soft shake of her head, Kitty gave him a wan smile. 'I will stay here. I'm grateful, but I cannot desert my duties. I have a working list for tomorrow.'

Heading to the door, Stanley spoke over his shoulder.

'Don't give up. Stay here in the hope Michael will return,' he said softly.

Kitty followed him into the hallway, and they stood beside the surgery door. She pushed it open.

'I am not going to abandon my patients. I noticed Michael's diary is clear; he had planned everything. There are no entries as of yesterday.'

'What I don't understand, Kitty, is why he left it until the last minute to tell you, and not discuss it properly. Do you think he has returned to the clinic for treatment?'

Shrugging her shoulders, Kitty pulled a pained face.

'Who knows? If he was in distress, why didn't he tell me? Why put me off travelling with him? I'm not sure I even know him. We've hit a brick wall.'

She walked to the desk and flicked through a pile of papers.

'I will deal with these, and then offer my resignation with immediate effect, and make use of your storage offer. I'll go to Yorkshire, find out what Smithy knows. He's his oldest friend and confidant. He might have an inkling about what is going on inside my husband's head. It will give me time with Trixie and the children, then I will pay a visit to Cornwall to see Meryn, Wenna and Pots before returning home to Parkeston. It is only fair that I speak with my uncle. He helped me through life after my parents died, and seeing him might help me work through this nightmare. A week with him, and reconnecting with my roots, might help me understand Michael's predicament.'

Stanley gave a nod.

'I don't think rushing off to Liverpool or London will give you the answers you need. There is a chance he has found a flight out via the medics. Don't use the time as a holiday, use it to clear your head. Sort out what you want from Michael, and what you can do to help him,' he advised.

Kitty gave a soft smile.

'Who knows, I might have heard from Michael by then, and we can regroup and resume life properly as a married couple,' Kitty said, hoping her words would come to fruition sooner rather than later.

Chapter Six

As the beautiful wildflower-laden hills of Yorkshire whipped past the train window, Kitty tried to compose a conversation opener. Explaining to Smithy and Trixie that her marriage was over was not going to be easy.

Since leaving Fell Hall and reassuring Stanley she would stay in touch, Kitty could best be described as lonely and bewildered. How had it come to this? And now she was travelling to seek comfort and advice from her closest friends.

As the train pulled into the station, her heart began pounding with anxiety, when usually it raced with excitement at the thought of catching up with her friends again. During their telephone call, she had told Trixie that Michael was away, and she felt the need to see them again after such a long, hard winter. When she stepped down onto the platform, Kitty could see Smithy waving enthusiastically at the far end. She waved back and took a deep breath as she walked towards him. The warm sun settled on her face, and she tried to focus on the positive side of the visit.

'Hello, stranger,' Smithy said as he took her suitcase, offering a friendly peck on the cheek. He smelled the same as Michael's clinic, and she felt a tight lump in her throat. She moved her head, as if stretching her neck.

'Train seats will never be comfortable,' she replied, and, back in control of her emotions, she linked her arm through his.

'Take me to your wife and children. I can't believe you have another little girl! At least I didn't have to deliver her in a barn during a Christmas storm.'

Both laughed at the memory of when Kitty had found Trixie in labour in a barn on Christmas Day in 1944. It was not funny at the time, and circumstances with getting help due to the thick fog was a nightmare, but in the end, mother and baby were home, safe and warm, thanks to Kitty's quick thinking.

'Rose and Florence keep us busy, and I would not change a thing. Trixie is a marvellous mother; I am a lucky man. A son would be a wonderful addition, but I've been told that two is enough.'

Smithy did not sound disappointed, but Kitty wondered if, deep down, he was. If Trixie would expand her family in the hope of producing another Douglas Smith, the world would never object to that addition. He was one of the best doctors she knew, and his care and compassion for Michael after his head injury went beyond friendship; it was almost brotherly.

'You've seen the power of women during the war, sons and daughters, both the same in my eyes,' she said gently, trying to redirect the conversation, 'and knowing the genes your two have, those girls will rule the world.' Kitty hated the thought of him being disappointed when he was already blessed with two children.

Smithy bellowed a laugh. 'Please, no, ruling the home is bad enough.'

The greeting from Trixie was warm and inviting, and Kitty no longer felt alone. Rose and Florence entertained her, but in her heart, they also created a smidgen of pain. How she longed to have a child of her own, and enjoy the sense of family life.

Once the children were in bed, Smithy left the two women to chat.

Curled up on two large horsehair sofas in a comfortable room in the large house, both soon settled into times past. It was Trixie who brought the conversation into the present.

'You told me Michael is on a course, Kitty,' she said, shifting in her seat, 'but I think something else is going on. You have lost your spark. Yes, you laugh and giggle, but'—Trixie shook her head—'I think something is wrong. You can tell me, Kitty. Do you need help?'

Trixie's words were the unplugging of the dam Kitty had built behind her bravado, and she burst into tears. No amount of dabbing them away stemmed the flow. Trixie jumped from her seat, went to her friend, slid onto the sofa beside her and pulled her into her arms. For several minutes, Kitty allowed herself the luxury of a good cry on Trixie's shoulder before she moved from her arms and composed herself.

'Michael has left me – left the country. He's…'

Trixie stopped the conversation by rushing to the door, 'I'm getting Smithy. Just wait a minute, he needs to hear this,' she said.

Kitty watched her friend leave the room, and something told

her that Trixie or Smithy might already know something about her situation.

A few minutes later, both of her friends walked into the room, wearing the same concerned expression. Smithy's face had a slight flush, and she guessed Trixie had disturbed him while he was enjoying a whisky nightcap.

Rising to her feet, she looked at them both, then addressed Smithy.

'Did you know how he felt?' she asked him.

Without showing any sign of not understanding her question, Smithy took a moment before replying.

'He came to me asking advice about transferring his British licence to Canada. He did not mention leaving now; he made it sound like something you were both possibly planning for the future,' he said. The red flush of his face brightened.

'I don't think that's the truth, Smithy. I am so sorry, but I think he told you something,' Kitty said and gave Trixie a swift apologetic glance.

A heavy atmosphere of anticipation filled the air as they waited for Smithy to respond. Out of the corner of her eye, she noticed Trixie tugging at the strings of the apron tied around her waist and tossing it onto a chair – a gesture Kitty's aunt would make when she was annoyed with Kitty's uncle. A battle cry – defend yourself and cope with the questions.

'I … um, yes. All I know is that he applied for a position in Alberta near a place called Calgary. The last I heard, he had travel documents for both of you, and you were in agreement about leaving England.'

'In agreement? He sprung it on me last week, then told me he was leaving. On our anniversary. I had no idea about any of it.'

Kitty's voice rose a notch, then she remembered the children asleep upstairs.

'I'm sorry, Trixie. Smithy, please tell me everything you know. I know about trains to Liverpool and London, but that's all.'

By the time Smithy had finished telling her about Michael's visit in November, Kitty was sitting with a glass of whisky and taking in the news that Michael had applied for a private doctor's position in October, and been told that the job was his in the new year. Neither of the men had attended a medical conference, as Michael had told her they were going to, which was the reason why she hadn't accompanied him.

'I am sorry, Kitty. Had I known…' Trixie said.

'You would have done nothing, simply assumed I knew because I am his wife. You don't need to apologise, either of you. This is Michael's mess,' Kitty said firmly.

Smithy shook his head.

'He was excited about it all and wanted to surprise you, which is why he came to discuss it with me. I suspect he told a white lie because he didn't want you to worry. I am his confidante and doctor, after all. He did not want you to think he was coming to me because he had health issues. You always visit together.'

Kitty gave a shrug and huffed slightly.

'Then why did he not surprise me in November, or even for Christmas? Why did he tell me he was leaving before discussing it with me? And tell me he wants his children to be pure Canadian? Why?' she asked, her voice quiet with fatigue.

Trixie took Kitty's hand.

'Only Michael can answer that. For now, Kitty, I think you need to get a good night's sleep, and we'll see what we can do to help track him down in the morning. This is not a problem which can be solved when you're apart from one another.'

Chapter Seven

The following morning, Smithy invited Kitty into his office after they had eaten breakfast with Trixie and the children.

While she waited for Smithy to finish writing down a message from a patient, Kitty took a moment to look around the room. She noticed that, although the clinical equipment was neatly arranged, just like in Michael's office, Smithy's room had a sense of cosiness – slightly shabby but radiating comfort. It struck her that Michael had never personalised his surgery rooms. He had taken over the practice from the previous doctor without making any adjustments. She thought back to their home; he had never placed items he treasured and enjoyed anywhere other than in the bedroom, nor was there anything personal in his office. Was he intentionally avoiding truly settling in Britain after the war?

'I telephoned a colleague who had offered a reference for Michael, and he said that Michael was particularly interested in applying for several positions in Canada, some of which he had never mentioned to me. He also spoke about contacting an old friend about setting up his own surgery near a recent oil strike.' Smithy pushed a piece of paper across the table. 'Michael wrote down the name of the place in case our colleague was interested. I find it strange he never said anything to me.'

Kitty glanced around the room again. 'Maybe it's because he knows you have everything you want right here in Yorkshire,' she said bluntly and picked up the piece of paper.

'Do you think this is where he is headed?' she asked.

Smithy looked at her, his stare soft with concern.

'I don't know, Kitty. I am hurt he never confided more. Michael never struck me as one who would seek riches, but if he is trying to start a new life, build a practice and a home, then maybe he is looking to invest. Did he have enough savings to do that?'

Taken aback by his words, Kitty's mind shifted to their finances. Michael had an account for the surgery, and they saved their personal money in a tin. They called it their rainy-day tin. While not of great value, it contained enough that she had considered placing it into a bank account, but never got around to doing so. Kitty guessed that when she returned home, the tin would be gone.

'I suspect he's probably taken what little we had in our rainy-day tin to tide him over,' she said, resigning herself to the fact that if he had taken the money with him, she would only have her small wage as a district nurse.

'Kitty, Michael loves you. We both know he is not the greatest communicator – look at how he surprised and annoyed you by arriving back in England unannounced when Rosie was christened. Remember, he shared his reasons with you, and you eventually got married. I suspect what he is doing now is ensuring you have everything in Canada he wants you to have. He's not going to leave you, and he certainly would not have married you if he meant what he said about pure-blooded Canadian children.'

Kitty felt a surge of annoyance coursing through her. It was understandable that Michael's best friend would be protective and supportive of him, but it baffled her that he didn't comprehend how hurtful Michael's words had been to her.

'But you know what he said, Smithy. He wanted "pure Canadian children" – his words were just that – and he can't have a pure Canadian bloodline with me now, can he?' she replied, her voice rising with indignation.

Smithy paused for a moment deep in thought before smiling at her.

'I'm not wanting to upset you, Kitty, but this is a typical Michael and Kitty situation,' he said. 'Just because he wants his children to be born Canadian doesn't mean he wants a Canadian woman to fulfil that wish. He has always wanted *you* in his life, to bear his children, but instead you introduced the idea of divorce, and it's complicated everything. Kitty, think carefully – did he ever say anything that hinted he also wanted a divorce?' Smithy urged, his tone kind and encouraging.

She went over the conversation between her and Michael for what seemed like the hundredth time.

'No. In fact, he looked defeated when I said it, and then he seemed to give me an opt-out too. Have I got it wrong, Smithy?' she asked.

'When he is ready, Michael will reach out to you. I am certain of it, and I urge you not to do anything hasty.'

Smithy kissed the top of her head as he pulled her close.

'We'll find him, Kitty. We will.'

Kitty did not reply. Smithy was fighting Michael's corner, and he would not see the cracks in her marriage, ones Kitty was beginning to notice more as she spoke about her situation.

Later in the morning, after washing dishes and a huge pile of children's clothes and nappies, Trixie and Kitty took time to stop and chat, mulling over their times together during the war.

'I still remember Ma Smith and Belle the day we all first met. What a pair they were,' Trixie said and laughed.

'And Belle turned out not to be Annabelle Farnsworth, the German spy, but a heroine for Great Britain named Lizzie. She was never nurse material.'

Kitty giggled. 'The trouble she got herself into was unbelievable at times. I wonder if it was an act. I despised her attempts to steal Michael, and her snobbery, but now that we know the truth, I understand her and have come to admire her.'

Trixie raised her eyebrows and gave a smile.

'What went on in Birmingham was the start of our journey, but we now know she had already started hers.'

Sipping her cup of tea, Kitty thought back to 1940 and the years that followed. So much had happened. When they heard that Belle was to hang for being a spy against Britain, it was beyond comprehension. Then, when she received news that Belle had left her an inn in Cornwall and her worldly goods, Kitty was bewildered. After stumbling across a disguised Belle in Liverpool, now calling herself Lizzie, Kitty's confusion was justified. When the truth was revealed to her, she listened and accepted that she had to remain silent for the sake of the country. It was a burden she needed to carry until Lizzie told her otherwise.

'When I found out her secret, it knocked me for six. We still write to each other. She's happily married in America, doing goodness knows what, and I can't imagine her as a mother, but she is lucky and has her son,' Kitty said.

'Speaking of children, Kitty, I hate to say it, but you need to find Michael and discuss this situation. Both of you want to have children together, and this cannot be done without being together.'

Trixie gave a light laugh as she picked up her youngest child, preparing to feed her.

'I'm not laughing really, I am worried you're going to lose something precious because you are both stubborn.'

Kitty swung her a look, offended by her words.

'Stubborn?' she asked tersely.

Trixie leaned back in her seat and gave a brief grin.

'You know it, and I know it. I am not speaking out of turn. Both you and Michael need friends to guide you when your relationship struggles.'

To this Kitty gave a nod of agreement.

'We do need friends, that much is true. We also need one another, because if he feels as alone as I do right now, then he is a very lonely, sad person,' Kitty said, dabbing away a rogue tear.

'If you do reunite with Michael and move to Canada, this might be your last chance to be with friends. Take the opportunity to see your uncle while you're waiting for Michael. Leave him messages with Stanley about where you are. I bet in a couple of weeks you will both be together planning a new life in Canada.'

Kitty held her goddaughter in her arms, gently stroking her back in circular motions.

'You seem so confident that we'll find a way back from this disaster,' she said to Trixie.

'I feel it in my bones. Words have confused things for both of you. Wait for him to contact you. Smithy is worried you might consult a solicitor about divorce. Please don't, Kitty.'

'Write to me and let me know what is happening,' Trixie whispered between sobs as she hugged Kitty goodbye the next day.

Kitty's stomach rolled, and her heart thumped. Inside, she knew she had to hold onto the hug from her friend to get her through the next tumultuous stage of her life.

How had it come to this? Was she saying goodbye forever? Dear Trixie, the sweetest and most loyal friend she knew. Even their mutual friend Jo, once Kitty's best friend, could not match the friendship Kitty and Trixie had formed since the birth of Rosey. The busy end of a baby delivery in a barn had brought them closer, and the friendship both Trixie and Smithy shared with her and Michael strengthened the bond. Strand by strand of emotion, Kitty felt herself snipping the ties to save her heart from breaking. She knew that if she found Michael, she would have to find the courage to admit her failure to understand his words, and hope he could forgive her for her reaction.

'I will, I don't want to leave, but if I get the chance to get my husband back, I have to take it.'

Trixie's squeeze halted Kitty's breath for a second.

'Kitty McCarthy, I believe you can achieve anything you set your heart on. The first time I saw nervous Kitty Pattison standing beside her kitbag, ready to become the best Red Cross nurse she could be, I knew you were someone to look up to, not like the loud and flashy Belle. That one strutted around with her airs and graces. And as for Joan Norfolk, our lovely Jo? Stubborn and more interested in cars and grease than lipstick and dancing, she was not who I aspired to be. I was timid and thought you were the most amazing person I had ever met. Calm, bright and caring – I wanted to be Kitty Pattison.'

Kitty had never heard Trixie speak so openly before. She looked at her petite friend, a mother whose dark-ringed eyes told of sleepless nights. She never thought she would envy Trixie, but she had to admit a small part of her was very envious now.

'And here I am, wanting to be you. Maybe not in terms of height, but I want what you have, Trixie.'

Trixie bent over, trying to catch her breath as a giggle turned into a belly laugh.

'I want to be as tall as you. I'd love to have an hourglass figure with athletic legs. Yet here you are, wishing to lose a few inches of height, gain several pounds and deal with leaking breasts!' Trixie drew breath and then softened her tone. 'I love you, Kitty. You truly desire something special and you deserve it all.'

Smithy joined them and lifted Kitty's suitcase from the floor.

'If you want to catch this train, we need to leave,' he said, stepping outside and letting the cold air blow in.

'Keep those babies warm. Don't stand on the step and wave. I want photographs and letters,' Kitty said quickly, giving Trixie a peck on the cheek and kissing the girls.

Once she heard the door click shut behind her, Kitty took a deep breath before getting into Smithy's car. Sobbing on the way to the station wouldn't be helpful. She would head home, then travel to her friends in Cornwall, visit her uncle, explain her situation and say her goodbyes. By doing so she would show Michael she was ready to join him in his search for a Canadian life together. Until she had answers from Michael, saying goodbye to family and friends in England was the only option Kitty felt she had left.

Closing the passenger door when Kitty was comfortable, Smithy climbed into the driver's seat and looked at her.

'Ready?' he asked.

'I am. I'll miss Trixie so much. I have a feeling in my belly that this is the last time I will see you all,' Kitty said softly.

Smithy coughed, and Kitty guessed it was his way of suppressing his emotions.

'I will do my very best to get you two together again one day, I promise,' he said.

Kitty smiled inwardly; he was such a thoughtful, loving man.

'I won't hold you to that promise, Smithy. As a village doctor and a father, you're busy enough, and it will be a difficult one to keep. Just write what Trixie might not, and if I find Michael, then I will ensure he does the same,' she replied.

As they pulled into the station, he gave her a swift smile.

'Trixie's heart is going to be broken. She loves you like a sister. Please don't lose touch with her.'

Kitty climbed out and hugged Smithy goodbye.

'I'll never do that with either of you. Go home and hug your three girls; you're a lucky man. Thank you for everything,' Kitty said with more bravado than she felt inside.

Chapter Eight

When Kitty opened the back door to her home once more, she felt a chill in the air. She wanted to call out Michael's name, but hesitated, noticing there was no sign of his return.

After unpacking and washing a few items, she made her way to the wardrobe, where they stored their rainy-day tin. Surprised to find the tin still there, she gave it a shake before opening it, and was surprised by the sound of coins clinking. Lifting the lid, she found a piece of paper that listed the amount inside. She saw that Michael had crossed out the amount of twenty pounds and written the remaining balance: ten pounds. He had taken only half of their savings, which was more than she had expected. Their savings had increased since she had last checked, so the vast amount of ten pounds was a shock.

Michael must have added to the tin after receiving paid-up accounts from private patients. He charged one particular wealthy family in the area a higher amount of money, because of their demands for extra attention. It had obviously paid off. The notes and coins in the tin were a relief for Kitty. She would pack up the house, inform the medical board and head for Cornwall over the weekend. It gave her a few days to get everything done. Stanley told her there was no news of Michael leaving as a paying passenger, so he asked a friend to look into what medical ships had sailed to Canada, as there was a good chance that Michael might find passage out as a medical officer. Kitty agreed it was a possibility and readied herself to move her things to Fell Hall. There was nothing more she could do until they found out how or if Michael had left Britain.

A rise in temperature took them by surprise, but Stanley and two lads whom Daphne had taken under her wing helped move Kitty's belongings out of the cottage. On the table, she left a letter for Michael, should he return, explaining whom she had informed about giving up the house, and that she was no longer the district nurse. She told him of her plans and that Stanley had their belongings at Fell Hall. She asked him to find a way to contact her so they could discuss what their future might hold.

She was unable to leave some of the plants Michael had gifted her, because of her emotional connection to them, so Frank, the orphanage's new gardener, lifted them and promised to plant them in an area where they would be protected from the children racing through the grounds.

By Friday, Kitty was heat-exhausted, mentally drained and emotionally overwhelmed. The conversation with the medical board had been difficult. They informed her that Michael had registered his notice in January, and she cobbled together a story about leaving her post to join her husband once he sent the new address. She was embarrassed that she did not know half of what they had discussed, but she tried to remain calm. It drained her of emotional energy, but fired up the need to visit her loved ones. After she had seen them all, she would focus on seeking out Michael and forging a way forward with him – or deciding to begin a new life.

Kitty settled into Fell Hall and spent her time helping with the orphans. Daphne clucked around her like a mother hen, and Kitty let her. It felt good to be mothered. She missed her aunt who raised her, and had almost forgotten what it was like to enjoy the nurturing. Wenna, in Cornwall, was the same, and Kitty knew she would be smothered with her love when she arrived. Meryn was like a little sister to her, but she was a loving girl, so Kitty had no qualms about unloading her feelings if she needed to. June was a day away, and Stanley was right; she had worn herself out with worry.

'I've decided to drive you to Cornwall,' Stanley said over dinner, his kindly tone suggesting to Kitty that he was determined. 'It will be an opportunity for me to catch up with a few RAF chaps I trained with, before they head out to India and oversee the last of the men returning home. There's another friend who has left the Force and is flying passenger planes for private companies. It will be a great catch-up for both of us, as well as saving you an uncomfortable train journey and fare. No argument.'

Kitty smiled at him. 'I am not going to refuse. That's very kind of you. It will make the journey easier.'

Stanley snatched up his newspaper and rolled it before tucking it under his arm.

'We'll leave at oh five hundred hours, we'll see sunrise and enjoy the drive down. I'll ask Daphne to make up a picnic this evening, and I suggest you pack and have an early night.'

'I'll be up. Are you sure? It's a long drive, Stanley.'

'You let me worry about that. Get some rest and I'll see you in the morning.' He gave her a wide smile.

Watching him leave the room, Kitty thanked her luck for having such good friends. Each one had helped and guided her throughout the years she had known them.

Thanks to Stanley, Smithy and Trixie's words of wisdom, she gained a deeper understanding of herself and Michael's relationship quickly. She also understood what they needed to do should they ever have the opportunity to come together again. All she had to do was hope Michael wouldn't decide to take her suggestion of a divorce and run with it; she knew now it was the last thing she wanted.

Despite the sun not rising for another hour, the temperature suggested it was to be another hot day, and the birds sang loudly outside Kitty's window. She lay for a moment, recalling the days she woke this early to prepare for work on the wards, or when a child cried out for its parents from one of the rooms in Fell Hall. Everything was a rush in those days, and life worries were overwhelmed by bombs and rescue missions.

Nowadays, all she had on her mind was Michael, and she could see no end to the thoughts of dread and upset. Having a long drive ahead of them, Kitty ensured she ate breakfast, after which she wrote a short note of thanks to Daphne for laying the table and filling a wicker basket with food for the journey and two large flasks of tea. Stanley was an avid drinker of tea, and Kitty was more than happy to share her ration with him.

During the drive, they watched the sun rise lazily on the horizon, and soon the sky was ablaze with sunlight. Stanley pointed out places of interest, and they stopped in Nottingham to eat their picnic in a shady spot within the grounds of Nottingham Castle.

Kitty admired the large building. 'The original castle was built here by William the Conqueror,' Stanley told her. 'It withstood the Wars of the Roses and survived the Blitz. There are tunnels beneath the castle – the military probably used them over the past few years when they moved in.'

Kitty ate her lunch, which consisted of corned beef sandwiches, apples and tomatoes. She poured them each a cup of tea and sat back, listening to Stanley talk about the kings who had fought over the castle.

'You certainly know your history, Stanley. I confess to learning more from you just now than when I was at school,' she said when they were packing up their things.

'I love learning about the past, although I think our recent past will soon be forgotten. Sadly, wars will always happen.'

'I think this one will be a lesson learned,' Kitty said and climbed into the passenger seat.

'They said that after the Great War, but look where that got us. I hope your optimism proves true, Kitty. I have established a meeting club for injured RAF men, and we all agree it is good to be given another chance at life,' Stanley said, pulling out onto the main road and heading for the city of Birmingham, where they stopped for a comfort break. The heat had reached its peak, and they were grateful for what breeze blew in through the open windows of the car.

'This is the hottest I have ever known early summer,' Kitty declared, fanning her face with Stanley's newspaper, wafting air his way at intervals. Beads of sweat sat on his upper lip, and she began to doubt that it was all due to the heat. She was concerned about the discomfort Stanley would be in when they arrived in Cornwall.

'I think we should split the journey, Stanley,' she said. 'I can afford to pay for us to enjoy a bed and breakfast – my treat.'

Stanley pulled the car over onto a small country road.

'So long as I can stretch the leg, I will be fine. Feel free to nod off if the conversation dries up, but we've managed eight hours of fruitful and entertaining chat,' Stanley said.

'How many more hours do you have to drive?' she asked.

'Roughly another five, maybe six,' he replied, 'It's what, one o'clock now?'

Kitty looked at her watch, 'one thirty.'

'Righto, I know the route and shortcuts, so I'll get us to Gloucester for around four, and we'll find somewhere to stay overnight. I know where I can refuel there, too.'

Silently, Kitty was relieved. Her back ached, so she knew Stanley would be suffering. He was a man who needed guidance in self-care. He often forgot his prosthesis would rub and cause blisters, and although the car was adapted to avoid the problem, the drive must be tiring for him too.

Mrs Charlesworth, the landlady of the bed and breakfast, took some convincing that they needed two rooms and appeared to assume they were embarking on an illicit affair. Kitty and Stanley climbed the few stairs to their rooms after listening to her explaining how to hit the taps at the right angle for hot water. They politely waited until she had gone downstairs before bursting into laughter.

'Just the place for our adventure. I hope her egg and chips live up to her tale of their excellence,' Stanley quipped.

'Shhh, she'll hear us and we'll be cast as giggling lovers. What an imagination she's got – and she doesn't hold back with the questioning. I wonder if she was a secret weapon of sorts during the war. She has certainly learned the art of interrogation,' Kitty said, making Stanley laugh loudly.

'I have other guests napping,' the landlady bellowed up the stairs, and they stared at one another.

'Well, they're awake now,' Stanley said and quickly slipped his key into the lock of the room adjoining Kitty's.

Her room was clean and well-aired. She drew a shallow bath and washed herself down. She knew if she sat and soaked, she would feel sleepy and miss her evening meal. A metallic sound vibrated through the pipes, and she grinned to herself. Stanley was enjoying hammering on the pipes.

Kitty noted Stanley walking stiffly on his prosthetic leg as they descended the stairs.

'I think you overdid the driving today,' she told him.

Stanley continued to the bottom step and turned around.

'Nothing a good night's rest won't cure,' he said, holding his hand out for her to step off the last step.

'Good evening,' a voice boomed from across the room, and Mrs Charlesworth strode towards them. 'I trust you eventually managed to get water from the pipes, sir?' she asked Stanley tartly, giving him an indignant stare.

'Me? No, I had no problems with my pipework. You, Kitty?' Stanley turned his attention back to Kitty and winked at her.

Kitty's insides were fit to burst with laughter, but she controlled herself and smiled sweetly at them both.

'The water was hot and I had no problems at all. I did hear rather a lot of noise, but was soon engrossed in my book,' she answered.

The landlady did not appear convinced, but ushered them to what looked like a cosy table for two in the corner of the room.

'She does unnerve me,' Kitty said, giggling when the woman walked away.

Stanley gave a theatrical shudder. 'Me too. She's determined to catch us out.'

A plate of greasy fried eggs and pale potatoes mushed in a heap was presented to them both. 'The potatoes did not like the hot fat,' Mrs Charlesworth said as she ungraciously placed the plates on the table.

'Oh, that often happens to me,' Kitty said, 'I am always caught out. My brother lifts an eyebrow, but wasting food isn't done in our house, is it, Stanley?'

Kitty watched as the woman's face blanched and she swivelled to and from them several times. As Stanley was about to cut into the egg, his plate was whisked away.

'No, no. This is not good enough. I can see the gentleman has been injured, and he deserves better. I have a nice chicken pie and vegetables on the go. Give me a few minutes, and I will bring them to you. I can't have you thinking I serve food like your sister, sir.' The landlady gave what Kitty assumed was a laugh, but it sounded more like a horse snorting at hay. She watched as her plate was snatched up, and looked back at Stanley.

'So, she has ways of punishing the naughty lovers – greasy egg and mushy chipped potatoes. How clever of your sister to mention she serves up the same,' Kitty said, and they both smothered loud laughs.

After enjoying a baked apple and custard, followed by a sherry for Kitty and a rum for Stanley, they listened to the landlady tell them about the improvements she planned for the hotel – a building she had inherited from her parents. By the time the evening was over, Stanley and Kitty had received an invitation to stay with her again.

Outside their respective bedrooms, Kitty grinned at Stanley.

'I needed this adventure. Thank you – this evening has been such fun. Rest your leg and I will see you in the morning.'

'When I mentioned an early start, Mrs Charlesworth said she would serve breakfast at six o'clock. Do we risk it?' Stanley whispered.

'Absolutely we will. It will be hours before we eat again. Night, Stanley. Rest well,' Kitty said as she entered her bedroom.

As she climbed beneath the bedclothes, inhaling the scent of freshly washed linen, she realised it had been many hours since she had thought about her situation with Michael. The day had filled her with renewed energy, and she fell asleep feeling content, ready to face her future.

Chapter Nine

After a hearty breakfast of perfectly cooked bacon and eggs, proving the chips last night had been intentionally bad, Kitty insisted on paying for the rooms, and while Stanley put their bags in the car, she went to pay her dues.

Mrs Charlesworth fussed behind the reception desk with a duster and turned to her with a smile.

'Off now? May I apologise for my rudeness when you arrived, dear? My first marriage ended after my husband ran off with a younger woman. I tend to jump to conclusions. I noticed you both wore a wedding band, and when you said you weren't married, I did my usual – made you feel uncomfortable,' Mrs Charlesworth confided, pulling an apologetic face.

With a slight shake of her head, Kitty smiled.

'Stanley's wife passed away five years ago, and mine, well, he's seeking a doctor's position in Canada, where he was born.' She spoke more cheerfully than she felt about the situation.

Mrs Charlesworth clasped a hand to her mouth and then

waved it with childlike glee, smiling. 'How wonderful, married to a Canadian doctor! How romantic. I take it you will be joining him? What a wonderful opportunity for a young woman – to see a new country and learn new skills!' she said with great excitement.

'Well, if it all turns out as we both hope,' Kitty replied, wishing she could also express her excitement.

'I wish you all the best, my dear,' Mrs Charlesworth said.

When Kitty placed the money on the counter, Mrs Charlesworth counted out half and pushed it toward her. 'I will only take what is owed for your room. Please return your brother's money to him. I won't take from a man who fought for my freedom and lost a leg doing so,' she said, and before Kitty could respond, Mrs Charlesworth was walking back around the counter to the front door.

She pulled it open and continued, 'This heat will be the death of me! Now take that money to your brother, give him my good wishes, and have a pleasant journey, and a very happy life.' She turned her attention outside and waved. 'Goodbye, Stanley! Do call again, especially when your sister is living in Canada.'

As Kitty got into the car, she whispered, 'Mrs Charlesworth has a way of extracting information from you – you end up revealing everything before you even realise it. I swear, that woman must have been one of our best interrogators.'

Kitty waved at Mrs Charlesworth, who was still watching them.

'She has a soft spot for you; she wouldn't take the money for your room because you fought for her freedom,' Kitty said.

'Oh, that was kind of her, I had best go thank her,' Stanley said, easing himself from the car.

'Be careful; she also knows you're a widower. I think she has her eyes set on getting a new husband, you lucky man,' Kitty teased.

She watched as Stanley shook Mrs Charlesworth's hand and smiled. The woman was openly flirting, fanning herself with her hand and giggling.

Stanley limped swiftly to the car and into his seat and drove away faster than usual.

'Slow down, Stanley. She's not following.' Kitty laughed as he adjusted his speed.

'I thought she was going to eat me alive!' he said, his voice breathless.

The approach to Cornwall brought back memories of when Kitty first entered the county. Although she had been brought up by the sea, the Cornish coastline took her breath away. Its natural ruggedness, clear blue waters, golden sands and gorgeous flowers lifted her spirits. The twisting and winding roads did not have the same effect, but each narrow road they travelled through offered its own celebration of colour and fragrance. As they neared the inn her heart beat with excitement. With the American forces no longer moving around the villages, the place was less busy and much quieter.

After a few miles, she decided to discuss a subject on her mind, thinking this was the perfect time to do so.

'Have you thought about a new life partner, Stanley?' she asked carefully, fully aware of his love for his wife.

'Not really. Who would want a cripple for a husband?' he said flippantly.

His words pained Kitty; she had never realised he saw himself in such a way.

'Well, that is not a term I would use for a start – I consider it outdated and unkind,' Kitty said severely. 'You have a lot to offer,

Stanley, and I don't mean money and family estates. I mean kindness, love and humour. You work hard at anything that comes your way and are an intelligent, interesting man.'

'You're making me blush,' Stanley said, glancing at her and winking. 'But I don't want another woman in my life, I want an adventure. Shake off the war and do something different. Mountain climbing, something fulfilling.'

Kitty sat quietly for a moment. 'Wanting an adventure' made her think of Michael and his quest.

'Mountain climbing – that would be a challenge. How about doing it in Canada if I go to find Michael?' she said slowly and clearly, a sudden thought making sense to her. He turned to her.

'I, well, um, let's take our water bottles Mrs Charlesworth gave us and sit over there. That way I can concentrate on what you've suggested before we get to the inn. I need to rest my legs for a while, and besides, it will be harder to talk once you and Wenna get chatting,' Stanley said, laughing. He pointed to a tree with a shady patch of grass beneath.

Stanley slowed the car to a halt and turned off the engine.

Once settled on a blanket, they drank the water, which was warm but thirst-quenching.

'That suggestion in the car, what made you mention it?' Stanley asked.

'It was the remark about mountain climbing, and looking for adventure – you might find it in Canada, with me and Michael to keep you on the straight and narrow,' Kitty replied.

Stanley leaned back against the tree trunk.

'It is something to consider. Especially when you are settled – or do you mean for me to join you looking for him if we find he has left Britain?'

'Either. I am not sure why, but I had this sudden feeling it is the place for you to get out of the rut you are in – I don't mean it rudely, but aside from meeting your chums and playing cricket with the orphans, what is it you are doing with your life?'

Stanley gave a light laugh. 'I am still in the RAF, but I agree; I don't do much with my personal life. I suppose I could seek a transfer or a collaborative project out in Canada. I hadn't thought of opening up my world until you mentioned it. The only woman I have needed since Jenny died is Daphne, and the only one I love having as a friend is you. Let's get back on the road and chat about the positives and negatives of it all.' Stanley struggled to his feet. 'I'll chat it out with my friends this week, and see what can be done.'

A stunned Kitty sat in the car listening to Stanley's enthusiastic ideas. He would ensure the orphanage remained, and release funding for its upkeep, and for his new life, from another estate Kitty never knew he had – Jenny's family home. Her parents were dead, and after her passing, he inherited it all. A large rambling house in the Cotswolds, and a cottage in Wales.

Chapter Ten

As they drove into Mawnan Smith, Kitty's memories of her stay there flooded back, some good, some not so good. The difficult ones she accepted as her transition into learning more about life outside her sheltered one.

It was here that she turned Belle over to the authorities for aiding and abetting Germans entering the country. Little did Kitty realise it was a ruse by British Intelligence to lure and capture them. The real Belle – Lizzie – had left The Stargazy Inn to Kitty for being a friend. Confused at the time, Kitty – not wanting the tie to the property – handed it over to Meryn, Wenna and Pots.

Pots had run the place for years; for Meryn, it was her home, a safe haven where customers were kind and understanding about her family and hearing loss. Meryn had lost her ability to hear and speak during the mineshaft fall that injured her and killed her mother. Heartbroken, Meryn's father left Cornwall and abandoned her at the home of his old friend, Pots, when told Meryn's condition was permanent.

Pots had been on the brink of leaving his spiteful wife, and, although he was an older man, he was not going to leave Meryn with her, so he took Meryn with him to the inn, and cared for her like a daughter.

On the drive through Cornwall, Kitty and Stanley's conversation had led to many ideas, and both were enthusiastic about the prospect of finding Michael. They made plans, and everything began to take definite shape. They chose to discuss their move to Canada properly when they returned home. Kitty felt hope fill her heart where dread had once sat. She felt alive again, and Stanley had certainly found renewed energy. She also felt a twinge of sadness. Her visit to her friends could be the last time she saw them. This trip was now her farewell visit.

When they pulled up outside The Stargazy Inn she noted how clean the yard was and how the whitewashed walls gleamed in the sun. Even the barrels awaiting collection were stacked neatly and washed clean. Wenna and Meryn were both good at keeping house, and their pride in the inn showed. Kitty had made the right decision to hand it legally to them.

Gathering her bags from the back of the car, Kitty watched as Stanley stretched to ease his back. She could not imagine life without him; even if they could not find Michael, she wondered if they could find a way to start afresh and heal their past lives. But before she could remind herself to be positive about finding Michael, a voice boomed out from the inn's doorway.

'Hello, my lovers. Get inside and cool off.'

Kitty recognised the strong Cornish accent as Wenna's. Conwenna Veryan, who had saved Kitty from an enemy attack and befriended her on the first day she arrived in Cornwall, now stood with her hands on her hips. She had not changed in the three years since Kitty had last seen her.

'Wenna!'

Kitty called out her friend's name, dropped her bags at her feet and allowed herself to be swallowed up by Wenna's embrace.

Behind Wenna, a face peered round and gave Kitty a wide smile.

'Meryn Tremayne, look at you!' Kitty said.

Her friend slipped around Wenna and held out her arms, and they both hugged.

Kitty held her back at arm's length to ensure Meryn could see her face.

'How are you?' she asked, ensuring her words were formed for Meryn to read.

Meryn pulled a paper pad and pencil from her apron pocket.

I am very happy to see you again. I have missed you.

She handed Kitty the pad, but she didn't need it. Meryn had written to Kitty several months before telling her she was learning sign language, and Kitty decided to learn too, as a surprise and support for Meryn. So she replied with her hands: *And I have missed you. Let's get inside from the heat,* she signed.

Meryn's face lit up with pleasure, and she threw herself into Kitty's arms.

Stanley gave a light cough. 'Hello, everyone. I am going to head off and get a rest before I catch up with friends. I will leave Kitty in your capable hands and bring my friends to meet you all in a day or so. Tell Pots to keep a barrel cool,' he said, adding a cheery laugh.

Kitty released herself from Meryn's stronghold hug and

turned her attention to Stanley. She kissed him on the cheek and then touched his arm.

'See you in a day or two, Stanley. Please drive carefully and make sure you rest that leg. Thank you for getting me here. I need this break – we have a busy time ahead of us.' She hugged him.

'You just collect your thoughts. I'll try and find out more about Michael's whereabouts, and then we'll get this darn mess sorted,' he whispered, knowing she did not want Wenna to know the situation until the end of the week. Kitty wanted to make happy final memories before saying goodbye.

After everyone waved him off, Kitty stepped inside the inn. Pots was behind the bar chatting with customers. He had not changed, although Kitty did think he looked smarter than before he and Wenna were married.

'Always chatting, Pots,' she joked, and the room rattled with laughter from the customers, with several teasing comments about him only working when his wife was around.

Pots' smile was wide and welcoming, and he shook his head.

'I daren't stand still or the wife will find me jobs to do elsewhere,' he joked back and winked at Wenna. 'It's good to see you, Kitty. I have a lemonade with your name on it here.' Pots tapped a glass bottle misted with condensation. 'I keep it in the ice bucket for Wenna while this heatwave is still going strong. Meryn makes it for us. She's a good girl.'

Kitty was so pleased to see and hear that Meryn was happy and settled. She still felt badly for introducing Meryn to Lewis. When she first met him – an American soldier – he'd seemed kind and thoughtful; he had taken Kitty under his wing when Michael was injured, and helped with Michael's transfer to the French hospital. When Kitty introduced him to her circle of friends, Meryn fell in love with him, and it hurt Kitty to the core that he had left Meryn high and dry during the wedding preparations, having been found out to be a womaniser with a wife back home. Especially when they had encouraged her relationship.

Meryn's true love had been Bobby, another American. He was the father of her child, and word came that he was married when Kitty first met Meryn. Kitty and Pots chased Bobby away before they found out about Meryn's pregnancy. Then Meryn wrote to tell her Bobby was back in her life to support Kedrick, and proved he was not married. Kitty hoped he would not cause her young friend more pain, but Meryn's recent letters about him were upbeat.

Kitty sat chatting for an hour, then Meryn tapped her arm and briefly nodded towards the door.

'Bobby and Kedrick,' Kitty said with a beaming smile. In the doorway was a smiling black American soldier, still in uniform, and Kedrick. Kitty looked at the little boy and waved. She turned back to Meryn.

'Kedrick's grown so much! And Bobby's back in his life, how wonderful.' Meryn nodded and signed to him that his auntie Kitty had come to visit for a few days.

'Hello, Kedrick! Come and give me a big hug; I've missed your hugs,' Kitty exclaimed. With encouragement from his father, the little boy went to her. He was shy at first but Kitty soon brought a smile to his face with the gift of a small, knitted rabbit. He hugged her and she lifted him and swung him around, both of them giggled with joy. 'My word, what a big three-year-old you are, a strong man like your daddy!' she said.

Then she turned to his father. 'Hello, Bobby, it's good to see you again. Thanks for coming back to help Meryn.'

'Kitty,' he replied with an awkward smile, shaking her outstretched hand. 'I would never have left her if I hadn't been encouraged to stay away. Someone lied about me being married to put her off. I've always loved the girl, and I did wrong by her, but that is in the past. I have put in a request to remain in Britain – for us to be a family.'

Kitty felt her face flush. She had played a role in him being encouraged to stop seeing Meryn when she heard the rumours about him being a married man. Poor Meryn, caught up in Lewis's lies, and clinging onto a second chance at love, only to be let down again. At least Bobby had proved he did love her and waited for the right time to show his support.

'I hope it works out for you. She deserves happiness and he's a beautiful child. You have another chance at love; I won't stand in your way.'

Bobby grinned. 'She looks to you as her big sister and Wenna as her mother. It looks as if we're family too,' he said.

'It looks that way,' Kitty said with a smile.

Meryn gestured for them to follow her to the private residential side of the inn. Once they were inside the large kitchen, the familiar aroma of baking pasties filled the air, bringing back fond memories for Kitty. She heard Wenna laughing in the bar, and a wave of relaxed pleasure washed over her. Everyone was settled and happy again.

That evening Meryn, Bobby and Kedrick took a walk around the village, and Wenna and Kitty sat in the garden enjoying the fragrant breeze cooling their cheeks and shoulders.

'How's Meryn doing?' Kitty asked Wenna, who was frantically fanning her face with a pamphlet encouraging British soldiers to remain in the regular army. Kitty wondered briefly how many would do so.

'She's a good girl and a wonderful mother. Kedrick is a bright button and as good as gold. He thinks Pots and I are his grandparents and gives us so much joy. Bobby is – believe it or not – good for her too. War turned him into a man. Even Pots has warmed to him.'

Kitty gave a soft sigh. It would make leaving so much easier, knowing her friends were all happy.

Chapter Eleven

Feeling refreshed after a good night's sleep, Kitty looked across the bay from her bedroom window. The clear waters looked inviting as they lapped around the remains of equipment that lay abandoned by the American army which had launched from Trebah in 1944, a time in her life she would never forget.

She shuddered at thoughts of that day. Her and Michael had scrambled across the foreign beaches rescuing the injured. Kitty tried to push back the memories. It was the time Michael was so badly injured that he did not recognise her. She reminded herself he had recovered, and no matter what lay ahead, the man she loved and married was alive – something for which she would be eternally grateful.

Being here in Cornwall was the time to enjoy the company of her friends and paddle in the water with Kedrick. Happy memories were required to settle over the ones that haunted her occasionally.

Equally happy sounds from the kitchen made her smile as she

stepped inside. Wenna, Bobby and Kedrick sat around the table preparing sandwiches, and Meryn decanted lemonade into bottles. Pots stood by the back door puffing on his pipe. The scene warmed Kitty's heart. There was peace in this home, the settled calm of a united family made from fragments of others.

'Morning!' she said cheerfully, and then tapped Meryn on the shoulder, to sign.

'It's going to be a hot one,' Pots said as he accepted a mug of tea from Wenna.

Kitty nodded. 'I'm going to enjoy a paddle today, there's cooler water at Roker Beach and Dovercourt Bay.'

Wenna placed on the table a large bowl of scrambled eggs, a plate of bacon and another with big wedges of fresh bread. Everyone sat down and ate. Kitty filled her heart with the memory, reminding herself to buy a notebook and write everything down. Simple moments to be treasured whenever she felt alone or lost in a personal struggle. Kedrick slipped down from the table and edged onto her lap. No one stopped him, despite Meryn's strict table rules. It was a loving gesture towards his honorary aunt. This was a time for relaxing, enjoying small moments, and Kitty realised it was not just her making memories.

After chores were finished, everyone strolled leisurely along Blackberry Lane towards the sea. Kedrick skipped ahead with his bucket, ready for his beachcombing adventure. The silver shadows danced on the surface of the turquoise blue water, and the sky was clear of clouds.

Kitty slipped her arm through Wenna's, watching Kedrick jump and leap, free from worries and cares. A brief memory from her childhood with her parents before they were killed, and the warmth of the sun on her skin felt the same. She must have enjoyed a day much like this – was it before or after her baby brother was born? She tried to remember, then wondered if it was a memory mixed up with one of her uncle and aunt when they took her into their lives.

'He's a happy little soul,' she said.

'He is that. He's a dream child. Not a naughty bone in his body, and he rarely cries or has a tantrum. Meryn is a good mother and manages well. She rarely asks for help. I admire her.' Wenna sighed. 'Kedrick has the sweetest singing voice, but again, she never shows any sign of frustration that she can't hear him as we do. To hear him sing, she places her hand on his chest – she says the vibrations have a rhythm, and she reads his lips.'

'Oh, that's beautiful, what a wonderful way of appreciating a song. Oh, there he goes!' Kitty said as Kedrick ran full pelt down the slope to the sea, with Meryn chasing him. Again, laughter rang out, and Kitty felt the pull of England and doubted her decision to move.

They walked to the cove where Meryn had suspected Belle of smuggling and reported back to Kitty. They sat on the rocks where she and her friend Jo had spent time together, before they were shipped off to various Red Cross hospitals or medical camps. Cornwall had a special place in her heart, and a small spark of sadness settled inside her chest. Did she really want to leave England?

For the rest of the week they roamed around the villages, prepared picnics and enjoyed the summer days relaxing. In the evenings they sat in the bar or outdoors enjoying the company of other villagers. On the last evening, Kitty could no longer put off telling them all. This would be the last time they would be together. Wenna insisted they call time early and close the bar, so as to enjoy the evening in the residential garden with Kitty.

Bobby and Stanley had joined them, the two men sharing a room overnight to ensure Kitty and Stanley set off early in the morning.

Kitty sat in a deckchair watching Kedrick, and Bobby run around the garden after a ball, with Stanley joining in as best as his prosthetic leg would allow. The laughter filled her ears. Meryn, Wenna and Kitty sat sipping strawberry lemonade. A blackbird tweeted in the late evening and Wenna called for Kedrick to get ready for bed.

When he was washed and changed, the little boy rushed straight to Kitty and flung his arms around her neck. He smelled of fresh air and soap. His warm lips on her cheeks seared her skin with a loving kiss. A precious moment rushed through her body and into her heart.

'Bye bye, darling. Be a good boy for your mummy, Nanny Wenna and Grandy Pots. Listen to Daddy, he is a wise man. Don't forget to keep sending me those lovely drawings. Night-night, sweetheart,' Kitty said and held him close, keeping her tears in check.

Once the adults were seated and a calm chatter about everyday life began, Kitty knew it was now or never to share her news.

'I have something to tell you all,' she said.

Wenna swung her a look, then immediately looked at Kitty's middle.

Kitty shook her head. 'No baby news, Wenna,' she said with a light laugh. 'This is my last night with you all before I leave England,' she added quickly.

Meryn stared at her and frowned.

'Michael, well . . . where do I begin?' Kitty said. 'Michael wants to live in Canada. He's gone a ham-fisted way about it by leaving me.'

There was a gasp from Wenna, Pots and Bobby. Meryn jumped from her seat and pulled out her notepad. The conversation was going faster than she could express herself.

Why did he leave you? Looking for a house? Another woman? she scribbled at great speed.

'No, I don't think there is another woman. I am not sure about the house hunting, but I do know he wants his children to be Canadian born,' Kitty said.

'Why didn't he take you?' Pots asked, his voice carrying a hint of annoyance.

'I don't know, Pots. He sprang it on me one breakfast, told me he wanted his children to be what I took to mean *pure* Canadian. I think I reacted badly. I told him we needed to divorce,' Kitty replied.

'Divorce? Are you out of your mind? I have never met such a solid married couple,' Wenna said loudly, and Pots hushed her with a pat of his hand.

'I thought he meant he wanted children with a Canadian woman, and we couldn't get through the conversation properly. I went to stay with Stanley, and Michael disappeared. Stanley and Smithy are trying to track him down. Stanley?' She looked at her friend for support. The conversation was exhausting her emotions. The explanation and the thought of the goodbye to follow were overwhelming.

'Michael discussed with Smithy and colleagues about

venturing into an oil investment in Canada,' Stanley told the hushed audience. 'Apparently, a town or city out there has struck oil, and it is the ideal time to set up a medical practice and invest in a home. We suspect Michael is heading there, but truthfully, we don't have a clue. I have medical RAF friends who are making enquiries in Canada, and Smithy has sent word to the hospital where Michael was a patient – he mentioned Michael might be under stress and heading to Calgary. Just in case – well, in case he does need medical help. We're waiting for replies, and that's all we can do to help Kitty.' Meryn studied his face, then looked to Kitty.

Kitty gave her a nod of confirmation.

'This investment…' Pots said.

'Husband, quiet!' Wenna said firmly, 'This is no time to talk about investing money. The girl is leaving us. Did you not understand? This is the last time we'll be together.'

Bobby gave a polite cough. 'Does this mean you're prepared to go out there if they find him, Stanley?' he asked.

Stanley nodded. 'I am. I will go wherever Kitty needs to go. I have made arrangements this week to sell properties, and to ensure Fell Hall will always be an orphanage. I gave it up to a board of governors a few years ago, but it still needs funding. This will leave me with money to support us both. Although, in fairness to Michael, he left Kitty with a full purse,' he said.

Kitty looked around the table; the shock was obvious.

'I appreciate I've dropped this bit of news at the last minute, but I didn't want it to overshadow my whole visit. You are my family of sorts, and I need to go, so please, be happy and write to me,' she said quietly.

'I'll not be happy, but I'll write,' Wenna said.

I will write, and try to be happy for you. Bobby and I will save and one day, when Kedrick is older, maybe we will be able to come and see you, Meryn wrote.

'I've secured Kitty and me a place on a flight to Toronto. The Canadian government are flying out Brits to the country, and well, my rank and name helped me get the two of us on the plane. I said I was escorting a Canadian hero's wife out to join him. We'll have a lot of papers to complete by next week, and I might have to fudge a few lines on where Michael is based, but I will get her to him, I promise. Then, it will be up to him. Whatever they decide, Kitty will always have me in her corner,' Stanley said, his voice warm and reassuring, and Kitty knew she was in safe hands. She smiled at her friends.

'Stanley is like my older brother; he has helped me so much as you all know. I don't know if I will ever come back here. It is time for me to start a fresh life, and a new country is an invitation to try a different one. The worst part is that I have to go back home to my uncle and explain this all over again.'

Chapter Twelve

After a painful farewell to the small family in Cornwall, Kitty told Stanley her concerns about moving abroad.

The long drive home provided her with the perfect opportunity to weigh the pros and cons of her situation. By the time they arrived back at Fell Hall, she had received reassurance from Stanley that he would support and fund her return to Great Britain if she felt she could not stay in Canada.

His support meant Kitty felt more confident about breaking her news to her uncle and on impulse packed fresh clothes and set off on another journey. This time to her childhood home. From London, the train chugged and stopped at various stations before pulling slowly into Parkeston Quay, the port station near the main town of Harwich in Essex. A short walk away was her old school, and her uncle's house in Hamilton Street.

The afternoon was fading into early evening, but it was still bright and warm. The familiar smells of smoke, fuel and sea rushed her senses into action, and a tremor of anxiety pressed home.

She was not here for a holiday, but to share life-altering news. Along the short walk down Hamilton Street, she heard children laugh and neighbours call to one another over the fences. It was a comfort blanket around her nervous shoulders; a welcome reminder that she was not a stranger to the community and that her news would not be private for long.

Hesitating at the back door, she wondered whether to knock or step inside. This was her first visit home since her uncle's marriage after her aunt passed away. She chose to open the door and call out.

'Cooee. Anyone home?'

'I'm in the back room,' a woman's voice replied.

It was Doreen, her step-aunt. Kitty put her bags to one side, and walked through the narrow kitchen and into what Doreen referred to as the back room, where Kitty had sat eating many delicious meals, played games and shared time with her Aunt Lil and Uncle Frank over a jigsaw. The room's colours made her take a deep breath as she stepped inside. It had been redecorated, and its familiarity had gone. Her aunt's knick-knacks were no longer on the mantelpiece, and the table was round, not a long pine one scrubbed for years to a shine. Doreen had made it her home, and rightly so.

'Kitty! Well, you're a sight for sore eyes. I thought it was next door coming to get her ironing. Come in, sit down. Frank will be home shortly, he's just closing the hall.' Doreen gave Kitty a warm embrace, leaving the fragrance of peach blossom talcum powder in the air as she moved. Lily of the Valley had been the fragrance that lingered in the home when her aunt was alive. A pang of loss nipped at Kitty's heart.

Kitty sat in a chair she did not recognise, and a sense of no longer belonging overwhelmed her as she glanced at the unfamiliar items dotted around the room. Items her late aunt would have classified as garish.

'This heatwave has made Frank happy. You know him, he loves to be outdoors. He spoke about going out on one of the fishing trawlers to earn a few shillings. I think he and your dad used to when they were younger. My boy is visiting soon, and he will go out with him, they get on well.' Doreen careered through the conversation without giving Kitty the opportunity to speak. The mention of her uncle going out to sea, knowing Kitty's parents and baby brother had drowned on a boat trip, had obviously not registered with Doreen as insensitive. The woman lived for gossip and offloaded many a scandal to Kitty. Unable to deal with more news of bed-hopping neighbours and the sins of others, she excused herself and used the outside lavatory. She took time to stroll around the garden, noticing the plants they had put in as a family were still in the same place, and was glad that her uncle's domain was untouched by his forceful second wife.

'Who let you through the gate?' Kitty's heart skipped when she heard her uncle's voice. She turned around and watched him prop his bicycle against the wall.

'Uncle. It's good to see you. I thought I would surprise you, but now I realise I should have called ahead,' Kitty said as her uncle removed his bicycle clips from around his ankles, pulled a comb from his pocket and combed back his oil-creamed hair. Kitty smiled inwardly; the actions warmed her heart; some things never changed. She recalled days like this when she was younger, waiting patiently to see what treat he had brought home for her.

'I'm only here for tomorrow, then I must head back,' Kitty reassured him. 'Are you coping with the changes inside?' she tentatively asked. 'I know how you dislike change, and well, I can see there's a lot that's happened since I was last home.'

Her uncle shrugged. 'Doreen, like Lil was, is a homemaker. Their tastes are different, and sometimes I wonder if Dor is colour-blind, but she's a good woman. Kind and loving. I am happy, if that's what is worrying you. I am very happy,' he said and tapped her arm with affection.

'That's good to hear,' Kitty said. 'I came home to speak with you about something important.'

'Is it something that can be discussed over a brown ale indoors?' Frank asked with a wink.

Kitty laughed. 'Some things never change,' she said.

Once inside, her uncle picked up her bag.

'I'm glad this is not heavy. I've been saving something for you, and you can take it back with you,' he told her. 'Dor, Kitty is staying for the night, love.' He was still very much in charge of business in his home.

'I guessed as much and just popped a pretty eiderdown on. Not that it's cold, but it's nicer, don't you think?' Doreen directed her question to Kitty.

'Thank you. I am sorry I have arrived unannounced, but I need to speak to you and then get back to Brancepeth.'

When all three were sitting comfortably, and polite conversation was out of the way, Kitty's uncle looked at her with concern.

'Where's Michael, working?' he asked. Kitty heard suspicion in his voice.

She shook her head.

'No. He has finished at the surgery. We no longer live there.'

Kitty took a moment to compose herself and think about what she was going to say next. 'I am staying with Stanley, and Michael… Well, Michael has disappeared.'

'Disappeared? What the bloody he—' he spluttered.

'Frank…' Doreen warned.

'We think he has gone to Canada.' A wave of embarrassment swept through Kitty. She could not reassure her uncle about where her own husband was.

'You think he's gone to Canada,' her uncle said slowly. 'Did he run away?'

Again, Kitty took time to reply. She sipped her drink and placed the glass on the table, her hands shaking. She could no longer hold off from breaking her news.

'He told me he wanted to return to Canada, where his children could be born Canadian.' She shook her head at Doreen, whose face had suddenly lit up with the mention of children. 'We had planned to have a family, but he said he wanted them to be pure Canadian, and well, that's not going to happen with me in the picture, so I suggested we divorced.'

Kitty's heart banged against her ribs, and her breath released in a rush. Her uncle's face was a vibrant red, and Doreen's was pale.

'Divorce?!' her uncle shouted.

'Frank. The windows,' Doreen said and rushed to close the sash window facing the garden.

'Now the neighbours will think I've asked you for one. Keep your voice down, dear. It's not going to help Kitty. Now sweetheart, why did you think divorce is the answer?' she asked Kitty, her voice calm and inviting an answer.

'Because I am British, not the Canadian I thought Michael

longed for. But Stanley, who has been marvellous and looked after me for weeks—'

'Weeks? So, this is not a new thing then? Michael has been gone for weeks?' Her uncle paced the floor in frustration.

'His friends have tried to find him for me through letters and telegrams, and we have an idea after talking to his colleague. He is most likely in Canada, seeking a place to invest in oil and start up his own surgery,' Kitty said.

'That's all well and ruddy good, but what about you? You're homeless with him giving up his job, and husbandless. Do you have money or has he taken it all?' Her uncle's voice now had an edge of anger to it, and Kitty was beginning to regret telling him.

She shifted in her seat. 'He took half of our savings, and left me a good sum of money, more than I was aware we had. There was no note.'

Doreen encouraged Frank to sit down.

'I bet he was shocked at the mention of divorce, dear. Are you sure that's what you want?' she asked softly.

Kitty shook her head.

'No, the last thing I want is to lose Michael. Stanley made me see sense. We went over the conversation Michael and I had, and he thinks Michael meant he just wants his children born in Canada, and for us to live there. He's not wanting a Canadian wife. But he went before I could ask him.'

The silence in the room was uncomfortable. Now she had to tell her uncle about the next stage of her journey to reconnect with her husband.

'We have a plan – me and Stanley – we are going to Canada in a week's time. He's funding the trip, and escorting me across the country to where we think Michael might be. Stanley has put his affairs in order, and will find a place to live. If we can't find my husband, or if he does not want me in his life…' she paused, fighting back tears at the thought 'I will either return to England or stay there. Stanley is going to live there and climb mountains, apparently.' She gave a small laugh.

Doreen gave a soft gasp, and Kitty's uncle simply sat looking at her.

'Am I dreaming this?' he said, and ran his fingers through his hair, disturbing its neatness.

'Sadly, you're not. I'm sorry, uncle, I never dreamed I would be leaving England to look for Michael, but I am his wife, and I have to correct my misunderstanding. If he still wants me in his life, then I will be doing the right thing.'

'He should have left a note,' Doreen muttered.

'He should have taken better care of my girl, that's what he should have done. He promised me.' Kitty's uncle walked across the room. 'And as for you suggesting a divorce…'

'I'm sorry,' Kitty whispered.

'I suppose it is the right time to give you the suitcase. Wait there,' he instructed and left the room.

'I'll look after him,' said Doreen. 'He has grown used to you not being around, but it is going to be different with you out of the country. You must promise to write and let us know what is happening. It will help him.' Kitty could see how much her uncle's new wife loved him.

Carrying a small suitcase into the room, her uncle looked at her.

'This is filled with your childhood. When we were sorting out the attic, I came across it and was going to give it to you the next time we were together. It's the right time to give it to you now, considering…' He laid the case on the table.

He clicked the locks open and stood back for Kitty to open it.

It was packed full. On top was a white knitted item. She lifted it out and shook it.

'It was your christening blanket. Your mum knitted it. We buried your brother in his,' he said sadly. 'Lil wanted to give it to you, but the moment never arose thanks to the war. We thought it might upset you if we gave it to you when you were little, so, rightly or wrongly, we held it back.'

Several items brought back a fleeting memory, but when Kitty lifted out a red beret, she held it to her nose and sniffed.

'This was Mummy's,' she said, not registering the word she had used. 'I remember she wore it every Sunday when we went to church and for our walk along the promenade.'

Her uncle coughed; it was an emotional moment for them both.

'She left it behind the day they … well, she said it might blow away on the boat,' he said.

Doreen touched Kitty's shoulder. 'Put it on. I bet it will suit you. She would want it worn. It looks like good quality felt.'

'It was a present from your father that he gave her when you were born. He bought you this, and your brother that,' her uncle said as he handed her a small teddy bear and pointed to a wooden boat. 'He was a thoughtful man. He always walked in with a packet of baccy and flowers. Generous soul.'

Kitty went to the mirror and smiled. 'I remember my mum used to plait her hair too.'

'It was to keep the beret in place; she had a small head and had to grip it in place, which is why she didn't take it that day,' her uncle said.

Kitty placed the beret on her head and knew she would have to pin it in place, too. Then she laughed. 'I remember now. She plaited my hair and let me wear it to church the week before…'

Kitty gulped back the emotional memory. 'I had begged her and begged her to wear it, and she said it could be my birthday treat!'

Doreen clapped her hands. 'How wonderful, what a lovely memory. Now you can wear it with pride. Wear it to Canada, take her with you.'

The atmosphere lightened.

'There are a few items of your father's in there. A couple of silver fountain pens, a leather wallet – our father gave us one when we first went out to work – a woollen scarf our mother knitted for him, and booties she knitted for you and little Ian. There's a lock of yours and his hair, simple things. I've wrapped the breakables. Lil and I didn't know what to keep for you, and we probably got rid of things we shouldn't have, but it was a difficult time,' her uncle said, his voice heavy with sadness.

Kitty walked to him and kissed his cheek.

'You did everything right for me and by me. I could not have asked for a better childhood after losing them. Your brother had the best brother and sister-in-law, and I had the best second set of parents.' She kissed his cheek again. 'I can't take a lot to Canada, but I will take this case and the memories that go with it. All I ask from you is for a pipe of yours, and something of Lil's, and please, a little something from you, Doreen. That way I will never feel far from my family.'

Chapter Thirteen

After they had spoken about her future, her uncle insisted he would talk to Stanley about wiring her a sum of money when she arrived in Canada. He had saved it for her cousin, his son, who had been killed in action. He wanted Kitty to have it to help set up her new life.

Kitty was touched when Doreen gave her a small package.

'Don't open it now or we'll both be in tears again. It's just a little something to build your heirloom chest,' she said.

With their blessing to go, and a promise to return if Canada did not provide the life she hoped for, Kitty went to bed. She lay back and thought about life as a child in the house, and gave thanks for her uncle and aunt. Doreen could never replace her aunt, but she certainly had a place in Kitty's heart.

The following day was painful. The goodbye hugs were long.

'Right, I have work to do. Have a safe journey, my girl, and don't forget to write. I'm off, Dor.' He pecked his wife on the cheek and patted Kitty's as he walked past her. Choked with emotion, Kitty tried hard to hold back the tears. Doreen was crying enough for them all.

'I'll make sure he has his favourite supper. He'll be all right. Now, don't miss your bus, dear.' Doreen hugged her again, and Kitty took a moment to inhale her step-aunt's violet perfume. A woman she barely knew, but would always be grateful for. She had a big heart and it was obvious she loved Kitty's uncle.

Kitty took a bus to Dovercourt Bay station, and placed her bags with the left luggage porter. She visited a florist, made a purchase, walked the hill to the seafront and along the promenade, where she placed the flowers on the water in memory of her family. She took a moment to stand beside the old lighthouse where she and Michael had once kissed. The warm, gentle breeze stroked her cheeks and dried her tears. A walk up the incline to Dovercourt Park gave her a view of the promenade below, and as she looked across the water, watching the flowers drift out on the tide, planes flew overhead, casting shadows on the blue-grey sea.

A farewell flypast could not have been planned any better than that moment. She stood a while and watched them dip and dive across the water. There was no fear, no running for cover as in the past, and, as she looked about, she noticed others were watching the pilots in awe as well.

There was a long way to go, but life was moving forward and away from the horrors of what was now known as World War Two. She watched a group of boys fling their arms wide and run around the green, pretending to be planes. Instead of using the firing gun sounds, they laughed and whooped loudly in joy. Two young women waved their handkerchiefs in the air, and an older man stood saluting, his back straight and his shoulders broad. Kitty guessed he had fought against the enemy in the Great War.

She also stood in gratitude until she could no longer see the planes on the horizon. She walked on, taking in the views across to Felixstowe, past the stone lookout and the Stone Pier, then continued into Harwich town. Kitty smiled hello at anyone who gave her the time of day, and passed the many public houses where the fishermen gathered after their hard work at sea. She watched from the Ha'penny Pier; the post-war clean-up was still taking place, and nothing would be the same again. All they could do was hope that everyone would pull together and that world peace would bring sense and prosperity to a shattered world.

At peace with herself, and seeing that all was well in her hometown, Kitty took from her pocket the package Doreen had given her and tugged the twine free. Inside the box was a silver bracelet. A simple delicate chain, which fitted around her wrist and caught the sunlight as she twisted her arm. It was a thoughtful and precious gift.

Eventually, it was time to take the train back to London, then on to Durham. Thankful that she would not endure such a painful parting again, Kitty clung onto her small case as if it held gold bars. It was heavy but precious, and she was not going to leave it behind. Her treasures would travel with her. When Stanley met her at Durham station, he did not mention the extra case or the weight. He asked a few questions about her trip, the health of her uncle and Doreen, and hoped she did not meet too many obstacles when she told them she was emigrating.

Kitty liked that about Stanley: he understood the need to let her grieve leaving her family, and would find the right time to boost her back into life.

At the orphanage, the atmosphere was lively – as always – with children and staff preparing for bedtime. Unlike state-run orphanages, the rules here were not strict, allowing the children's laughter to fill the air. For Kitty, observing their playful antics and the staff's warm responses brought her joy, as it demonstrated that happiness had returned to the children's lives, giving the place a sense of home rather than just an institution.

Stanley asked one of Daphne's adopted sons to take Kitty's bags to her room and ushered Kitty into his private sitting room.

'The boys have thrived with Daphne taking them under her wing,' Kitty commented as she closed the door, 'much like the Gaskin brothers when I first came here. They were a cheeky pair, now they're moving into adulthood, and there's nothing they don't know about farming. They were lucky with their adopted parents. I love receiving their letters.'

'That pair of scallywags kept us on our toes, but they have grown into fine young men. I am glad they still keep in touch. I have to ask, how are you, Kitty? You were quiet in the car.' Kitty heard the concern in Stanley's voice. She shrugged.

'I'm sad when I think of the goodbyes I have made, as they might be my last. I intend to commit to Canada, and my uncle, well, he's not getting any younger,' she replied.

Stanley went to the drinks cabinet, took out two crystal glasses, poured a generous measure of brandy into each and handed one to her.

'Drink; it will help you sleep. You're doing the right thing, but you are allowed to be sad, too. Tomorrow, we've an appointment for our medical card, and then we must collect your passport. I also have an appointment with a solicitor in Durham. This is to ensure that if anything happens to me, you are protected and financially secure.' Stanley raised his glass.

Kitty looked at him in surprise.

'I am not your responsibility, Stanley. I am Michael's wife. I appreciate – no, *more* than appreciate – your help, but you cannot spend your money on me,' she said with passion.

Stanley leaned back in his chair, shook his head at her and then leaned forward, keeping eye contact.

'Jenny would want me to do this for you. She was fond of you, as I am, and it's played on my mind. I owe you a lot since you moved my bed around at the hospital, encouraging me to walk and giving me the incentive to live again. Without you, I would not be as able and independent. Let me do this for you. I have no children, wife or siblings. But you're like a sister to me – just like we told Mrs Charlesworth, only it's not a lie – I do think a lot of you and want you to inherit my worldly goods.' He spoke with conviction. 'All I ask is that you give me a decent burial when the time comes.'

'Enough! We have to live first,' Kitty almost shouted, his words frightening her.

'You're right. I can't wait to see your face when we land,' Stanley replied, and his laugh lightened the mood. 'The first official passengers will fly next month, in August. My friends are now pilots for the airlines, transporting them – and us. We're on the trial trip for one of them.'

Kitty knew Stanley well enough to recognise when he chose to change the subject; there was no point in continuing the discussion. His mind was made up, and nothing she said would change it. She refrained from mentioning that he might meet someone in Canada and want to leave them his legacy, knowing he would argue that it was unlikely to happen. Instead, she joined him in the new conversation about their upcoming trip.

'I am nervous, but excited at the same time. I'm putting my

trust in him – and you. What am I doing, Stanley?' she said with a giggle.

She still could not believe that in a matter of days she would be inside a plane looking down on the world.

'You, my dear, are going to find Michael and live happily ever after. If that doesn't work out, you will have a comfortable life exploring Canada with me by your side. That's what you're going to do,' Stanley said. They spent the rest of the evening discussing what might happen once they landed in their new country.

In her bedroom, Kitty laid out her clothes. She had several dresses that were heavy with their underskirts, and decided to leave them for Daphne and the other ladies to alter them for the children. She lifted out her mother's beret and set it to one side. She would wear it with pride when she landed in Canada.

She unwrapped a photograph and gazed at her parents, the handsome couple smiling at the camera holding hands. Her mother's belly was rounded, and Kitty guessed she was the child inside. Her aunt had often told her she had inherited her father's eyes and her mother's heart-shaped face, and now she could see it was true.

Although the photo was black and white, she could see they both had the same hair shade and knew it was the same as hers, thanks to her aunt. It saddened her that this picture had not been part of her life until her last visit home, but she understood how difficult it must have been for her uncle. The two brothers had been very close, and he was heartbroken over his loss. Her aunt and uncle probably tucked the photograph away in the case and forgot about it. Bringing Kitty and her cousin up was their priority. Then, when their son was killed, his photograph was the one they focused on. She had promised to send her uncle one of her in Canada, and wondered if it would replace her wedding photograph on his mantlepiece. He was angry with Michael, despite her asking him not to jump to conclusions and to remember she had played a part in their separation.

'Well, Mum and Dad, I am taking you on the journey of my lifetime. I am confused, frightened and sad, but I will hold onto courage and hope with you and Stanley by my side.' She kissed the image.

It was sad that she did not have a photograph of her baby brother, but she had a nugget of a memory when they let her hold him soon after his birth. She had never known him as a brother, just as a baby who appeared at breakfast one morning. He was gone from her life just as quickly as he arrived. At five, she had not understood death or loss. She did understand confusion and sadness. It had taken a lot of patience on her aunt's part to help her through those feelings. When her cousin died, her aunt was torn up with her own grief, and Kitty had to deal with her own sadness as best she could. It felt as if she had lost another brother. The loss of her aunt was another traumatic moment for Kitty and she wished she had her aunt's voice of wisdom whispering in her ear as she wondered whether she was doing the right thing in going to Canada.

She closed the small suitcase, zipped the new valise Daphne had given her and stored them with her kitbag. Everything was in place. The formalities of the following day would make it official, and Kitty would learn more about her husband's country and begin an unexpected adventure.

Chapter Fourteen

While she pottered around her bedroom, Kitty thought back to the conversation she had had earlier with Stanley and how she had been worried about not knowing what would be at the other end of their flight.

In his usual reassuring way, he had reminded her that they were born not knowing what the world they had arrived in was like, so it would be a learning curve for them both. They must remember not to forget one another's needs and expectations, in order to make the path smooth for them both.

A letter from her uncle sat on her dresser. It was marked in capital letters that it was not to be opened until she had arrived in Canada. Writing letters was not like him, so she suspected it would be an emotional read. She was tempted to open it beforehand, but she did not want to break her promise to her uncle, so she put it in her handbag's side pocket – out of sight, out of mind.

Was that how it was with Michael? She was out of his sight, so it was easier for him to put her out of his mind. It disappointed her that he had not written. All post would have been redirected from their home to Stanley's, but nothing had arrived. She had written to him every day, expressing her emotions at the moment of writing, describing the process she was going through in order to find him, and what she wanted to explain to him when she did. Not having anywhere to send them, she tied them together and kept them in her suitcase. One day, she hoped to give them to him, along with an apology for being so hot-headed and putting their marriage in a dire situation. She knew he had played his part by walking out, but if she apologised, and he realised that he meant so much to her that she had given up her life in Great Britain to be with him, they might have a chance to start afresh.

From downstairs, the trill of the telephone in the hallway made her jump. She listened for children calling out, disturbed in their sleep, but all she heard were footsteps and muttering from one of the orphanage staff. Kitty glanced at her clock; it was ten forty-five.

Who on earth would be telephoning at this time of night?

She listened to Stanley's muffled voice as he spoke down the telephone. He did not call out for anyone or put the telephone down, so she guessed it was private to him and had nothing to do with a new influx of orphans. Knowing she was not needed to help with anything, she readied herself for bed.

Kitty undressed, washed the heat from her skin and slipped into her cotton nightdress. She went to the window to enjoy the cooler air. Stars and the moon shone against a navy sky, and she stood wondering if Michael was also looking at the moon, and thinking of her. During the war, when they were apart, their letters often mentioned looking at the moon at a particular time and sending love to one another through the stars. She closed her eyes and let a tear trickle down her cheek before batting it away, but others flowed. It would be easy to cry away her days and sob through the night, but she had to remain focused and in control. Her emotional state was fragile, but her heart was strong and her mind determined.

Downstairs went quiet, and Kitty settled into bed, leaving the curtains open. She could still see the stars and focused on a formation close to the moon. Soon her eyelids felt heavy, and she gave in to sleep.

About an hour later, a noise disturbed her, and the sound of a car on the gravel drive startled her awake. She slipped out of bed and peered down. A figure stood looking up at the sky before facing the front door, where a light blazed across the driveway. She couldn't make out who it was – not even if they were male or female. Kitty thought back to the war, when the light would never have happened – or, if it had, a member of the Home Guard or police would have soon called for it to be turned off.

The outline of Stanley holding out his hand suggested that one of his old colleagues or a friend had come with a message or to stay overnight. She watched as Stanley ushered them indoors.

She listened for voices in the hallway, but heard nothing and guessed they had gone into the large sitting room at the back of the house. When Stanley couldn't sleep, he often sat in there reading. Climbing into bed, Kitty fell back to sleep until the cockerel and other birds called out the start of the following day.

Rousing herself, Kitty remembered Stanley's late-night visitor and wondered if another guest would be at the breakfast table. Instead of keeping her dressing gown on to go down and help Daphne and the others prepare the children's food as she often did, she dressed herself in one of the few dresses she had held back, then slipped quietly downstairs to the kitchen.

'Morning, Daphne, another warm night,' she said as she tied a pinafore around her dress.

''Twas that,' Daphne replied, stirring a large pot of porridge. Kitty smiled: come sun or snow, Daphne always insisted porridge was the best start to the day for the young children.

'I wonder if they have porridge in Canada,' she said suddenly.

Daphne stopped stirring and looked at her in amusement.

'Ee bairn, I think they must. Many Scots are living there now, and they would insist on it. You can't get through the day without a bowl of porridge, a sprinkle of salt and sugar, and warm milk,' she said, her face serious.

Kitty tried not to smile; the thought of a row of Scottish men and women demanding porridge oats was enough to give her a cartoon vision.

'It's oats. Canada must grow oats,' she said.

'I wonder how many other things they might not have that I enjoy,' Kitty sighed. 'I hope they have—' She jumped when a female voice cut in from behind her.

'Oh, they will have plenty of exciting things for you to find – there's a whole different world out there.'

She swung around and came face to face with her friend Jo.

'Jo, what are you doing here?' Kitty exclaimed as she looked her up and down in amazement. 'You look incredible, wonderful.'

Joan Norfolk looked more feminine than she had ever seen. Car-greased overalls or uniforms were all she'd seen Jo wear over the years. This Jo wore a black skirt suit and white blouse. Her hair was longer and pulled back into a neat bun. She also wore coral lipstick and mascara. The new image was a surprise, but Kitty could see her dear nursing friend had not lost her mischievous grin.

Kitty went to hug her, but to her surprise Jo took a step back, then tapped her jacket and moved it to one side before embracing Kitty.

'Gun. Sorry, I forgot it was there. I'm so used to nodding off between shifts with it in my pocket,' she whispered out of Daphne's earshot.

Kitty looked at her, puzzled. 'Gun?' she asked. Jo shook her head as Daphne moved around the kitchen.

'A fleeting visit, I'm afraid – official bodyguard duties for a VIP in London, hence the new fancy uniform. I can't say much more except that I now work in a new, important security role. I telephoned to speak to you, and Stanley briefed me on what had happened. I have twenty-four hours off, but must return in good time to fly home.'

'VIP? Are they American?' Kitty asked in awe.

Jo tapped the side of her nose.

'Can't say, but I live a good life in the United States. Sorry I can't bring the orphans doughnuts anymore. No Donut Dollie war duties for me.' Jo laughed as she spoke. Kitty knew her American connection with the entertainment and coffee van was how Jo was approached to work with the French Resistance. She eventually met Virginia, who preferred to be called Gina during her work in France. Their friendship became so strong that Jo accepted an invitation to work for the American government and moved to Gina's home.

Daphne walked over and smiled at her. 'The memories of your visits and the children licking their lips are still with me. Are you here for the night?' she asked.

Jo shook her head. 'No, thank you for asking though, but it took me over five hours to get here. I will have a couple with Kitty, and then head back.'

'A pot of tea and a bowl of porridge coming right up. I might even find you a slice of Victoria sponge to take with you.' Daphne handed them each a tray of food and drink. 'Go to the back sitting room; it's quiet at this time of day. The staff are dealing with the children.'

Doing as she suggested, Kitty set the table while Jo took her gun to her car and stored it away.

Kitty and Jo sat and ate their porridge by the window, looking out at the vast garden filled with flowers, fruit trees and vegetables.

'I remember when you first came here. I thought Stanley was a posh snob, but he soon proved he wasn't. Jenny was a lovely woman. And you're always happy here,' Jo said, pushing her empty bowl away from her.

'It's my healing place. Whenever I need help, I come to find Stanley; he never lets me down with his wise words. He's been incredible since Michael disappeared, and now he's moving to Canada with me, it will—'

Jo raised her hand to stop Kitty talking.

'Wait, Stanley never said Michael had left you – disappeared. He said you were moving to Canada, and I assumed you and Michael were going together. Is Michael out there now? What's going on, Kit?' Jo's voice was filled with concern. 'I rang to say I was on my way to visit you both, but the operator said the line was disconnected. I checked with Stanley, and that's when he told me to come here, that you were living here. I assumed he meant both of you.'

Kitty looked down at her hands.

'It's a long story, but basically, Michael wants his children to be pure Canadian, and I am British, which means they won't be what he wants. I mentioned divorce, and although he looked shaken up about it, he seemed to have decided it is the right thing for us both, because he disappeared on me,' Kitty said in a rush.

Jo finished drinking her tea and stood up from the table. She walked over to the window and looked outside.

'You guys were okay when I left,' she said, 'married, and settled.'

'You sound very American, Jo,' Kitty said, deflecting her friend's words.

Jo tutted.

'Divorce. It sounds dramatic, Kitty. No wonder he ran,' she said bluntly.

Kitty jumped to her feet, making the dishes clatter against one another. She watched Jo turn to look at her.

'This is not my fault! It was a misunderstanding, but I did not care what nationality my children would be; he did,' Kitty said loudly.

Jo pointed her finger at Kitty and waved it about. She used this gesture when they trained together; it was always over a situation between Kitty and Michael. Jo had a way of working things out with Kitty without allowing her to break down in tears, facing the issue and working through it together.

'That's because you were in your own country, and your

children would be British. It never bothered you that their father would be Canadian, but Michael must have considered it, and although he was happy with an English wife, he possibly wanted to reconnect with Canada. Maybe it's why he wants to return – to reconnect, I dunno, with himself?'

Kitty opened her mouth to speak, but Jo stopped her, and Kitty remained silent as her friend continued. 'Listen to me. As orphans, you were the luckier one of the two. He has nobody in the world. All he has is his Canadian identity, which is tucked away in England. Who knows – maybe he's feeling lonely for his fellow countrymen. He's been here a long time and even joined our army to fit in with his colleagues. The injury and subsequent return to Canada during the war must have sparked his desire to rediscover himself. But I know he loves you. When you mentioned divorce, he probably took it to mean the marriage was over.'

Jo sighed. 'Jeez, it's easier watching over the presi—my boss. Sorting out affairs of the heart was never my forte. I am too outspoken. Listen. Go to Canada. I am across the border in the US, so if it doesn't work out, I am there for you.'

'Stanley's moving out there with me,' Kitty said bluntly.

Jo sat down, clearly shocked.

'What? He's moving with you? Is this your reason for wanting a divorce? You and Stanley?' she asked, biting her lip and frowning.

'No!' Kitty said, shocked that Jo asked the question. 'He wants something more from life than sitting around here. I was going to look for Michael, and a joke about mountain climbing triggered a serious conversation about starting over in Canada.' She gave Jo a look of disbelief. 'Whatever happens, Stanley will be part of my life out there. He's a good man, but he hasn't had a life since Jenny died. He's like my big brother, you know that. He and Michael are good friends, too. There's no romance or hidden agenda. How could you ask such a thing!'

Jo put her hands up in surrender to Kitty's outburst.

'I apologise. But it comes from a good place. I hope you make a go of things and find Michael. Please write to me when you arrive. When do you sail?' she asked.

Chapter Fifteen

Kitty shuddered at the memory the word 'sail' had triggered. The journey to complete rescue missions in Operation Overlord, on the Normandy beaches in 1944, was not a pleasant sailing day out. Nor were the days when she learned how her parents died.

'Fly. We fly out in two days. It's on one of the planes the Canadian government is using to fly out British immigrants in August. Stanley's friend is the pilot on his test flight out of Heston Aerodrome – somewhere in Middlesex.'

Jo gave a low whistle.

'He's got his uses,' she remarked with a smile.

Kitty giggled. 'He does, and he is also a determined man. He approached everyone with connections to get us onto the flight.'

'I can't believe he is giving all of this up,' Jo said, expressing with her hands that she meant the house. 'Has he got property in Canada?'

Kitty laughed. 'Neither of us has anywhere to stay yet.

We have a long train journey first, and then when we have arrived in a town – city, I don't know; all I know is its name, Calgary – once we get there, we'll find lodgings to begin our search for Michael, and a place for Stanley to settle. We think that's the area where Michael's headed, because of an oil investment,' she said.

'Michael, an oil baron? Am I dreaming all of this, Kitty? It's like something out of a novel,' Jo said with a shake of her head, frowning. 'Will you be okay? I mean, the last time we spoke, you upped and left at the hint of you joining us in America. Are you sure you can cope with being hundreds of miles away from your uncle? If Michael rejects you and Stanley stays, you will be alone in dealing with everything. You're strong, but I'm worried, Kit.'

Just as Kitty went to respond, Stanley called her name from behind the door and knocked.

'Come in, Stanley. It's quite safe,' Kitty said and laughed. She was relieved that he had halted the conversation.

Stanley entered the room and glanced first at Jo, then at Kitty.

'Morning. Enjoy your surprise, Kitty?' he said, smiling. 'Did you get any sleep, Jo?'

'It's a lovely surprise, although I've shocked Jo with my news,' Kitty said.

'I slept well enough, but it is too quiet for me. I'm used to noise and voices. City life,' Jo replied, and just as she did so, the children filed downstairs, chatting amongst themselves.

'The children understand their mission,' Stanley joked and sat at the table.

Everyone laughed as the noise grew louder in the hallway.

'Daphne is feeding me before I leave. If you're still hungry, there will be enough for ten on this table soon. You are most welcome to join me.' Stanley offered Jo a seat.

'I've eaten, thanks. I hear you are joining Kitty on a new adventure.'

'Got to pass the medical first,' Stanley replied.

'I'm sure you will pass. Kitty is fortunate to have you at her side. Other war brides are sailing out to the unknown alone.'

'I hadn't considered myself a war bride until Stanley brought home the first batch of papers. We've had to bend a few rules because we don't know where Michael is, so keep your fingers crossed I don't get sent home on a turnaround flight. I have a booklet about how to help myself integrate as a war bride. It says I must keep busy and live as a Canadian, and that's fine with me. Now, I should get these to the kitchen,' Kitty said, collecting the crockery from the table. Jo moved in front of her and opened the door, then returned to Stanley.

Kitty left them chatting and returned to the kitchen to wash their dishes. She noticed a cloth bag with a note for Jo from Daphne – a few British homemade treats. Kitty smiled and thought about what she would miss when she moved to Canada. The pampering love she received from Daphne was definitely at the top of her list, along with some of her tasty dishes. She made a mental note to ask Daphne for recipes to take with her.

An hour later, she and Jo said their farewells. Kitty was grateful for the visit as it was an opportunity to rekindle their deep friendship face to face. Writing letters never allowed her to explain why she ran out on Jo at the end of the war. It was hard to explain that she had feared Jo would die when she worked for the Resistance, and then seeing her move on with Gina, and worrying about their relationship and what legal issues it would bring about for Jo in America, was too much to take in, and Kitty had walked out on her.

Jo had drawn a rough outline of her schedule for the rest of the year, and a telephone number where Kitty or Stanley could reach her. She told them she had connections with Canadian security forces and promised to approach them if Kitty struggled to find Michael, but would only act if Kitty asked. She invited them both to visit her and Gina for a celebration she called Thanksgiving, a few weeks before Christmas.

Kitty's life was to change in much the same way as had Jo's. Jo admitted that she might have struggled without Gina's influence. Kitty found it hard to think Jo would struggle anywhere in the world, but understood the nerves behind making such a drastic change in lifestyle and leaving all that you know behind.

'Feeling ready to complete the challenge of emigrating?' Stanley said, touching her shoulder as they watched Jo drive away.

Giving a last wave as Jo drove out of view, Kitty remained staring ahead, holding her back straight and flexing her neck. Jo's visit, as welcome as it was, had added to the pressure on Kitty. She had no clue how far her money would go in Canada, and if she would ever be able to afford to travel outside of the country. Her thoughts were all over the place, with obstacles and questions popping up daily.

'I hope I see her again. We have a long way to go before I will cross any border out of Canada. Michael is my priority, and so are you,' Kitty said.

Stanley gave a loud tut. '*You* should be your priority until we get there and find him. I am mine. I will secure a home for us until we find him. I don't want you fussing over me either. I will cope. I have proved that already.'

Kitty leaned her head against his shoulder. 'I understand,

Stanley. I struggle with not caring for others. It almost feels selfish to think only about myself. I will try, I promise.'

Stanley patted her shoulder. 'You allow the nurse in you to take over your life. It is not selfish, it is self-preservation, and important.'

'Let's get ready for the medical and fetch my passport. It is time for me to toughen up,' Kitty said, turning around and facing the house.

'Kitty, you're one of the toughest women I have had the pleasure of meeting. I am proud to call you my friend,' Stanley said.

'Stop. No more trying to make me cry, Stanley,' Kitty said and gave a semi-forced laugh before she became emotional again. Being overwhelmed and frightened was exhausting, and she made a promise to herself to gain control, do as Stanley suggested and begin looking out for herself. But to do that she needed to regain the emotional stamina that got her through many missions during wartime.

Chapter Sixteen

Having performed star jumps, touched her toes and proved her health was at its peak, Kitty sat waiting for Stanley to appear from his medical room.

Her nerves twitched; they both knew she would have to travel alone if he were turned down from entering Canada. Stanley had told her the flight would take over ten hours. His friend had warned him of extremely cold winter temperatures and bears wandering the forests, all of which he relayed to Kitty. He wanted her to know the obstacles ahead and not go into the journey without understanding the risks and dangers. Michael had been the same when they went into crumbling buildings during the war and crawled near split gas pipes to rescue people.

On the first formal rescue, he warned her of the consequences of a bomb attack and gave her the option of remaining in the medical tent. Kitty had never feared the rescues; she understood the risks and put all thoughts of possible death or injury to herself to the back of her mind.

It had to be done for the sake of those trapped in the buildings. Now she used the same mental strength to move forward in her search.

Stubbornness, her uncle had called it when she was younger. Kitty had never stepped away from helping others, and after Stanley's advice earlier, she had decided to think of the trip to Canada as another mission. One that would help her fix her life, and find out if fate had a plan for her, or if she would walk away from a disastrous search.

A door clicked open further down the corridor, and a stern-faced Stanley stepped out of a room. He limped more than usual, and Kitty feared the worst. She rose from her seat but did not approach him, knowing he would dismiss her concern as fussing.

She stayed quiet as he joined her.

'They gave me the green light to go, but didn't make it easy. Apparently, I will be able to learn to ski if I am careful, so that mountain climbing idea I had won't be off the menu,' he said and earned a shush from a nurse when his belly laugh echoed down the corridor.

'A green light and skiing? It's really happening, Stanley. This time next week, we'll be at our destination and looking for somewhere to stay. I can't believe it!' Kitty said in a hushed voice.

Stanley stretched his legs and back, then smiled.

'Once we have your passport, we're finished with the planning. It's good to have friends in high places,' Stanley said and gave her a grin.

'You have a lot of friends in high places, and luckily for us, one who is happy to be thousands of feet in the air,' Kitty replied.

The warm air when they stepped outside reminded them that

the heatwave was still in full swing. Taking their time, they strolled to the car parked in the shade.

'Will you be able to drive in Canada?' Kitty asked, the question suddenly popping into her head as he adjusted his seat.

'I thought the same, especially as I am not taking this beauty,' he replied and stroked the steering wheel of his beloved car.

'We will eventually live in cowboy country, so maybe a horse and cart will be the answer,' Kitty joked, 'and I don't know the first thing about horses, apart from the fact that they eat hay.'

'It might be something to think about if we live on the edge of a town. Although I think I can do everything with a wooden leg, I know I can't ride a horse again. I tried, and bruised my pride,' Stanley replied and swung her a wide smile.

'I'd bruise more than that. I am not sure horses and I are meant for one another. I've never ridden, so it's a challenge to face later down the line,' Kitty said. 'I can't believe we are talking about a horse and cart, and cowboys.'

'Well, we might be talking about mucking them out in a few weeks, too!' Stanley quipped.

When they collected her passport and stamped entry papers, Kitty realised how much Stanley's surname meant in certain quarters. She felt a sense of great importance when she entered a room with him; people were eager to please.

'They practically fall at your feet, Stanley,' she said after the last appointment of their day.

'My grandparents were well known in society, and the name carries a lot of weight. It opens doors. It's all snobbery, but useful,' Stanley said, and Kitty took his laugh as one of embarrassment.

'Well, it would have taken me an awful lot longer to get

through those doors if you hadn't organised everything, so thank you.'

'I think we should celebrate with tea and cake over there,' Stanley said, pointing to a pretty tea room on the corner of the street.

'Definitely, then it is home to finish packing. I want to spend time with Daphne before we leave; she has been a wonderful friend since I first set eyes on Fell Hall, when you came out of the hospital. I want to ask for a couple of her traditional recipes, your favourites,' she said.

'Let's hope they will still be my favourites after you have cooked them,' Stanley said with a jovial lift to his voice. Their to-do list had been fulfilled; now, all they had to do was travel, begin the physical journey in search of Michael in Canada using what little information they had.

By the end of the day, they were armed with a large pile of papers to add to the ones sitting on the Fell Hall dining table.

Stanley laid out a map of Canada and pinpointed the flight route and where they would land.

'Malton Airbase is here'—he pointed at a place on the map—'near the city of Toronto. That's where we land. We'll stay in lodgings overnight, then take the Canadian Pacific Railway train across country. We'll pass through Winnipeg, I think. Here's Calgary. Alberta is its province – there, in the west,' Stanley said, tapping various names on the map.

Kitty peered at the map and traced her finger along a route line he had drawn.

'It all seems very simple and easy on paper, but I am wise enough to know it won't be an easy journey.' Kitty said, more as a reminder to herself than to Stanley. 'But at least it's not on horseback.'

Stanley laughed. 'I love your positive outlook on everything, Kitty. It will get you through a lot – even horse riding and driving a car one day.'

Kitty huffed in fun, 'I am not sure I will manage either without having a nervous episode.'

'Well, it's our last night here – make the most of the comfortable beds and washing facilities in the house. The hotel in London will be pleasant enough, but after that—'

Kitty cut Stanley off.

'After that I will be wondering why I left England. And on that note I will go and enjoy a rose-scented bath and remove all thoughts of living in a tent in the wilderness,' Kitty said and kissed him on the forehead. 'Thank you for everything, Stanley. Get some rest too. Tomorrow will be another long drive for you – thank goodness Jack will take over halfway.'

'He can't wait to get the pedals removed,' Stanley said with a hint of sadness in his voice.

'It was a generous gift to him, Stanley. Maybe when you have a new car, whatever brand they have over there, then we can take a photograph with that fancy new camera of yours,' Kitty said as she left the room.

As she climbed the stairs to bed, her heart went out to Stanley; he would not only be leaving his car behind, but, in a sense, parting ways with Jenny. Her grave and family home would no longer feature in his life. When they were settled, Kitty decided to ensure he had somewhere to visit to reconnect with his wife and uphold his tradition of flowers for anniversaries. Kitty had already tucked away a few special items Daphne had set aside for him, but Stanley was determined not to take physical reminders. Neither woman wanted him to regret it after setting up a new home, but there would be times when he would miss the comfort of his wife at his side.

Chapter Seventeen

1st July 1947

The large plane stood on the runway, waiting to transport excited and nervous passengers. Some were trainee pilots, and others, like Kitty, were new to air travel. Stanley was chatting to his friend, the man responsible for getting them there safely.

He looked sensible and calm, which reassured her.

'Kitty, over here,' Stanley called. Kitty's feet were rooted to the spot in the queue to board, and she hesitated. Both Stanley and the pilot approached her, obviously sensing her nerves.

'This is Pete, he's…'

Kitty stepped towards the man Stanley was introducing and held out her hand. 'He's the brave man taking me to my husband, thank you,' she said with more bravado than she felt.

Pete took her hand and gave it a hearty shake.

'Mrs McCarthy, I've heard all about you and your kindness to my friend here. I would like to invite you to view the cockpit and meet my crew,' he said.

Taken aback, Kitty smiled at him.

'Please don't ask me to fly the thing. I am not steady-handed enough today,' she said, laughing, 'but thank you. How fascinating, I would like that – oh, and call me Kitty.'

Pete let go of her hand and shook Stanley's.

'Once we're seated, one of my colleagues will fetch you. Go and get comfortable, and don't let him take the window seat. He's seen enough of the sky. This trip is yours to enjoy,' Pete replied, playfully nudging Stanley.

As she climbed the steps to the plane, Kitty's heart pounded and her legs felt like lead. This was it, the moment she stepped off English soil, possibly never to return.

'It's not too late,' she whispered to herself.

Stanley's hand touched her back.

'This is it, Kitty. Soon you will be in Michael's arms again.' His words switched on a light of courage inside her, and Kitty stepped into the plane.

Looking down at the ground after take-off was exhilarating, but she was unsure how to describe the moment when they left the runway. Stanley guided her through deep breathing to stave off any threat of nausea, and soon she was looking out at the soft clouds skimming past the window.

Had she actually done it – left behind all she knew – or was this a dream?

Was this Michael's way of forcing her to move to Canada?

Kitty sat in her seat, allowing thought after thought to pound through her head until a new voice whispered. It was the brave Kitty, the woman who had battled against one of the most horrendous enemies the world had known.

It is done. You chose this journey; Michael did not force you. He opened a door, probably not realising what he had done. Focus on enjoying the flight.

A member of the crew fetched them to join Pete in the cockpit. The array of dials fascinated her, and the thrum of the engines vibrated through her body. Kitty stared ahead, looking out at the sky in awe.

She watched in wonder as Pete and his co-pilot manoeuvred the plane, and felt privileged to enjoy the moment.

'Your ears might pop,' Stanley said as the descent into Malton was announced. Kitty stretched herself. Ten hours felt longer than she had expected. She and Stanley had taken a nap, and she was glad she was more alert for the arrival than she'd anticipated.

'I think my head will explode with so many thoughts running through it right now. And my heart, well, that's fluttering enough to keep the plane in the air!' she replied.

Stanley reached over and took her hand.

'Once we're out of the airport, we'll be free to take a breath and find the house. I am told it's comfortable. We'll be able to rest and let our bodies catch up with themselves. Don't be afraid, this is a time to celebrate our courage.'

'You've always got courage,' Kitty replied, gripping his hand as the plane bounced onto the tarmac.

'Not as much as you think. I draw from you, too,' Stanley said.

'Welcome to Canada. And can I say that is a pretty shade of red,' the hostess said to Kitty, looking at Kitty's beret.

'Thank you, it was my mother's,' Kitty replied touching her head, hoping the beret would be her good luck charm. It was hot, so she imagined she would need to take it off sooner than she had hoped, but at least she had worn it as she had promised herself she would.

Kitty took a deep breath as she stepped onto the disembarking platform before descending the stairs and stepping onto Canadian soil. A place she might call home for the rest of her life.

She smiled when she saw Pete standing at the bottom.

'Welcome to your new home,' he said. 'I could not resist greeting you personally. Good luck, Stanley. Shout me when you have a place to stay, and I will visit you.'

After the greetings, then farewell from Pete, they left the airport, to face their new life together. Kitty took her beret off, and tucked it away safely, then gave herself a virtual pat on the back.

You made it, Kitty. Well done.

'Now, where do we go from here?' she asked Stanley. The world around her looked very different to the one she had left behind. Vast areas were given over to farmland, and as they walked closer, they saw small log cabins and brick buildings. Stanley approached a neat one-storey building surrounded by sun-scorched land and beckoned her to follow him to the front porch. Kitty looked around at the property, an elderly but tidy home of someone who took pride in keeping it freshly swept, with pretty flowers in pots, well-watered. Stanley turned the front door handle, and Kitty waited for him to call out to someone, but he turned to her instead.

'This is where we're staying for the night. It is basic, but it is owned by someone Pete knows. Their parents are long gone, and the woman married someone from another city. She lets it out for the summer. Pete said his colleagues bring their families to stay when they fly short runs.' He stepped inside. Kitty waited.

'Phew, it will need airing, it is hot inside,' he called out.

Kitty picked up her travel bags; their heavier items had been transported to a collection point at the railway depot.

'It's quaint,' she replied as she stepped inside. The furniture was of good quality, the wood finely turned. She smelled beeswax polish and lavender. She opened a small window onto the back of the property and looked out at the dry ground, which backed onto another small property.

'It is, and that out there is a modern bathroom. It was built last year, according to Pete, but has been built to match the house. Hence its appeal to his colleagues. I am going to make use of it and will pump water from the back porch when I get back. Go and choose a room for yourself – there are two off the kitchen.' Stanley pointed to a door. 'I've seen them both and am not bothered, but I know you ladies, decoration matters.'

Kitty laughed.

'I am so tired I am not bothered by damask or floral bedding, but thanks.'

When Stanley returned, he brought a large jug of cool water, which Kitty sipped. 'It's sweet,' she said. 'I had expected it to taste of dirt – dust.'

'They seem to have their own spring or borehole. The bath has a copper heater so that the water will be warm. It flows from a tap, so that makes life easy. I was expecting to carry bucket loads down for you to bathe this evening.' Stanley said teasingly.

'Oh, I will be bathing, don't you worry. But what about food?' Kitty asked.

'Pete's friend said there is a shop – store – not far down the road. We can go and fetch some now and then settle for the evening,' Stanley suggested.

'I hope it's not far. Do you have your stick handy?' Kitty

asked as she looked around the area from the front porch. She saw homes, but no sign of shops. 'Did this use to be a farm? There's a lot of land surrounding it.'

Stanley joined her, stick in hand, and nodded. 'From what I understand, several farmers sold to the airport developers. The daughter kept this place, and couldn't part with it. I could happily live here.'

'Me too, but only if there is somewhere to buy food,' Kitty said with a giggle.

Having turned a corner at the end of the street, they saw and waved to only one person. Eventually, they came across a general store and stepped inside.

The man behind the counter gave them a wide smile.

'Mr Walker-Fell, I assume. I'm Albie,' he said loudly. He bent down behind the counter before Stanley had time to reply. Kitty and Stanley looked at one another, bemused.

The man appeared again and produced a wooden box.

'As she does for all her guests, Mrs Cooke ordered a basic box for you – a gift. I will take it to your car,' he said.

'Many thanks, Albie,' Stanley said, 'but we're on foot, it will be a while until we have a car,' he said. The storekeeper looked at them, smiled, then nodded.

'Wait here,' he instructed.

Kitty looked around the small store, picked up a jar, and read the label.

'Jelly, forty-nine cents,' she said and showed Stanley. 'I think it is strawberry jam.'

Stanley smiled. 'We have a lot to learn,' he said, just as the storekeeper returned.

'My boy, Albie junior, will take you home. He's delivering nearby, and an hour early won't trouble my customers. Good luck with everything,' he said, disappearing out of the back of his shop again.

Stanley turned to Kitty and gave a theatrical whisper. 'I think we've just been served and dismissed. Let's go and find our transport.'

Outside the store was a dusty-looking truck with boxes in the rear. A youth sat in a front seat leaning out of the window, and Kitty smiled. Then she realised he was the driver and the passenger side was opposite to that of the cars in Britain.

'It is very kind of you to help. Please thank your father – he disappeared before we could speak to him,' she said, waiting for Stanley to sit beside her.

'Pa's deaf. He's not one for small talk; he gets embarrassed. I'll tell him. Okay, you guys ready?' Albie Junior asked.

'Ready,' Stanley replied.

By the time they arrived back at their lodgings, they had learned who sold their farms, and that Albie junior wanted to work at the airport, but his father needed his help with the store.

Stanley and Kitty listened to him chatter; he more than made up for his father's semi-silence, and Kitty was grateful to him. She was too tired to hold a long, polite conversation, so she interjected with the occasional encouraging word. He had the same soft accent as Michael, and hearing it had reminded her that she still had the toughest assignment to carry out: to find her husband.

Chapter Eighteen

After a simple meal of scrambled eggs, crusty bread and warm milk, Kitty bathed and readied herself for bed.

Stanley sat on the back porch enjoying the evening air. Once Kitty had finished pottering around her room, she joined him.

'The stars are certainly out tonight. I don't think I have felt this peaceful since Michael left. Everything has been a whirlwind,' Kitty said with a sigh, putting her feet up on the small wooden stool opposite.

'Make the most of it because we have a busy journey ahead. But I agree, having a moment of peace is good.'

They sat silently until the night air cooled, then Kitty excused herself and went to bed. It took a while for her to settle, but the time change and the rush of the past few days soon caught up with her, and it wasn't until Stanley tapped on her door in the early morning that she realised she had fallen into a deep sleep.

'Ready for the next part of this mission, Recruit McCarthy? Rise and shine!' Stanley called out cheerfully and laughed.

Kitty listened to him walk away and stretched out in bed.

Was she ready?

She wasn't sure, but one thing she did know was that it was something she had to do, and there was no turning away from tracking Michael down. Even the few hours she had experienced in his country made her want to find out more about whether she was suited to what looked to be a completely different way of life.

Ensuring the small home was as clean as they found it, Kitty and Stanley waited on the porch for the taxi – pre-booked, thanks to Pete – to take them to the main railway station in Toronto.

Pete also advised Stanley on tourist spots and places of natural beauty to stop and enjoy. Kitty felt somewhat anxious; they were not on holiday. She was keen to get to where she hoped Michael was living.

'Don't we need a straight through route, Stanley?' she asked.

'If Michael has settled into a new job, then he will be there when we arrive. There are some places we'll never have the opportunity to see again. One long journey isn't possible, so stopping on occasion makes sense. Be patient, not many more days and we'll find him,' Stanley said encouragingly, and Kitty eventually settled down to the idea.

Toronto's Union Station bustled with passengers, and Kitty found the noise overwhelming after the previous evening's silence. She stood in awe as they approached their train waiting at the platform. Stanley gave a low whistle.

'That's a spectacular beast of a machine,' he said, looking up at the enormous locomotive.

'It's huge! I wonder what the inside is like. I hope the seats are comfortable,' Kitty exclaimed. The train looked majestic; it towered above any she had seen in Great Britain, and when the steam was released, she had an instant image of dragons and dark tunnels.

Stanley pointed to their cases and two crates as porters loaded them onto the train.

'They're still intact. Fingers crossed for the other end,' he said and gave a thumbs-up to the men loading them into the large carriage. Although Kitty and Stanley had chosen to make stops along the way, their goods were to be transported to a storage unit in Calgary. Stanley's colleagues were knowledgeable about all aspects of travel across the country, and their useful information made the journey plans easier to organise.

Stanley took a while to step onto the train, and the conductor stood patiently waiting. He then helped Kitty, and she gave him her brightest smile. Her excitement grew with every second that passed, holding back the anxiety.

Looking out from their window seats, they waited patiently for the train to embark on its journey to many towns and cities new to Kitty and Stanley. They chatted excitedly about what they might see. Looking to one side, they watched a small gathering of people selling items from wicker baskets. Kitty noticed some women were wearing breeches and clothes she had only seen men wearing in Britain. Horses were tethered nearby.

'I can see myself redesigning some of my dresses into dungarees now we're here, especially if I am expected to ride horses and work on a farm. No more fine dining for me,' Kitty said with a laugh, reminding Stanley of how he mentioned becoming a farm owner during a conversation the previous evening.

'I think you will stand out in the crowd in rose pink satin ones, or better still, lemon print,' Stanley teased.

Kitty absorbed the moment. It was light-hearted and

something to treasure during the hard times – she was no fool and guessed she would face many.

The shoosh and whoosh sound of the steam from the train's smokestack echoed down the platform, and the deep vibrating sound of the departing whistle was a signal that their journey was about to begin. Kitty listened to the chug and trundle as the train built up speed, and she adjusted her eyes to the scenes outside her window. Breathtaking views of mountains, and at their base, pine trees and ravines housing fast-flowing rivers with enormous rocks. Her mind was snatching each spectacular image and storing it away. Stanley quietly looked out of his window at an awkward angle, seeing what she had already witnessed. 'Come and sit beside me, Stanley. See it properly without stretching around.'

Stanley chose a point when the train slowed for a large bend in the track, manoeuvred himself beside her and leaned forward to see out of the window.

'It's wonderful. Some of the mountains still have specks of snow on them. Oh, look, over there!' he said, pointing to a small group of deer wandering, nibbling at the ground as they moved elegantly between shrubs and trees.

They both exclaimed and shared their joy at what they witnessed as the train wound its way across the country. They enjoyed good food and drink, and Kitty relaxed into the views and listened to the conductor share stories of the places they passed whenever he walked the carriages. He was extremely proud of his country and all it offered.

A loud whistle blew, and the conductor returned to announce the next stop: Winnipeg.

'It is named after Lake Winnipeg. But its name is Cree – and means something like muddy waters,' he said with great authority in his voice.

'Cree?' Stanley said. 'Is that the people of the area – do we say tribe?'

'They are Canadian-born – the land belongs to their ancestors. My grandfather is Cree born,' the conductor replied.

Kitty smiled up at him. 'My husband spoke to me about his ancestors on his mother's side. Sadly, he never knew where they lived. I think his father enticed her away from her family.'

'Ah, family mysteries. I hope you find out yours, sir,' the conductor said, directing his words at Stanley. Both she and Stanley realised he thought they were married.

'I'm escorting my sister to be with her husband, whom she's talking about. We will certainly try and learn more of what you have told us, thank you,' Stanley said, closing the conversation. Kitty felt a warm glow of belonging whenever he used the term 'sister' – it had occurred a lot over recent weeks. Their loss and need to be part of a family had brought them closer, and no one would ever doubt they were siblings from their behaviour towards one another.

The conductor nodded, touched his cap and continued calling out relevant information as the train shuddered to a halt.

'Do you want to walk the platform for five minutes?' Stanley asked Kitty.

Kitty guessed he wanted to stretch his hips and leg muscles, so she agreed.

A smoky veil lingered the length of the station, smelling of soot and oil. Walking arm in arm, they chatted about the difference between the three places they had come across along the way. They both liked the idea of farm-style living. The buildings they could see in the distance were not log cabins, but more in keeping with a modern city rebuilding itself after the war. As they approached the end of the platform, Kitty spotted a dark-haired child and waved. The little girl waved back, smiling, her large, dark-brown eyes twinkling with joy. Stanley grinned.

'Wherever you go, you attract the little ones,' he said affectionately.

'Just as you do with loud, noisy mechanical things,' Kitty replied, pointing at the train, which gave another ear-piercing sound, preparing itself for departure and making those standing nearby jump with surprise.

Chapter Nineteen

Although not ideal, Kitty welcomed the overnight sleep in their private carriages. The care and attention given to them suggested to her that Stanley had paid more for the tickets than he let on. He had only asked her for a portion towards the travel, ensuring he had the comfort he required, but not at her expense. She appreciated his discretion but would ensure she and Michael repaid him.

She washed and changed her dress to one more suitable for travelling in hot weather. The next leg of the journey was to be longer than the previous one, and the temperature was rising, although it was only six o'clock in the morning. A gentle tap on her door and a polite voice from the sleeping car conductor alerted her that breakfast would be served in the dining car, and she smiled. It was time to start another day. They were getting closer to finding Michael.

'Thank you,' she called softly, slipping her feet into her comfortable sandals. The sway of the train was gentle and slower than usual, and Kitty guessed there was a station ahead. She looked out of the corridor window, and something in the sky caught her eye. A large black and white-headed bird with a yellow beak soared and dropped between the tree tops. Its graceful glide and wide wingspan made for fascinating viewing. Although her stomach told her to head for the dining carriage, Kitty could not take her eyes off the bird.

'A Bald Eagle,' a deep male voice said beside her, and she turned to see a passenger also looking out at the bird.

'It's huge, yet so graceful. I can't take my eyes off of it – it's mesmerising,' Kitty said, glancing at him briefly, giving him a polite smile, then returning her gaze towards the eagle.

The man gave a soft chuckle.

'I remember the first time I saw one as a child, I fell in love too. They are a spiritual bird. Whisper your secret words and hopes its way; the bird will take them to the heavens for your ancestors to hear them.'

'What a lovely idea,' Kitty said quietly, thinking of words she would love the eagle to share for her.

The man turned to her and replaced his fedora. He looked like a smart businessman.

'It is a fact, not an idea. Try it and see,' he replied seriously in a soft voice, politely touching the rim of his hat before moving further down the corridor.

Kitty's stomach grumbled, and her thoughts returned to Stanley, who was probably already eating breakfast. Reluctantly, she moved away from the window and went to join him.

'Morning,' Stanley said as she walked to their table. When she was seated, a dining car waiter ensured Stanley's used silverware and crockery were removed and Kitty's fresh ones were perfectly arranged on the pristine white tablecloth.

'This train is like a moving fancy hotel,' Kitty said as she pulled her white lace gloves from her hands. She had chosen to dress in some of her finest clothes while travelling, as she had a sneaking feeling she would have little use for them in Calgary.

'They certainly look after their passengers,' Stanley said, 'I have eaten more ham than I dare think about, and the waiter still wants to bring me more.'

Across from her table, Kitty spotted the man who had spoken to her in the corridor and smiled. He nodded her way.

'Making friends?' Stanley asked as he layered a generous portion of butter onto a slice of toast.

'It's a gentleman I met earlier when we both stopped and admired the bald-headed eagle flying along with the train. I think it is good luck after what he told me,' Kitty replied and picked up a menu to browse. The waiter took her order of ham, eggs, tea and toast, and she returned her attention to Stanley.

'Where are we heading today? Do we stop anywhere?' she asked.

Stanley took out his map from the inside of a folded newspaper on the seat beside him. Kitty smiled. He always looked so natural and at ease scanning a map, and this one of Canada was his constant companion, as well as a source of fascination for her. Names such as Sioux Lookout, Portage la Prairie, Saskatoon, Saskatchewan, Chilliwack and Medicine Hat excited her imagination. The conductor mentioned that he was born in Saskatoon and showed them prime Saskatoon berry-picking spots he used as a child, which they had studied on the map the previous evening. He pointed out several stop-off points as well and recommended some to Stanley.

'I think we're stretching our legs at Edmonton, before heading for Red Deer, where you and I will stay overnight and enjoy a break from travelling. We'll take a different train from there and catch up with our goods in Calgary,' Stanley said.

Kitty knew the schedule was running smoothly and she was not concerned about timing, but, again, the cost of what Stanley had planned for them and the money she had given him did not add up, and she could no longer ignore the situation.

'Stanley, about the funds,' she said in a semi-whisper, not wanting to offend him by publicly talking about money.

'What about them?' Stanley asked, looking up from the map but keeping his finger on a place of interest to him.

Choosing her words carefully, Kitty gave a little shrug.

'I don't think I have given you anywhere near enough to cover my expenses on this trip. I do not want you to be out of pocket. Can I offer you a bit more?' She hesitated, feeling slightly awkward. The last thing she wanted to do was to upset him at the start of the day.

He coughed and continued scanning the map as he spoke.

'There will be less in the pot when you inherit it. I want you to find joy in Michael's country before you catch up with him. It would be good if you could reassure him that you would be happy living here. I plan to make him realise you're willing to learn, to become a Canadian.'

'I can't be that, my blood is British – English,' Kitty said.

Stanley picked up his pencil and drew a circle around whatever had drawn his attention, and looked at her full in the face.

Kitty waited for his response.

'Paperwork will tell you different in a few years – you will belong here. As for blood, well, there has been enough of that spilt over recent years. The reuniting of the two of you is far more important. And, I will tell him the same when I see him. All

I ask is that you forget worrying about repaying my money, learn what you can and fall in love with Canada.' Stanley spoke firmly, and Kitty knew the conversation was over.

'Thank you, Stanley. I will never forget this, and I promise to try my hardest to learn all I can,' she said softly and returned her attention to her cup of tea, reflecting on his words. What she had seen of Canada from a moving train had already excited her. The vast lands offered so much more. She wanted to smell the pine in the forests as the conductor described, and to learn basic skills as a housewife. They had had a housekeeper when she and Michael worked at the surgery and on the district, and their meals were prepared, so Kitty had had little to do as a housewife. Her years at home with her aunt were not spent in baking and cooking, but in studying and caring for people in the community.

In her new home, Kitty wanted to learn to bake mouthwatering pastries, reproduce Daphne's recipes for hearty meals, and make pickles and fruit jams. She wanted to start married life again, push aside the rescue missions and help Michael create a new adventure for himself. Yes, she could try to become at one with Canada, to accept her life in England was over, but first, she promised herself to enjoy Stanley's gift.

Chapter Twenty

Edmonton was another busy station, and, as they had done at Winnipeg, Kitty and Stanley walked the platform nodding and smiling at the people around them.

Kitty looked at posters, browsed magazines and read pamphlets that looked useful and informative about her new country. She made a selection and then glanced at the array of chocolate bars. There had been no such sight in wartime, and now she stood in front of a counter with so many to choose from, she was spoilt for choice. There were several names she did not recognise, and some she did.

'Did you know there was a candy bar protest and strike in April?' said the man she assumed was the newsstand and confectionery booth owner.

'A strike? I bet the children were annoyed,' Kitty replied, giving him a polite smile.

The man threw back his head and gave a guffaw.

'It was the children who went on strike. They were angry

their candy bars had risen by three cents from five cents, and refused to buy them.'

'Did they win?' Kitty asked.

The man gave another loud laugh. 'No, but I am sure they felt they'd had their say.'

Kitty held out a chocolate bar, a brand she recognised. 'So, this is known as a candy bar. Candy?' she asked.

'It is, what do you call it?' the man replied.

'From now on, candy bar, but I knew it as a chocolate bar,' Kitty said, happy to learn something new.

The man reached into a large jar and handed her a lollipop.

'This is maple candy. It is the sap from a tree, a treat going back many years, and something truly Canadian. Enjoy a treat from me,' he said, grinning.

'Thank you so much. That is very kind of you. When I eat it later, I will think of you and the children who went on strike.' Kitty paid for her goods and placed the lollipop in her bag, carefully tucked away, before rejoining Stanley outside.

'I've got a lollipop for teaching the shopkeeper something new. Chocolate bar, instead of candy bar,' she said and giggled.

'Storekeeper is his title, I think. Something else for us to learn. Shops are stores,' Stanley replied. Just then they were stopped by the storekeeper as he approached Kitty holding out another lollipop.

'One for your husband to enjoy, too. They're not something you will want to share,' he said, giving Kitty a jovial wink. Neither she nor Stanley corrected the man about their relationship; it was easier to let him have his moment of kindness.

'Thank you, sir, that is very kind of you,' Stanley said, accepting his gift. 'I have a collection of newspapers to pay for – I see more oil has been found near Calgary.' He tapped a picture on the front of one of the newspapers.

'Leduc, yes. There's riches to be had for the right investors there,' the man replied.

'Isn't that where we're headed, Stanley?' Kitty asked.

The storekeeper pushed back his cap and smiled at Stanley. 'Wise man. If you have money to invest, do it now. Good luck to you both,' he said and walked away to serve another customer.

Back on the train, they sat in their private carriage. Kitty recorded all she had seen in a new notebook – including recipes from her magazines – while Stanley wrote letters to people back in England. Both lollipops were demolished as they wrote.

'These lollies are going to be my downfall. They're delicious,' Kitty declared once she had finished hers. 'I think we're moving. Just as well, or I may have been tempted to run and buy some more.'

'Yes, we're on our way, and I agree that lollipop was rather tasty,' Stanley replied. 'Not too much longer and we'll be able to look for some in Red Deer. There's bound to be candy stores there.'

Kitty smiled at him for using the Canadian terms. They were determined to introduce the new words into their vocabulary, and Stanley did not hesitate to use them. Sometimes Kitty was less confident.

Their bags were packed and ready to be transported to The Buffalo Hotel in Red Deer, and all they waited for now was the conductor's merry announcement that they had arrived. After talking with Stanley, Kitty accepted that she had little chance of changing his mind, so she permitted herself to experience holiday excitement, knowing it would be best to be rested and restored for the emotional outcome waiting at the end of the journey.

'Red Deer. Next stop, Red Deer,' the conductor called out. Kitty gathered her things.

'Time to enjoy fresh air, and I understand there is a movie theatre – picture house to you and me – in town. Plus several places to eat. The conductor is a fount of knowledge,' Stanley said with a laugh as he packed away his belongings.

'Movie theatre. I must write that down when we get to the hotel. I have a washroom for a bathroom, and a faucet for a tap. Dungarees are called overalls in Canada, so I will learn to make overalls and coveralls from my pretty dresses instead.' Kitty laughed, smacked her forehead with a palm and pulled a confused face.

'It gets confusing, but we'll get there,' Stanley reassured her.

'I knew I would have to learn new traditions and regulations, but there are a lot of words, too. Michael must have done the same when he came to England, because he only used British words like "tap" and "cinema",' Kitty said. She followed Stanley as they exited the station. 'Gracious, I was not expecting such a busy town.'

'I'm not sure, but I think it is a city,' Stanley said. 'We need to head to the east-west main street – apparently there are two. We're looking for Ross Street.'

Both stood and looked down the long, wide street ahead with buildings on either side. People leisurely wound their way in and out of the stores.

'The hotel is not far – I'm told it is a short walk, but no doubt it will take us a bit longer with window shopping,' Stanley said.

'I need a few new handkerchiefs and would like to embroider them now that I have my aunt's small sewing basket. So I fear it will be more than window shopping for you,' Kitty said, giggling.

'It's a good job I am a patient man,' Stanley replied, making Kitty giggle again.

The sooty smell from the station still hung in the air, but as they walked away, Kitty noticed that the air was getting fresher and carried tempting aromas from the nearby restaurants.

They enjoyed a warm welcome and comfortable rooms when they arrived at the hotel. When staff serving them tea in the dining room learned she was married to a Canadian doctor, Kitty found herself the centre of attention, with questions about how they met, which led to questions about her journey through the war as a Red Cross nurse.

She told them about transporting the German Nazi Rudolph Hess from Scotland to London, when he was injured on a peace mission to Great Britain. She described her time working in a prisoner of war camp, nursing German soldiers, working with Canadian soldiers on the Normandy beaches, and many more of her wartime achievements, including helping Stanley with his rehabilitation, plus Jenny and the orphanage.

Stanley gained praise for his pilot duty, and admiration for his determination to ski after losing his leg, and for giving up his home to war orphans. Everyone was kind and encouraging when she said she was meeting her husband to start a new life, and Kitty recorded as much as she could remember to relay to Michael, especially the requests to thank him for his service.

When they sat eating their evening meal, Kitty reflected upon her past.

'It is not until I say it aloud that I realise what I have achieved since leaving home. Even though I was twenty at the time, I was so naïve and wary about everything at first, but then, thanks to

Michael, I gained the confidence I never knew I had. Nowadays, in peacetime, it all seems surreal.'

Giving a nod, Stanley finished his meal and set down his cutlery.

'I often reflect on the orders I gave and received, and their outcomes. I will admit conscription was the best thing that ever happened to me. Yes, I lost a leg, but I didn't lose my life or my career. I lost Jenny, it's true, but I always had you from the beginning of my return to a normal life. And here we are, both experiencing something bright and new together.' His voice carried an emotion that Kitty had not heard before. Their journey had brought them closer together.

'I think we are twins from a past life,' she said. 'We certainly have the same thoughts and willingness to support one another. Although you were the wealthy version of me.'

Stanley gave a hearty laugh.

Making Stanley laugh always felt good, and it helped Kitty keep her spirits lifted.

'Believe me, the world would not cope with two of me,' Stanley quipped back.

They linked arms as they strolled through the streets, walking off their large steak meal, and chatted about memories made in England. They spoke about their childhood days and the events that altered their ways of life. Stanley's parents were both wealthy, but he spent years away from home in boarding schools. Kitty did not envy him those times. Although she only had her parents for a few years, her childhood was happy thanks to her aunt and uncle. She listened to Stanley and reflected on the saying that money can't buy happiness. She felt torn: it didn't buy her happiness as a child, but as a grown woman on a journey through

Canada, money helped her enjoy a comfortable lifestyle, if only briefly.

She penned a letter to her uncle and Meryn, sharing her news to date and describing her discoveries as best she could, but the flavours of foods and the smell of the town drifting on the evening air were not so easy to capture. She made the letters upbeat and leaned towards the positive when mentioning Michael.

By the time they had enjoyed two days at Red Deer, Kitty had learned more to help her feel at ease, apart from the roaming bears and what to do if she ever encountered one. The instruction not to run went against what Kitty thought was the most logical thing to do. Stanley joked about him not standing a chance as he couldn't run, and Kitty ended all talk about bears. Their light-hearted, relaxing break helped them both, and soon they were back on the train and heading for Calgary.

Chapter Twenty-One

The train journey ended, and Kitty stood waiting in the busy centre of Calgary, while Stanley searched for someone to guide them to rooms for rent.

She wondered if Michael was in the city. A place where men gave her smiles through blackened, grimy faces. Men who worked the oil wells. Everywhere she turned, there were men on horseback and women on small carts laden with household items. She guessed, like her, they were new to the city and ready to lead new lives in a prosperous place. While waiting, she scanned the area for Michael, hoping that he would turn a corner and find her standing there. But all she saw were the weary faces of strangers.

Stanley returned wearing a frown and looking concerned.

'Everywhere is full. Even the expensive hotels. I should have cabled ahead and booked somewhere.' His voice was loaded with frustration.

'Is it just here, or are there other towns nearby?' Kitty asked.

'There's a village where a woman has lodgings, but it is out of town.'

'How do we get there? If it is short-term, then at least we have a roof over our heads. By the looks of the traffic, hundreds of people are looking for somewhere to stay or live,' Kitty said.

'The man who told me is her cousin. He said he could take us, but we should not expect anything luxurious,' Stanley replied. 'I am not sure we should leave the city – we don't know the area yet.'

Stanley removed his hat and rubbed his head. Kitty could tell he was worried and sensed he was anxious because he had promised to keep her safe and comfortable.

'We have to think about this, Stanley. We're both going to need somewhere overnight, at least. I am prepared to take the risk if you are. We can try again tomorrow,' she said, keeping her voice upbeat.

Stanley gave a nod. 'That's true. We can regroup in the morning if the place is unsuitable,' he said, returning to speak to the man. Kitty waited a while, then someone called her name. Turning, she saw Stanley and a younger man sitting on a horse-drawn cart. The man, in his twenties, jumped down from the cart and shook her hand until Kitty thought he would shake her arm from its socket.

'As I told your husband, don't expect anything like a luxury hotel, but Mim keeps a tidy house. She's widowed, and having another woman arrive, she'll be mighty pleased. I'm Ted. Let's get you on the road.' He spoke with the energy of a child at Christmas. He helped her onto the cart, talking continuously, but neither she nor Stanley had the opportunity to explain that they weren't married.

As they travelled along, Kitty guessed Ted had not told

Stanley how far out of Calgary his cousin's home was – a good hour had passed and they were still travelling at a trotting pace. The sun bore down, and a thirst grew in the back of her throat from the dusty roads. They passed the odd homestead and cattle; the miles of flat lands with intermittent rolling hills, she learned, were called the prairies. The large mountains in the distance were impressive, their tips sparkling in the sunshine with sparse lingering snow. They created a magnificent backdrop, with their shadows darkening the rolling hills at their base – a giant embrace of stone surrounding land that needed tender loving care is how Kitty would describe it in her letters home. The Rocky Mountains – the Rockies. All around her were stark reminders of how small she was on the planet.

Ted told them the winters were harsh and the weather variable. The farm land had originally attracted a few settlers, but now Calgary was of interest because of the new oil find that had attracted attention around the world.

When the cart turned off the dusty road two hours later, they finally came to a village he called Cochrane, still within the province of Alberta. They bumped towards a sprawling single-storey wooden lodge, and Kitty was convinced her backside would be bruised when they reached where they were sleeping that night. She doubted Stanley would refuse to stay, no matter how rough the place was; they were hot and tired, and if he was anything like her, he was disoriented and bewildered by Ted's failure to tell them how far out of Calgary they would be staying.

'Here we are, Riverside Ranch,' Ted said.

Although it was large, Kitty had expected 'Ranch' to mean something bigger; and 'Riverside' was more contained than she would have imagined. The log cabin was surrounded by wooden posts forming partial fencing on one side of the land.

'Mim bought this place after her husband, Dan, died, and with my help – but only when I can – she has made it a home. Five years of hard work would make many a man question his strength. I admire her for her refusal to give up,' Ted said with pride in his voice. 'As you can see, the fencing needs attention. It was damaged a few months back, when a rogue cattle drive rampaged through – foolish settler thought he was John Ware reincarnated.'

'John Ware?' Stanley asked politely.

'A black slave who drove cattle from America to Canada – he's well known for his techniques and strength. He settled this side of the border, had clever ideas on irrigation and ditching, and loved his cattle as much as his wife and children. He has a history here.' Ted clicked his tongue at the horse, slowing it down as they arrived at their lodgings.

'He sounds fascinating,' Kitty said, genuinely interested, and made a note to learn more about this man who made Canada his home too.

'Hello!'

A tall, well-built woman stepped off the large porch and down the steps, waving to greet them. Ted jumped down from his seat, and she hugged him like a mother hugs a child. Kitty guessed the woman was close to forty, roughly twice his age.

'Oki! Welcome to Cochrane,' Mim said in a voice so loud it made Kitty jump.

Stanley slowly got down from the cart, and Kitty clambered down to join him.

'Thank you,' Stanley said, holding out his hand. 'I'm Stanley and this is Kitty – my, um, sister.'

Ted swung them both a look.

'Well, if I haven't made things awkward for you. I thought

you were husband and wife. There is only one spare room,' he said, looking embarrassed.

Kitty switched her glance to Stanley, who grinned at Ted.

'We won't turn away somewhere to stay the night. It won't be the first time we've had to share a room,' Stanley said.

'What he means,' Kitty quickly interjected, 'is that I was his nurse and I slept in a chair beside his bed.'

Ted looked at Kitty. 'My apologies – I…'

'It's an easy assumption to make. It isn't a problem,' Kitty said.

'For sure. There's the double bed, and I have a fold-away out back in the barn.' Mim offered her solution with an air of 'problem solved'. Kitty knew neither she nor Stanley wanted to let Ted or his cousin down. The money for their stay would obviously mean food on the table. The area had few luxuries, and the barn she'd mentioned needed repair because of its age.

Kitty stepped forward and held out her hand. 'Thank you, Mim. We accept your kind offer. Stanley needs a separate bed, as I am sure you can appreciate.'

'Well, Ted, do your duty by my guests and get their bags inside. I will fetch the fold-away. Make use of the outhouse for washing and other natural doings. We have running water thanks to our borehole leading from the Bow River,' Mim said with a voice of authority, looking at each person as she spoke. Kitty guessed she was a woman who was used to giving orders and people obeying them. She looked forward to getting to know her.

Inside the bedroom, Stanley looked over at her and shrugged with amusement.

'I will let you know if you snore,' he said in a whisper.

'Same here,' Kitty said and shook her head, trying not to laugh too loud.

Stanley sat on the edge of the bed.

'It's a long way out of the city. Longer than I expected. Saddle sore is not just for the cowboys who work the land, I can tell you.'

Kitty gave him a knowing look. 'Not a topic for the table, but I agree. I'll not sit comfortably for a week!'

Stanley chuckled, then yawned.

'We'll cope for tonight, and tomorrow I will ask Ted to take us back to Calgary, and we'll find somewhere we can rent ourselves. And we can make enquiries about Michael.'

Just as Kitty was about to reply, Mim returned with the fold-up bed.

'I dusted off a few spiders. A seasonal worker left it behind a couple of years ago,' she said at the bedroom door. 'I'll fetch your bedding, then we'll eat.'

When they regrouped around a large table on the back of the property, Mim served their meal. 'Homegrown beef, potatoes and cabbage,' she said, plating up large portions of delicious-smelling food.

While they were eating, Mim encouraged them to talk about their lives in England. Ted was interested in what they wanted from life in Canada, and Kitty hoped they might finally be getting close to finding her husband.

Chapter Twenty-Two

Kitty explained the dilemma of not knowing where Michael was, blaming it on letters crossing paths, not the fact that her husband walked out and left her alone. She would not taint his reputation if he were in the area, and she accepted she was at fault for misunderstanding the situation.

'I had my mind set on a small farm, something I can manage with a handful of men,' Stanley said.

Ted showed interest in the idea.

'There's land for sale. In Calgary, prices have increased since the oil strike. Good agricultural soil can be found in this area, and as for manpower, some settlers look for regular work. This is the land of ancestors, and you must show it respect; always ask the right people for advice. Right, Mim?'

Mim finished eating and wiped her mouth on her napkin. She picked up her glass and filled it with a cold light beer from a jug. Kitty got the impression that Mim was not a woman to be rushed into anything and was a deep thinker.

'We all have opinions, and I keep mine to myself. Ted is right about respecting the land and seeking the right advice from the right people. Be wise and humble – it will lead you on the right path, for sure.' She began gathering the dishes. Kitty went to help, but Mim shook her head. 'You are paying guests. I cannot afford to give you free lodgings.'

Her response was blunt but honest, and Kitty sat in her seat again, not wanting to offend.

'What advice can you give Stanley on looking for land, Ted?' she asked, returning the conversation to Stanley's ideas.

Ted leaned back in his chair and puffed out his chest with an air of importance. It amused Kitty, but she tried not to let it distract her from her question. Stanley had great ideas and ambition, but on seeing the vast land and potential struggles, Kitty was worried he would invest in haste and live to regret it.

'It depends on what you want from your purchase, Stanley. A large working cattle farm is a big investment and expensive to upkeep,' Ted said.

'I wasn't out to become a farmer as such. I want a homestead much like this, a project that will keep me from becoming bored, and a substantial roof over my head. Kitty and her husband could live with me until they find the right home for themselves,' Stanley said, his voice sounding tired.

Kitty wondered if the realisation of what he had hoped for and what would be available had disappointed him.

'We just need to find a place to rent for the short term, and then see what is available for you, Stanley. It is very early days and we're lucky to have found Ted and Mim. I'm sure they won't mind us asking advice,' she said, offering a smile to both men, then to Mim, who had returned to the table.

'We can share what we know for sure,' Mim replied and

pulled out a white clay pipe, stuffed it with tobacco and lit it. Kitty hoped her mouth wasn't wide open as she watched, fascinated and surprised. The fragrant, earthy smell wafted around them. Mim looked at her, and Kitty guessed she had stared too long.

'Skullcap,' Mim said, 'It settles my nerves. I took to it after my husband was killed.'

Kitty gave her a polite smile. 'I'm sorry if I was rude staring at you like that, but it is unusual for me to see women smoking a pipe. My uncle gave me an old pipe of his as a keepsake, but I can't see me smoking it – he enjoyed it though. I meant no offence,' she said apologetically.

'None taken. It's a remedy I use when I am troubled. I do not smoke cigarettes,' Mim explained.

Unsure what to say, Kitty remained quiet.

'Were you born here?' Stanley asked, and Kitty was grateful for his question.

'Ted was, but I was born outside of Calgary, in nineteen hundred. My father never returned from a hunting trip a week after I was born. When I was five, my mother moved us to Edmonton, bringing my newborn baby cousin with us – I still don't know why. But her mother was not the kindest of women, so maybe Mom took her to save her.'

Mim puffed on her pipe, and her audience waited patiently. Kitty wanted to hear more. Mim had a way of telling a story, and her voice soothed. The contents of her pipe relaxed her starchy side.

'I met Dan after my mother passed away in thirty-nine. We had just over four years together. His heart failed him.'

Kitty quickly calculated in her head that Mim was forty-six or forty-seven. Mim continued her story, and Kitty noticed Stanley looked as interested as she was. Ted must have heard the story before, but he sat listening politely like them.

'I never had children, but when Ted's mom ran away and left me to bring him up, I didn't hesitate. Ted is my son by fate's choice. We're happy in our ways, eh, boy?' Mim addressed Ted.

'Yup, we work. Mim says jump, and I ask how high,' Ted replied, and everyone laughed.

'I think it is a wonderful outcome for you both,' Kitty said.

'As he said, we work. Both are as odd as my shirt's buttons, but we work,' Mim replied, looking down at her checked shirt with mixed buttons of various sizes.

Kitty giggled then stifled a yawn.

'I've either bored you silly or you're exhausted. Use the outhouse and get yourself some sleep,' Mim said, and Kitty took it as a command rather than an offer. Like Ted, she did as she was told. She snuggled beneath the cover on the fold-up bed waiting for Stanley to return to the room. He looked out of place in his red dressing gown, an expensive wool garment with a velvet collar.

'What are you doing over there?' he whispered.

'You can't sleep on this, it is far too narrow and your hips won't thank you in the morning. Go to sleep, Stanley. I think we'll have a busy day tomorrow,' Kitty whispered back. 'Night, and sleep well – Cowboy Stan,' she teased and turned to face the wall before he could respond.

Chapter Twenty-Three

Kitty tossed and turned in her bed, unable to sleep as long as she had hoped. Stanley's soft snores reminded her she no longer had her husband beside her for comfort.

Despite her efforts to suppress them, feelings of inner pain and worry began to resurface. Knowing that her husband was living nearby – or at least trying to find his fortune – while she wasn't by his side filled her with a sense of failure.

Could they make it work if she found him? Would he appreciate the effort she had put into trying to find him? Would he reject her because of her divorce outburst?

Questions flooded her sense of calm whenever she tried to switch off and settle.

By early morning, she was still as tired as when she went to bed, but she slipped out of the room and down to the outhouse. Flies irritated her, and she swatted them away with a fury they did not deserve. Tension built in her neck and shoulders, and she had no desire to return to the house immediately. She walked a few yards, then stood watching the sun rise slowly across the land and creep over the side of the mountains.

She closed her eyes and imagined the eagle flying on her behalf. Slowly, an image emerged of her doing the flying, lifting wings that were free of burden and feeling the wind on her face, blowing away her troubles. Kitty raised her arms and moved them to capture the feeling within her own body.

Her mind took her high above the tip of the highest point of the Rockies, skimming across the dry lands. There, she swooped between the fir trees, brushing against them and releasing the pine aroma into the morning air.

Slipping off her shoes and standing barefoot on the land, absorbing Mother Nature's powers, while still moving her arms, Kitty turned her head skyward and felt the gentle warmth touch her face. She was beyond caring if anyone saw her; her mind and body no longer belonged to her. She had put her trust in the soul of an imaginary eagle, and they flew as one. Slowly, they descended, and soon Kitty felt the land beneath her feet again.

She crouched down and touched the land that Mim relied upon to survive – a place she loved. Suddenly, Kitty wanted the same. She wanted to return to a simpler life, where although she would work hard, she would rest well and enjoy the rewards of a mind at peace.

As a wife, she had to ensure her husband's comforts and needs were met, but what about hers?

Did Michael—*had* Michael taken them into account?

Was he seeking a home for them with her in mind, or had he selected something which suited only him?

Without her at his side, how would he know her feelings about Canada, how within hours it made her feel connected to something raw and untouched? Was it tiredness that made her want to put the outside world aside and learn to lead a new life without the rush of modern living? Her nursing days were intense and stretched her energy and emotions to their limits. Her life had already been busy and stressful; she had never slowed down after the war.

A noise disturbed her quiet moment, and she turned around, unashamed that she was crying and barefoot.

'We women carry our troubles until The Mother enters our souls and gives us inner strength,' Mim said, looking at Kitty with knowing eyes.

Kitty cuffed away her tears, making no attempt to smile at Mim, who stood in a loose shirt over male britches and was also barefoot.

'I don't know what came over me. Something took me flying like a bird – in my head – but it felt real,' Kitty said, her voice barely a whisper. She looked back at the mountains, now a golden tan where the sunlight touched. A bird swirled to its highest point as Kitty had only moments before.

'The wise ones of the tribes whose lives were taken and your ancestors, they all hear you. They showed you how to release your mind. Only those with an open heart and mind will hear and feel them in the soil and our hearts. You have connected early with your new land, Canada, but she tells you this is where your heart wants to beat,' Mim replied.

'Were you born to a tribe, Mim? I hope I am not rude in asking?' Kitty had already wondered, as Mim's skin tone and hair colour suggested she was connected to someone with an indigenous bloodline. Kitty sensed that Mim came from an old Canadian family.

'You are not rude. Inquisitive, and that's understandable. I was and am one of the First Nations. The Siksika are my people, but my mother turned her back on her family after my father disappeared. She wanted what a white man offered, which was nothing in the end. I had to work in the city to survive her drinking habits,' Mim said.

'I am sorry,' Kitty said. Mim shook her head, her long, glossy hair waving free from the plait it had been bound in the previous day.

'When I met Dan, he was alone in the world, and he encouraged me to find why my heart cried out for space and to leave the city behind. He encouraged me to use my real name, Akomimm, which means love. My mother had changed my name to Louisa. Dan always called me Mim.'

'Dan sounds wonderful,' Kitty said.

Mim nodded.

'He was. Dan wanted me to find my roots and for us to live as my ancestors had taught for years. He never made it, and I could only afford this place. I know I can return to my people, but I am too independent now. They help me when I need extra hands during the busier season. I live freely, and since I am happy, they put no pressure on me to return. I no longer wear the chains that my mother bound me in. I am where I am meant to be, that's for sure.' Mim looked into the distance after she had spoken.

Kitty exhaled the sigh of a heavy heart.

'I am so sorry you were taken from something so precious, and to lose the love of your life. I am tired and heart-weary with worry about my husband. Our marriage is troubled, so I am here looking for him to let him know I want to live in Canada too. There are no letters crossing between us, it's a start from scratch situation.'

'And your "brother"?' Mim said. Her eyes told Kitty she knew the truth.

'We didn't lie to you. We're as good as brother and sister, but not in blood. We've been through terrible times together, and neither of us have siblings – mine died with my parents. Stanley and I have a bond which will never be broken. Michael understands – he likes Stanley.'

Mim pouted and raised an eyebrow.

'I doubt any husband will understand you sharing a bedroom with another man. Best keep that to yourselves,' Mim said. 'When you settle, come my way again. I feel your soul, and it is pure.'

After the conversation, Mim walked to the outhouse and left Kitty looking at the place that called her name. Mim encouraged her to feel the heartbeat in the soil and showed her she had a path to follow.

Inhaling the dusty aroma of the warm earth and other smells surrounding her, Kitty breathed to calm her mind, balance her unsteady fears and take the fresh air with her. Calgary would be hot and not so fresh.

'Morning. Sleep well? You were up early,' Stanley said as he walked past her with his washbag in hand. Kitty took a moment before she turned round and smiled at him.

'Morning. I was restless, but I know you slept well,' Kitty said, teasing him. She pointed to the outhouse.

'Mim's down there now. I watched the sunrise, and she stopped for a chat. She knows about us not being siblings, and gave wise advice not to mention it to Michael. I don't like lying to him, so if – when – we find him, I will be honest.'

Stanley shifted into a more comfortable standing position.

'I will reassure him. He knows he can trust me and what you mean to me. Being honest is the only way. Sadly, Michael wasn't, and look where it has led you. He should have told you his plans.'

'He wasn't dishonest, he just never involved me, but I understand what you mean,' Kitty replied.

'Go and get dressed, and we'll make a concerted effort to find him today.' Stanley said and waved at Mim as she walked towards her horses.

Chapter Twenty-Four

After the peace of Cochrane, Kitty's ears tingled with the noise of Calgary. Cars, trams and people surrounded her, and in that moment she knew the city would never be her home. Her busy days as a nurse in England, rushing from one bomb site to another, crawling through the rubble, listening to the cries of the injured, had taken their toll. Kitty stood watching the rush of busy lives swirling around her and closed her eyes, trying hard to shut out the noise. 'Okay?' Ted's voice brought her back to why she was there.

'I'm not liking this noise. Not for permanent living. I need to find my husband, and to tell him I can't live here.' She looked around her desperately. Stanley had gone to make enquiries about Michael at the post office nearby.

'Not live in Canada?' Ted asked, striking a match against a wall and lighting a cigarette.

'A town. I need peace. It's all too much!' Kitty's breath caught in her throat, and her chest constricted. She cupped her knees and breathed slowly in and out.

'Kitty?' Ted knelt beside her, his voice filled with concern.

Kitty did not respond; she concentrated on her breathing, the way she had taught many patients when pain relief was unavailable. Eventually, she regained control and stood upright.

'I'm sorry, Ted. I am fine. I think it is the heat,' she said apologetically.

'Stanley's coming,' Ted said, and Kitty heard the relief in his voice. 'Stanley, over here!'

Ted waved to Stanley and rushed to his side. Kitty guessed he was relaying the story of her episode because Stanley gave her a worried look and moved as fast as he could to be with her.

'Kitty? Ted tells me you are unwell?' he said.

Shaking her head, Kitty reassured him she was fine.

'Did you find Michael?' she asked anxiously.

Stanley shook his head, 'No, but I've been advised to try Leduc. It is the centre of the oil strike, and many interested parties are out there. Michael was here for oil investment, so it is a place he might visit.'

'I have to work,' Ted said, 'but I can help find someone to take you.'

Thirty minutes later, Kitty and Stanley were sitting in the back of a large old Ford pick-up truck surrounded by bales of straw, heading for Leduc. Kitty gave a slight giggle and cough when dust blew from the road and a breeze ruffled the loose straw skyward and over them both.

'If Michael is at the other end, I think he might run a mile. I must look horrendous,' she called out to Stanley above the engine's noise.

He grinned back at her. 'You have a few new hair accessories,' he said.

Kitty felt for the stray straw strands and tugged them free. She wiped her sweaty face and felt the fine grit clinging to her. She looked at her shoes, sensible brown lace-ups now scuffed and dirty, and could hear her aunt's and several hospital matrons' voices berate her for her untidy appearance. She no longer cared. Not tidy and clean, but happy and relaxed, those were the things she now sought. Her moment with the eagle and Mim had brought balance to her outlook on life, and seeing residents stressed and rushed made it more important for her to find the words to express to Michael what she wanted from their new life. If neither could agree, they would have to compromise.

She had come too far and learned something valuable during her short time in this country: she was not going to become a wife who obeyed the rules because society stated she should. She wanted to become someone like Mim, close to nature, a free spirit, and share her compassion with others. She wondered if Michael would open a medical clinic to continue his practice. He was a good doctor, and his skills should not go to waste. She also wanted a small homestead for herself, where she could raise their family. She was keen on country living, and if they could live near Mim and learn from her, that would be the ideal outcome. The old Kitty no longer had a voice.

When they climbed down from the truck, they followed the driver's advice and headed for one of the buildings on the edge of the large well pumps. The smell of oil and damp ground permeated the air, and Kitty knew neither she nor Stanley would want to set up home in the area.

'The smell,' she said as they walked.

'It smells of money to many,' Stanley said, 'I will definitely look to investing the money from Jenny's family home in oil shares. A valuable find for the landowner.'

The large log office had men coming and going, some gruff in their greetings and others intent on ignoring them. They were what some might call rough and ready, but Kitty could see they were willing workers. She doubted many had wives; they lived for oil drilling. Stanley flicked his head towards the office. 'We'll ask about Michael here. I'll ask about investing, too.'

Inside the office, a man sat head down, absorbed in reading and signing papers while smoking strong tobacco, and Kitty's nose was irritated to the point of a sneeze. The man looked up from his papers in surprise.

'What can I do for you?' he asked, blowing out a large puff of smoke, looking from Kitty to Stanley.

'Two things, we hope,' Stanley said.

'Ah, you are Brits. Welcome.'

'Thank you.' Kitty replied.

'Mrs McCarthy is looking for her husband, Doctor Michael McCarthy,' Stanley interjected. 'We lost contact during our travels and were told he was heading to invest in an oil find near Calgary, so we are assuming here.'

The man gestured to two chairs. 'Sit yourselves down. Doctor McCarthy? I can't say I have come across anyone of that name personally, but he might be registered in the claims office in Calgary,' he said.

'Thank you. Stanley is looking to invest, so we might be lucky on both counts,' Kitty said, giving the man a bright smile.

The man turned to Stanley.

'What do you know about oil drilling?' he asked.

'Not a lot. I know you have drilled – is it a hundred and thirty-three times? – and struck lucky this February, but that is about as far as my knowledge goes. A colleague of Kitty's husband told me that when he mentioned Michael was looking at opportunities,' Stanley said. 'I do understand a good investment opportunity though, and if I can make my money grow to finance my old age, then I would be wise to look into it, don't you agree?'

The man stood up from his desk and walked to a large map on the wall behind him.

'Our plans are to drill for more. The thirteenth of February was my mother's birthday, and when the oil strike hit and the burn-off happened, I told her the flame, which was sky-reaching, was in her honour. She took it as it was meant, a teasing joke, but after I lost her a month later, I am pleased she saw it happen.'

'I'm sorry for your loss. Are you the landowner?' Kitty asked, unsure what to say other than her condolences.

'No, I manage the field, and have worked on every drilling,' he said.

'Dedication has paid off for you,' Kitty said with admiration.

Stanley walked to the map and studied it for a while before turning back to Kitty.

'I think we'll return to Calgary, find accommodation and begin our search again tomorrow. I will find out more about investing. This is an important find; even I can see that.' He held out his hand to the man. 'Thank you for your time, Mr…'

'Lomax. Jimmy Lomax. Come by and let me know how you get on,' he said, addressing Stanley, then turned to Kitty. 'Sorry I can't help you, Mrs McCarthy.'

'Thank you for your time, and if you do hear anything, would you be so kind as to send a message to a lady named Mim in Cochrane? She lives on a homestead, and her nephew Ted will get word to us from there. She's our first friend in Canada,' Kitty said, shaking his hand.

'Then I will class myself as your second. Do not hesitate if you need advice or a second signature, I'm happy to help,' Jimmy said to Stanley and smiled at them both.

When they left, it dawned on them they had no way of getting back to Calgary, so Stanley returned to speak with Jimmy and they again travelled back to the city on the back of a truck taking some of the men for a few days' leave. It was loud and jovial when they spoke amongst themselves, sharing their intentions of finding lady friends and drinking all night. Kitty had been in the company of enough soldiers not to be shocked or offended, but their bawdy banter and lack of manners made her pity whoever had to deal with them after they had drunk themselves into a stupor.

Chapter Twenty-Five

Once again, Kitty stood in the centre of Calgary waiting for Stanley to find them accommodation for the night. She was thirsty and hungry, and the heat made her feel dizzy. She found a small patch of shade, hoping Stanley would return with news of Michael, but a sudden blackness overwhelmed her, and her legs gave way before she could call out for someone to help.

A rocking motion and voices brought Kitty out of the darkness. She opened her eyes and looked up at dark brown eyes peering down at her.

'She's awake,' Mim's voice called out.

Kitty went to sit up, confused as to where she was, and why Mim was with her.

'Thank goodness for that.' Kitty heard Stanley's voice.

'Where am I?' she said, her voice croaking and her throat feeling dry.

'Sip this,' Mim instructed and put a cup to Kitty's mouth. Kitty sipped a mouthful of cool water.

'Let's sit her up,' Stanley said, and Kitty felt her body moved so that she was sitting up with her head resting against pillows. Her head felt tender and she put her hand to the sore spot.

'What happened?' she asked.

'We assume you fainted,' Stanley said.

'No food, or water, and a day of travelling from what I hear,' Mim said in an irritated voice.

'I'm sorry, Kitty, I never thought to stop and eat. You said nothing, and our mission was to find Michael,' Stanley said.

'Mission. You weren't on a mission where you needed to keep marching on,' Mim said, sounding more annoyed.

'We were both focused on Michael and not ourselves.' Kitty said, 'It's not your fault, Stanley. My head hurts – did I hit it?' Kitty touched the side of her head and winced.

Mim nodded at her. 'You did, but that was down to Ted. He lifted you onto the cart, and your head fell against the top. He's upset and will come to see you after he has settled the horses. Just rest. You are back with me for the night,' Mim said.

Kitty shifted and looked at Stanley standing at the end of the bed.

'Stanley?' she said, waiting to hear if he had news of her husband.

'Nothing,' he said. 'There was nowhere to stay, which is why Ted brought us back to Mim. She's kindly taken you in, and I will go with Ted and stay with him back in Calgary, if you feel comfortable with that?'

Kitty did not say anything. She was unsure about being left alone. Mim was kind, but Kitty barely knew her.

'I want you to rest tomorrow, and while I'm in Calgary, I can keep looking for Michael,' Stanley said. It made sense and Kitty gave a slight tilt of her head.

'I suppose it will be fine. I've travelled alone and been with strangers enough. Mim is good company. Promise you will be careful,' she replied.

'I promise, and you do the same. I will see you late tomorrow and hopefully have news or somewhere for us to stay,' Stanley said and walked over to her. He dropped a kiss on her forehead and left the room. Kitty leaned back feeling exhausted.

'I am sorry about your head.' Ted's apologetic voice drifted from the doorway.

Kitty opened her eyes and looked at him. His face had furrowed lines from frowning.

'I am fine and safe, thanks to you. A slight bump on the head will soon go, and I have the luxury of this bed for the night. You've both been very kind. I won't forget it. Thank you.'

Ted waved a hand dismissing her thanks.

'I will take good care of Stanley. You rest, and Mim will entertain you tomorrow. There's a ditch to be dug down to the Bow, so that will keep you busy,' he said with a laugh, giving her a wide grin.

'I'll have it dug by the time you return,' Kitty replied, relieved that Stanley had Ted as company for the night.

Later in the evening, Kitty took a lamp to the outhouse, and when she had finished washing away the day's grime, she stood outside looking at the moon. Another day had passed with no news of Michael, but the crescent moon above the mountain's highest point reminded her that there was a chance he was looking at it too, which gave her hope.

'Where are you, Michael? Have we got it wrong? Are you in another part of Canada? Or are you still in Britain?' she whispered, but before melancholy set in, she went back to the cabin and was greeted by Mim, who was pouring broth into a large mug.

'Beef broth, it will see you through the night. Drink,' she said, holding out the mug.

Kitty took it and sniffed. 'It smells delicious,' she said appreciatively.

'Homegrown from my stock. We have good cattle and they keep this place going,' Mim replied. 'Let's sit on the porch. It is my favourite time of day, when I can relax and enjoy the company of the moon.'

They sipped their broth in silence. Kitty knew this was precious time for Mim and did not want to disturb her peace. She wondered how long it would be before she could sit on her own porch after a day of working on her own home, and preparing a meal for Michael.

'I take it you are not in the family way with the fainting episode? It made me wonder if you were. And what will you do if you don't find your husband?' Mim asked bluntly, breaking the silence, and Kitty was grateful she had not taken a mouthful of soup or she might have choked.

'No, no, I am not. With the Michael situation, we'll have to speak to someone in authority to help us find out if he left England and arrived here safely. Stanley has promised to support me and any decisions I make. It is early days, but I don't think I will return to Great Britain. I think I am where I am meant to be, and that one day Michael will find me if I can't find him.' Kitty's sadness threatened to break through the internal barrier she was building.

'I will take you somewhere tomorrow. It is a walk, but I think you are meant to see it. Now get some sleep and try not to worry,' Mim said kindly. Kitty noticed Mim's voice was no longer firm, as if she had softened towards her guest. Kitty was touched.

'I appreciate your friendship, Mim,' Kitty said. 'Thank you.'

'Get some sleep,' Mim repeated and Kitty smiled to herself She guessed Mim felt the same but was not one for emotional conversations.

Chapter Twenty-Six

Mim had woken Kitty and ensured she had fully recovered and was ready to hike. They went through Kitty's clothing, but Mim stated nothing was suitable except for a floral blouse. She offered Kitty a pair of thick denim trousers that belonged to Ted. Although they needed a leather belt to fit properly, they were perfect for the hike. The trousers felt heavy against Kitty's skin, but she appreciated that Mim had put thought into her outfit. They decided that Kitty's sensible brown shoes were not ideal, but would be more comfortable than an oversized pair of Mim's. Mim also gave her a wide-brimmed straw hat to wear.

'There, a prairie girl in the making,' Mim said as she placed the hat on Kitty's head and handed her an embroidered backpack. 'This was my mother's. I've put in a water flask, an apple, and a slice of bread to keep you going. We'll eat at the end of the hike.'

'I'm grateful to you for showing me something new. I know you are busy, Mim,' Kitty said as they left the cabin.

'I have business at the other end, so it is not a wasted day. I see something in you and want you to share some time with me, to begin understanding what life is like around Cochrane village compared to Calgary.'

'Not far now,' Mim called over her shoulder. Kitty arched her back; since before sunrise they had walked miles through the prairies along the Bow River banks.

Kitty felt invigorated, tired from a restless night, but renewed by walking through the open spaces. The thick trousers helped protect her legs from being scratched by coarse grasses, and she was grateful for the long sleeves of her cotton blouse when mosquitoes buzzed around her near the river. When their water flasks were empty, they filled them with the fresh, cool water as it flowed over the rocks, heading, Mim told her, towards the Oldman River. The pine trees shared their aroma as they crushed the needles underfoot.

'I will teach you how to make a poultice for blisters from the pine. You will be wise to invest in boots for the longer walks,' Mim said as Kitty adjusted her shoes for comfort, noting they had rubbed at a small area on the side of her foot.

'I have a lot to learn, especially when it comes to sensible clothing,' Kitty replied.

Mim gave a slight snort of a laugh. 'You have a whole new way of life to learn. Winter hasn't arrived yet, and that's a different kind of living. I don't know how cold Britain gets, but we dip miles below freezing here. I am hardened to it – you will have to adapt fast.'

Kitty fastened her shoes and stood up, satisfied she was ready to continue. As they walked, Mim taught her a few words in her native tongue. Kitty struggled at first, but then soon satisfied Mim with her pronunciation.

Further along the trail, they watched a man fish, flicking his rod across the silver-tipped river.

'You will learn to catch trout one day. Ted and I enjoy our days on the river during the season.'

Kitty giggled. 'I think we would starve if it were just down to me, but I look forward to trying.'

Eventually, they stopped walking, and Mim nodded towards a group of what Kitty now knew were tipis. Mim told her she was born in her mother's, and could remember the comfort and warmth she lost when they moved. Kitty was not surprised when Mim said she would not live in one again, as her home was the dream of hers and Dan's, but thought it a shame that Mim's mother had taken away the family legacy.

'We are near the town of Mitford,' Mim said. 'I sell my surplus fruit and vegetables there, but soon there won't be anyone around. It is a dying town. Many of them have moved to Cochrane and Calgary. Where the jobs are. The tipis ahead are the temporary home for some of the Siksika working here on the ranches and farms. This is my surprise for you. We will be visiting them today.'

'Gracious, are any of your family in them?' Kitty asked, looking at the homes and horses ahead.

'They are all my family, but I assume you mean direct blood,' Mim said. 'My uncle – my father's brother – is the elder accompanying the youths on their first summer working the prairies, and when I heard he was with them, I wanted to come and see him. He is a wise man, and a funny, kind uncle. He is happy I am where I am, and has not taken offence that I am not living with them.'

Kitty looked around at the children running and playing together. Several were barefoot, and she envied their ability to ignore the stones and jump surefooted without stubbing their toes. She saw mothers feeding their babies in a circle, all laughing and chatting together, and was reminded of her upbringing, where the mothers gathered on the doorstep with babies at the breast, beneath a blanket. She watched Mim approach a group of youths wearing only leather trousers and headbands with feathers, and an older man wearing a large headdress of feathers and leather clothes in brown and cream. They were seated in a semicircle, and Mim beckoned Kitty to join them.

'Oki,' she said, and addressed it to the elder as Mim had taught her.

The man said something in his own language, and Mim translated back.

'He said welcome and asked your name. Remember what I taught you?'

'Nitsiska'sim Kitty,' Kitty said slowly and shyly.

The man nodded, then addressed Mim, who translated with a gentle smile at the man.

'My uncle's name is Togquos. It means twin. My father was his twin.'

Togquos said something else, and everyone around burst out laughing. Kitty looked at Mim, puzzled. Mim gave an amused shake of her head.

'He has honoured you greatly, but only because of how I interpreted your name. I tried to explain that it wasn't exact, and he has a naughty humour – he said you look like a frightened kitten, but will soon become fierce like all good women. We laughed because his wife is fiery, and we say he is scared of her. He said that, as you are my friend and determined to live on the land, you must have a Siksika name; he has named you Sinopa. It means Fox Kitten.'

Kitty felt the blush burn in her cheeks. It was not embarrassment but pleasure at being honoured by Togquos. She bent her head deeply towards him as a mark of respect, unsure if she was offending him, but it felt the right thing to do.

'Fox Kitten McCarthy. In England, we call the children of the fox "cubs". I am a new cub in Canada, and am happy to be known as Sinopa. Please tell him I am extremely honoured. I will visit him again one day and show him how fierce I have become.' Kitty laughed, and Mim joined her, then translated back to her uncle. The laughter that rang out around her touched Kitty's core. She needed the uplift Mim had given her and would be forever grateful to her new friend.

Togquos clapped his hands, and within moments, an array of food and drink was presented. Through Mim, she answered questions about her life in England and during the war. She told them about how she lost her family, and met Michael, and how she and Stanley set up the orphanage to fulfil his wife's dying wishes. The people around Mim listened with interest and made noises of approval. Once they had eaten, Togquos had the children dance for her in honour of her work for children without family. He said she and Stanley had given them a tribe and a chance in life, and he greatly respected them. He instructed Mim to bring Stanley to him so they could meet.

A young teenage girl approached Kitty and gestured to Kitty's head.

'She wants to know if she can braid your hair,' Mim said.

'I'd like that, yes,' Kitty replied.

She sat watching Mim's people move about their home, everyone calm and serene. The young girl plaited Kitty's hair, then held a hand mirror so that Kitty could see the colourful strands woven through the plait.

'It suits you,' Mim said when Kitty approved the style.

A group of young mothers walked over to them and spoke with Mim.

'They want to give you a gift for your new home when you have one. I need to speak to my uncle privately, but the women will sit with you and chatter amongst themselves. I won't be long,' Mim said, returning to her uncle.

Kitty sat, feeling welcomed and calm. She wanted this feeling for life, but was sensible enough to know it would never happen. Life threw troubles at everyone's door; it would not miss hers when she had one.

The women spoke to her and amongst themselves, but Kitty could only smile, and it seemed enough for them to enjoy her company. The gift Mimi had mentioned took Kitty's breath away. It was beautiful as well as practical. The women shook out a folded blanket in woven colours of blue, cream, yellow and red, and it was handed to her with smiles all round. One woman draped it around Kitty's shoulders, and the whole group raised their voices in what seemed to be a song. Kitty began to cry tears of happiness, sheer joy. She felt a moment of connection to Mim's extended family and noticed her friend looking over, her face beaming with pleasure. A young girl wiped away Kitty's tears, her large eyes showing concern, so Kitty gave her the widest smile she could manage and touched the girl's cheek to reassure her that she was happy.

When they said their goodbyes, their bags were heavy with gifts for Mim, and Mim's voice was light and cheerful.

'I have asked them to move onto my land and help me repair my fences in their spare time. My uncle has agreed. It will save me money and provide security for my horses and cattle. I have offered him a cow in return. He is such a kind man, and I think he likes that I have reached out to them at last,' she told Kitty as they walked the river trail home.

'They're all kind. I am grateful to you for sharing your family with me, Mim. I had no idea you had such deep connections when I first met you. I could see by their clothes and my blanket that their sewing skills, working with hide and wool, are wonderful. Everything is a work of art.' Kitty said.

'It is a generous gift. They see something in you, a willingness to learn, a purity to try and a heart filled with kindness. They will be your friends for life if you let them. You must forget your life before Canada and embrace this new one. They will teach you how to survive the seasons, everything. The residents in the main town will also be friendly and generous to you. Open your mind and you will do well in Cochrane,' Mim said as they reached home.

Kitty looked about for signs of Ted and Stanley, but they were not home.

'Be patient,' Mim said in a calming voice. 'What is meant to happen will happen in its own time. Help me prepare the vegetables; work will take your mind off your worries.'

As late afternoon rolled into evening, it became evident that the men would not be returning that night.

'I am sorry, Mim. I know you were expecting us to leave today,' Kitty said as they sat quietly on the porch, looking up at the stars.

'I am happy for your company, Kitty, so don't fret. Your bed is still made up. Rest, and tomorrow will bring you news, good or bad, but for now it is out of your control,' Mim replied.

'That's true, and I'm grateful for your company. It's been a wonderful day, thank you. I can't wait to write to my uncle and tell him. He will be grateful to you for looking after me, too,' Kitty replied, her thanks genuine. Mim had given her an insight into something new, a sample of a different kind of lifestyle in Canada.

Chapter Twenty-Seven

Ted's voice was the first thing Kitty heard when she lifted her head from her pillow the following morning. She was surprised to hear him so early. She scrambled to her feet, grabbed her washbag and rushed to the kitchen.

'Good morning,' she said to Ted and Mim, who were seated, eating breakfast.

'Morning,' Mim said, and Ted nodded.

'Go and wash, then come to hear the news,' Mim instructed, and Kitty's stomach gave a slight flip. Something was wrong. Stanley was not with them.

Wasting no time, Kitty did not stop to admire the plains or mountains this morning. She barely noticed the golden sunrise or the pretty blue jay sitting on the fence post nearby.

Where was Stanley? The question pounded through her head as she rushed back into the cabin.

'Where's Stanley?' she blurted out as soon as she was through the door. 'Is he hurt?'

Mim rose to her feet and nodded towards a chair. 'Sit down and eat while Ted tells you.'

Kitty did as she was told and looked at Ted, trying hard to judge his face as he finished eating.

By the time he had pushed his plate away, and Mim had put a dish of fruit in front of Kitty, Kitty's patience was stretched thin.

'Well? Where is he, Ted?' she asked impatiently.

Ted looked at her. 'He got himself a car and is driving to a hospital in Saskatchewan. According to a doctor in Calgary, your husband expressed interest in a new health system and a course at the hospital. The doctor didn't know if he was a resident in Calgary or travelling the country looking for a position which suited him.'

Kitty stared at Ted in disbelief. Michael had been in Calgary, and they missed him.

'Was he passing through Calgary or living there?' she asked.

Ted gave a shoulder shrug. 'We don't know. I know Stanley wanted to get to him before he disappeared again, and there was no time for him to come and fetch you. He urged me to help him find a car to rent, then sent me here with the message. Stanley became concerned when the doctor suggested that Michael appeared tired and disoriented.' He threw Kitty an apologetic glance as she sighed with frustration at his news.

'He has paid Mim for a week's lodgings and asked you to stay where you are so he doesn't have to come looking for you too, and he said he has arranged storage for your other luggage.'

Kitty's heart beat at a furious pace as her anxiety level rose.

'He's right to be worried. Michael had a severe head injury during a mission. He was brought to Canada for neurological treatments during the war, and then returned to England when he was discharged. I'm worried, maybe he has relapsed.' Kitty stood up. 'How far is it to Saskatchewan?' she asked.

Mim went to her and put a hand on her shoulder. 'Kitty, do as Stanley asked and stay with me. He is a good man and obviously cares for both of you. He knows where Ted lives and works in Calgary, and will send a telegram if you are needed, I am sure.'

Kitty knew she had no choice but to do as Stanley asked.

'I can't do much else, and yes, Stanley would not hide anything from me, so I must put my trust in him to help Michael. I am sorry we've brought this to your door, Mim. And Ted, thank you for taking the time,' Kitty said, giving them both a grateful smile. Her mood was much lower than the day before, but she knew working alongside Mim would be the distraction she needed, so she asked, 'What are your plans today, Mim?'

Mim patted Kitty's shoulder. 'To wear you out so you sleep well tonight. Ted, you go back to work. We will be fine here.'

After Ted had left the ranch, Mim told Kitty to change into the clothes she had worn the previous day and, when she was ready, to join her by the horses.

Kitty went to her room and tried hard not to think about Michael. She sat in front of the mirror checking her hair and decided to replait it as she liked the style. The single plait reminded her of her aunt styling it the same way on the first day of school, and the memory of her mother's plaits keeping the red beret in place. Kitty's nursing hairstyle was a bun.

She was extremely concerned about Stanley, but Ted told her he had given clear instructions on places for Stanley to stop for a rest and had personally helped Stanley feel safe enough to drive without an adapted pedal. The truck was easier for Stanley than a horse.

Throwing off the sadness and worry that threatened to drag

her down, Kitty patted down her plait, cleared her mind as best she could and went back out into the fresh air to join Mim.

'This is Ipota. It means to fly. She is a fast horse who thinks she's a bird. Ever ridden a horse?' Mim asked as she brushed down a beautiful chestnut horse, whispering to it as she worked.

'No, and I am fairly certain I can't,' Kitty said, watching Mim remove dried mud and grass from the flank of her four-legged companion.

'Time to saddle up and learn if you want to live out here like I do,' Mim said and grinned.

Kitty stared at her in horror and guessed Mim was not joking. After she finished grooming the horse, she picked up a saddle and held it out to Kitty.

'Well, come on. Meet your mount,' she said, nodding at another brown horse chewing at the ground. 'Ponokamita means horse in my people's language. His name is Saahkómaapi, which means boy. I am not good with creating names,' Mim said, laughing.

Despite her low mood, Kitty also laughed. 'Saahkómaapi,' she repeated slowly. 'So long as he is a good boy when I try to put the saddle on his back.'

Getting close to the tall horse and putting the saddle on him made her nerves tingle, but Kitty was determined to try. Riding the horse was another life challenge, and Kitty knew she must try to prove herself capable. She was unsure why she felt she had to prove herself to Mim, a virtual stranger, but her instinct told her it would help her survive whatever disaster might be around the corner.

Chapter Twenty-Eight

After an hour of instructions and getting to know Saahkómaapi, Kitty was ready for her first horse ride. Mim warned her not to let her nerves get the better of her, or Saahkómaapi would sense it and play her up.

Clicking her tongue in the way Mim had trained him to respond to, she waited for the horse to take his first steps, which was as nerve-wracking as stepping onto Canadian soil on her first day.

With Mim's encouragement, Kitty attempted to regulate her breathing and remain calm. The moment Saahkómaapi moved forward, she felt the gentle movement of his powerful body, and, as instructed, she relaxed into the sway. They moved slowly around the yard, then Mim dismounted and opened the gate.

'You're doing well enough for us to walk around the perimeter. I need to inspect the far fences in that field over there.' Mim pointed beyond the next field.

'What if he runs off with me?' Kitty replied in a panic.

'He won't bolt unless you hurt him somehow. He's a gentle ride, which is why I have given him to you to learn on while you are here. Trust me, and trust Saahkómaapi, but it is important to trust yourself, Kitty.'

'Easier said than done,' Kitty replied with a smile.

They ambled along, taking in the scenery around them, and Mim showed her places and things of interest. Kitty was greatly impressed by Mim's knowledge and absorbed as much as she could.

Just beyond the boundary, Kitty noticed another lodge, much larger than Mim's, with two levels and a large front porch. The ground looked neglected, and the building uninhabited.

'Who lives there?' Kitty asked as they drew closer.

'It was an elderly man, but he passed away the year we arrived. His son is looking to sell it to the oil company, but I have objected because it's so near my home. I don't want to fall out with the son; we've known each other for years. Fortunately, I know the town clerk well enough and they keep me updated. If he is granted the right of sale, I will have a lot of pressure on me to sell mine, but I will only go when I want to, not when I am forced to by the oil companies.'

Kitty's heart bled for Mim. 'Is there oil here?' she asked, astounded at what she had just learned.

'No one knows. They drill and try, then move on. With Leduc's success, there is great excitement; the son is probably just cash-happy, and the oil company won't be interested. But if they decide to buy it, I may not have another year here. I keep looking for other places away from Cochrane, but my heart is in mine and Dan's land. I sit here by the river, and it takes my tears upstream. I will not cry on my land, it has to be my happy place. I have written and asked about purchasing the property, and am waiting. Hence letting out the room, to bring in extra income.'

Kitty listened to Mim open her heart. She felt moved that Mim could tell her about crying by the River Bow.

'I will object with you if it helps. I can write a letter stating the damage it would do to you as a widow,' Kitty said, her heart filled with a passion to help Mim.

Mim looked at her with tenderness in her damp eyes. 'You are a kind girl for sure. If I cannot buy the property, we can discuss it. Thank you.'

Kitty manoeuvred Saahkómaapi as Mim taught her, and approached the property. It was not surrounded by fencing. 'How much land is with it? I am not good at guessing acreage by sight,' Kitty asked.

Mim pointed towards a bend in the river and a cluster of pine trees.

'It goes beyond the trees, where there is another area. It is not large but a good size for a few cattle; he sold off most of it, which is mine. Hopefully, this place is too small for the mining company to buy,' Mim said.

Kitty saw the sadness in Mim's eyes.

'Let's hope it is too small and they sell to you,' she said, walking Saahkómaapi to the back of the property where the river ran past a large expanse of grass. She investigated the wrap-around veranda and came across a large back porch, similar to Mim's. Surrounding it were buds of late spring blooms amongst vast areas of overgrown greenery. She looked to her right and further down the river to Mim's home, thinking it sad that the farmer's son was not interested in such a beautiful place. Despite the weeds, the property needed minimal restoration. All it needed was a good clean to become a comfortable home like Mim's. 'I truly hope you stave off the oil companies,' she said.

'Me too, but I have work to do in the meantime. The team turned the cattle out onto another field this morning, and I want to check everything is okay. Take it steady and follow me,' Mim said, moving Ipota forward and away from the cabin. Kitty followed, realising Mim owned more land than she had first thought.

They looked down a slight incline into the pasture and saw Mim's cattle grazing contentedly in front of them. Mim waved to a man riding amongst them, and he returned the wave.

'All is good here,' she said and turned Ipota around. 'Let's head home and teach you how to remove the saddle and care for Saahkómaapi after a ride.' When they reached flatter land, she slowed down and dismounted.

'Stay where you are. I'm going to lead you into a trot. You are more than capable, and he trusts you; otherwise, you would have been on the floor by now. He likes to walk, but enjoys a trot. Remember what I told you about using your thighs and knees,' she said, moving Saahkómaapi gently, speeding him up, and giving Kitty encouragement and instructions on retaining balance and control. Eventually, she let go. 'Keep him moving, and I will catch up,' she said.

Kitty dared not speak. Saahkómaapi's body swayed faster, and she concentrated on staying in the saddle. It felt good to have learned a new skill that might be useful for her future or just for pleasure. She had never thought she would be on a plane one day, then travelling across a vast new country and learning and enjoying horse riding a few days later. The bond she felt with Saahkómaapi grew as they rode, and she had absolute faith in him getting her back to Mim's in one piece. How had her life changed so much in such a short time? She hoped Michael and Stanley would arrive and get to see her on horseback before the end of the week. When they looked for their own place, Kitty knew she would have to insist on keeping a horse somewhere.

When they dismounted, Kitty let out a large breath.

'That was incredible!' she declared. 'Thank you so much, Mim. I was so scared at first, and now I want my own horse!'

Leading Ipota towards her stable, Mim called over her shoulder, 'I thought you would be a natural. Saahkómaapi will appreciate the exercise. We'll go further tomorrow.'

Inside, Kitty felt a flush of pride. Mim's words were so positive, giving her more determination to keep practising while she had the opportunity.

Chapter Twenty-Nine

The next morning, Kitty woke up in Mim's home feeling grateful and a little less stressed – until Ted reported back that afternoon with a telegram from Stanley.

'It arrived this morning,' Ted said as he handed it to Kitty. It was not what she had expected to read.

Arrived. No record of Michael here. Will try other hospitals. Got a driver. Do not worry. S x

She handed it to Mim.

'This is not the outcome I'd hoped for, but at least Stanley will be back soon, and we can work out our next step, and get out of your hair,' she said and turned to Ted.

'Thank you, Ted. As soon as Stanley returns, we must decide on something more permanent. I am now wondering if Michael returned to where he was born – Haileybury. What a fool, I should have thought of it before!' Kitty said, frustrated that it hadn't occurred to her that Michael might return to his roots. They had followed him to where they thought he would be heading, but maybe he changed his mind even when heading for the hospital.

'Where is that? What province, whereabouts in Canada?' Ted asked. He looked at Mim, who shrugged her shoulders.

'Ontario, I think. Maybe I should find someone there to leave him a message. The local doctor, perhaps? I do know there was a fire there in the Twenties which killed his parents, but that's all I know,' Kitty said, pacing the floor.

'Stop fidgeting and sit still. It will help you think,' Mim said, pulling out a chair and sitting down. Kitty did the same.

'Has he relatives there?' Mim asked.

Kitty shook her head. 'No. He said when his grandmother died, he was the only member left.'

Mim thought for a while and then stood up. 'I have a map of Canada. Let's see how far away it is, and we can work out how to get you there when Stanley returns.'

Mim's suggestion struck Kitty hard. She questioned herself. Did she want to chase around the country looking for Michael? How many weeks, months or even years would she be unsettled and homeless? It wasn't what she had envisaged when she left Britain. She had hoped to find her husband within a day of arrival and begin planning for their future. She was exhausted from the fear of not surviving alone in Canada, and the desire to achieve, and had pushed herself hard this past week. Was that because she felt guilty about suggesting divorce, or to hide the pain that she could not find the man she married?

Sitting with her head in her hands, she began questioning her marriage. Was it built on true love, or on the passion and exhilaration they shared when enemy attacks threatened them and they looked death in the eye? Did she just feel compassion when he returned from his injuries? And had she confused it with genuine love between two people?

Was she this safe person for Michael, the woman who understood him and his mood swings? He did not stay in England to fight for their marriage, and made plans without sharing; he gave no hint and showed no sign of leaving their life in England. They made love, but was it lust rather than love? Were they simply two orphans clinging onto what they believed would eventually become a family?

She compared him to Stanley. He had brought them back together during the war, and now he was trying to do it again, prepared to give up his life in England. Their friendship was a strong one; they loved one another. Kitty loved him for his strength and kindness, and she knew from what he told her that he was determined to see her happy. He had not hesitated to help her try to solve her marriage problem. Michael's answer was to walk away. Had she made it easy for him to leave?

Stanley had picked up the pieces and was trying to put them back again, putting his own health and happiness aside. He was always there for her. For Kitty, that was love.

'Oh, this is hopeless. It is never-ending. Dear Stanley, he is out there and should be settling into his new life. I've ruined everything,' she said, confused and agitated. She jumped to her feet and began pacing again.

Mim tutted loudly.

'Sit down, Kitty. You are not helping yourself by getting upset. Stanley is doing what he is doing because he loves you. Is there someone in England your husband might contact if he can't contact you?' Mim said. 'Maybe you can write to them, tell them where you are, and let Michael come and find you.'

Kitty sat down again. She had written to Trixie and mentioned their location, but suggested they would move to look for Michael at some point.

'Our friend Smithy is the one he would contact. He knows we're here. When Stanley gets back, I will talk to him and send a telegram to tell Smithy and his wife Trixie we are not moving from the Calgary area, and if Michael contacts them, Smithy can pass the message along.'

Mim stood up and went to her, touching her shoulder.

'You can rest now. Do not trouble your mind any longer. It is in the hands of the guardians who watch over you. Please make this your home for the week. Sit and do nothing, or learn new skills. Either way, this is the place to do it; the land heals the heart. I will repay Stanley for your board if you help me with chores so I can cut down on labour costs in the fields.'

Later that evening, when she climbed into bed and lay back, thinking about how to move past feeling guilty, Kitty began to reflect on her relationship with Stanley. She had never questioned her feelings towards him, accepting him as a kind friend and brother figure, and her love for him was that of a sibling.

She loved her uncle, Smithy, even Pots, but her love for Stanley was different. Her love for Michael was different, too.

Stanley made her laugh and relax. He helped solve her problems without question. Michael had not made her laugh in a long time, and she rarely relaxed around him, constantly worrying about his health and moods. She solved *his* problems. He leaned heavily on her for decision-making.

Kitty sat up in bed and leaned back on her pillow, looking out of the window at the star-dappled navy sky, aware that she had spent the evening doing nothing but questioning herself. But she knew she needed to go through the process to help her understand what she was suppressing and what frightened her.

Being alone frightened her. She had felt like this after the death of her parents, and she never wanted to feel that way again.

She had watched Stanley deal with the trauma of limb injury and the death of his wife, then move on with his life, helping others.

Michael had recovered somewhat from his head injury and gained a wife, but was he satisfied with her? Was Kitty enough for him? Or was she too much? Was she responsible for putting pressure on him to want a family? Was she now a burden to Stanley?

For goodness' sake, Kitty. Sleep. You're not responsible for what either of the men in your life thinks or feels; from now on, you can only be responsible for yourself. Take some pressure off Stanley. Let Michael find his own way back to you. There is nothing more you can do.

Chapter Thirty

Over the following days, Kitty refocused and made herself useful.

Although her bed and board were paid for, she needed to find something to occupy herself. Walking around and seeing the sights was not an option for her; it would be a pleasure to enjoy with Stanley and, hopefully, Michael in the future. They had years ahead of them. The priority was homebuilding and supporting one another. All she had to do was wait for Michael to find her.

She thought about how hardworking her aunt and uncle were when she was growing up, and vowed to make them proud, although neither of them would see her. Kitty wondered if her aunt and mother had guided her through the recent challenges. According to Mim, when she returned to try to live a life with her uncle's teachings in mind, she followed one that helped her adjust to her mixed lifestyle and slowly leaned more towards her roots. She aimed towards a good and orderly life.

Kitty always aimed to live as a good person, but in Canada her life was far from orderly, so she made it her mission to transform her bouncing from one plan to another into something more suitable to the situation.

Armed with limited knowledge but having a vast selection in Mim's lush vegetable-growing area, she collected herbs and wrote notes about their properties.

After riding Saahkómaapi, learning something new about his personality and her abilities every day, she mucked out the horses, even though the smell sometimes turned her stomach.

When Mim was elsewhere, Kitty cleaned the house to lighten her friend's load. Following Mim's recipes, Kitty cooked and practised her bread- and pastry-making skills. She was surprised at how much she enjoyed cooking and baking. Her shortbread passed Mim and Ted's taste test, and Mim's uncle insisted she take him a weekly supply, which amused Kitty as she explained she was only staying for a few days.

Kitty completed every task Mim assigned her with a determination to succeed. Her goal was to be as self-sufficient as possible, knowing there was no guarantee that Michael would be found or that Stanley would stay. She didn't want to burden Mim, and since arriving in Canada, and having a break from commitments in England, she no longer wanted to return to nursing. Also, having witnessed enough pain and suffering, she felt unable to care for orphans and patients as she once had. She needed to focus on taking it one day at a time. Distractions would not benefit her new way of life. Her situation was not ideal for now, but it was one where she had wise guidance and support.

In the evenings, Kitty impressed Mim with her sewing skills by turning dresses into shirts and tops – more practical items for her new life. She altered more trousers Mim had given her that she no longer wore, and created working outfits more suited to the environment in which she worked. Mim asked her to repair some of her clothes and suggested that Kitty consider using her skills if she ever needed to supplement her income. This led Kitty to make small pouches from leftover material, which she stored away intending to sell or barter.

The household washing proved a heavy task. Helping Mim with the laundry, she used a large bath-like tub, a washboard and buckets, which made her realise how pampered she had been, having had a housekeeper and a copper boiler.

Hanging the washing on the line to blow in the breeze with the mountains as a backdrop soothed her busy mind. When the things were dry, Kitty folded them, inhaling the fresh air and the pine fragrance from the rinsing water. She found those simple pleasures helped soothe the ache she felt in her back and arms.

One afternoon, Kitty sat writing letters home. In her letter to Jo, she was careful not to reveal too much about her current living situation; knowing Jo, she would likely try to airlift Kitty back to Fell Hall or cross the border and insist she lived protected in America. Kitty imagined her friend's face when she read about her riding through pine forests. She hoped that was enough to show she was happy and settled.

In her letters to her uncle, Wenna and Meryn, she spoke about her upbeat days and mentioned that Stanley was following up on news about Michael. Nothing more. Nothing about feeling overwhelmed or frightened. Whenever those feelings reared up and made her want to give up on everything and return to England, she quashed them. Her promise to be responsible for herself was not something she would break. She had chosen to give herself a year in Canada, even if she had to remain alone; she would not work for anyone other than Mim or herself.

Kitty knew she had ventured into adulthood with a bravery others might not have experienced, and now she wanted to draw on that bravery again. It had been so easy to fall into a peacetime pattern with Michael that – aside from being his wife and there being no bombs – was no different from wartime. They dealt with sick patients, sat at home discussing new cures and returned to work the following day. Death and sickness were routine, and joy was limited.

New challenges and opportunities waited for her in Canada; it was the right time to follow through and grab them. Financially, she was concerned that her private money was not enough to support her, and only by learning from others could she have any opportunity to earn an income. Though unwilling to nurse again, she knew that going to a hospital and retraining was an option; it would be her last resort, but she would do whatever was necessary. Every day, she worked at unravelling her mind and releasing confusing and conflicting obstacles. Her soul healed through hard work and walking barefoot over the plains.

She talked herself through unpleasant tasks, forced herself to watch the skilled cowboys when they were branding cattle, and managed a few minutes watching Mim prepare a slaughtered cow for sale. Mim told her it was something her uncle had helped her overcome; if Kitty did not intend to farm in the future, it was not something she needed to learn in a week.

By the end of the week, Kitty was exhausted but satisfied she had not wasted time wallowing in self-pity. She had walked and ridden more miles than she ever expected, eaten unfamiliar foods and met with the women of Mim's tribe to learn the art of sewing hide.

Her back ached, her hands and feet were sore, and her heart was grateful. Life had turned her upside-down, shaking out the old Kitty and leaving behind a new version of herself, one that was learning to fill the emptiness with the tools of survival and was driven by a silent, suppressed anger at her situation.

Chapter Thirty-One

On the day they expected Stanley back, Kitty baked while Mim and Ted were busy with others fixing the fences.

Although Kitty enjoyed time alone and learning new skills, there were moments she would have loved to sit and enjoy a cup of tea with Michael, discussing their day and their future. She recalled conversations from when they first married and when they were at their happiest. The more she thought about it, the more obvious it became that by the end of their first year of marriage they had allowed work to take over their lives. Their intimate moments were few and far between; only the harshness of the cold winter had brought them closer. But it now seemed that wasn't enough for him; his mind had wandered towards seeking a new life that offered less of the ordinary. Michael never came back from work to a home filled with the aroma of freshly baked bread, as she had never had the time, not to mention doubting her ability to even be able to bake.

In the quiet of the kitchen, again it registered with Kitty that her marriage had dwindled into a monotonous routine. Only the patients varied; everything else remained the same. Without work, she doubted that she and Michael had much in common.

For the first time, she wondered whether he would have been happier if World War II were still raging. They would be working side by side in volatile situations, which triggered passionate moments, driven by the fear of imminent death. Their letters, filled with loving words, once offered hope for the future they had envisioned together; but the reality was not as expected, and Kitty could not see a way around their mistakes. Perhaps divorce truly was the only solution – a way to free themselves and discover their true desires. If parting meant they could come back together, having realised that they wanted each other all along, then that was what fate had to determine.

In the quiet room, Kitty felt a sense of relief at unravelling her muddled marriage problems and wondered if Michael was taking the time to do the same.

It dawned on her that the war had deprived them of many experiences most couples shared during the romantic stages of their relationship. The war brought frantic farewells and uncertainties, leaving no room for lengthy courtships. Time was never on their side, and when it was, Kitty and Michael had landed with a thud, moving around each other in a dance of the unknown. They had failed to find the rhythm to bring balance and harmony to their daily lives. They were not a couple made for the ordinary.

If they were to part ways, Kitty wanted to face Michael and apologise for not understanding his desire to return to his roots and find a partner who could give him children born in his homeland. If he too had realised they were bound together for the wrong reasons, she wanted to set him free.

At that moment, she understood that she loved the idea of being married to Michael, but had hoped the man he was before his injuries would come back to her. In that hope, she had allowed her natural caring instinct to nurture the wounded version of him. Now she understood that although he was no longer wounded, he had pursued a life he had previously wanted, only to discover that it did not fulfil his soul, and that Kitty was not enough.

Guilt had probably kept him at home with her, and Kitty's guilt at asking for a divorce guided her towards her own truth. Her heart longed for something different too – not a routine love within a routine marriage. She wanted a love that lived by impulsive, passionate reactions after a gentle touch or a whispered word.

Kitty inhaled the aroma of cinnamon, bringing her back to baking before her mind took her too deep into her feelings. She knew she couldn't deny herself the right to feel as she did, but it added another layer of guilt. She lifted out a batch of shortbread – from her mother's recipe that she had found amongst papers in the suitcase – and made large biscuits, which she learned were known as cookies, using Mim's family recipe. Four loaves of bread and a large beef pie sat cooling while she worked. It acted as a form of therapy, a soothing routine with a pleasant outcome. Baking was a quiet companion that helped her work through her troubles.

The temperature rose, and Kitty stopped to wipe her brow, wondering how she would manage her baking if it got any hotter. Mim mentioned that they experienced several weeks of hot sun, which might change to cooler days because of the unpredictable weather pattern. Kitty decided it might be wise to keep her baking days for the cooler ones.

Kitty dabbed her face dry and began folding flour and eggs into a bowl. She moved contentedly around the kitchen, imagining a day when she could bake in her own home.

'Now there's a sight for sore eyes, and what's that wonderful smell?'

Stanley's voice echoed into the cabin from the doorway, and Kitty's heart leapt with joy. She turned around to see him. She was surprised to see how exhausted he looked.

'You're back!' she said, rushing to hug him. Stanley held her tightly for a few seconds before gently moving her away.

'I am. It was a long and uncomfortable journey, but I managed to return in one piece,' he said, smiling at her. He glanced over at the food that was cooling on the counter.

'I can't believe you're cooking. Is the bread yours?'

Kitty looked at him and smiled proudly.

'It all is, and there's a lot more I can do since you left,' she said, carefully lifting the cookies and shortbread from their trays.

'Like what?' Stanley asked, leaning on the kitchen unit, waiting patiently to hear what she had to share. One of his good points was that Stanley always had time to listen.

'Well, there are several things, but one is sitting down with Mim's uncle, a tribal elder, and other young warriors, remembering not to point because it is rude – you know how often we point, and it is natural to us, but I don't want to offend, so sit on my hands a lot of the time.' She giggled. 'Oh, and I am learning their language, which has the longest words for the shortest translation. I'm known as Fox Kitten. Sinopa. Fortunately, that one is an easy name to say,' she said, in a rush of excitement.

Stanley laughed. 'I like it. Maybe we should start using it. It suits you, Sinopa,' he said.

'Where's your driver?' Kitty asked before peering out the window, trying hard to avoid the inevitable: a conversation about Michael. When they talked about him, Kitty hoped she would not sound uncaring, and Stanley would not think she was giving up too easily. She needed to explain that they had to slow down and find another way forward to enjoy their new life.

'On his way back to Calgary. I won't need him again. The next search will be in my vehicle – something more comfortable.' Stanley sat down in a comfortable chair with a loud sigh of relief. 'I will rest for a few days and think about where Michael could be; I can't find him anywhere in the two areas we thought he might stay. Goodness knows where he has gone. Six hospitals, several private doctors and a dozen oil investors can't help me either,' Stanley said, his voice no longer light-hearted.

'You tried, and for that I am grateful, Stanley. I have no words for how grateful I am. You have gone the extra mile and then some to help me. You look worn out. Eat these, and then rest.'

Kitty handed Stanley a large beaker of water and placed shortbread and cookies on a plate.

'Maple syrup cookies and cinnamon shortbread. Eat and enjoy while I clear up, and then we must discuss our living arrangements. We should be thinking about somewhere permanent, but we need our own space. All we've done is rush around, pack up our lives in Britain, fly here, travel days on a train, and then try to find Michael in the city. You took off to travel miles across the country, but it has to stop for your health's sake. Look at you, you are exhausted.'

Stanley shrugged off her suggestion that he was tired.

'I can give it one more try. Look further afield, on the other side of Calgary,' he said. Kitty watched him bite into his cookie, wondering when he had last eaten a decent meal. She felt so guilty for expecting so much of him. For far too long, she had taken one of her dearest friends for granted.

'I am sorry, Stanley. I am so sorry I came to you about my failed marriage, burdening you with my troubles and putting you through the search from hell. I am also sorry I said those words to Michael, but I am not sorry that you're back here and free to decide what you want to do now.' She heard Stanley give a heavy sigh.

'You have not put me through anything I didn't want to do. I can't bear seeing you heartbroken and worried. We need to work out where to look for him next,' he replied, his voice insistent and determined.

Kitty closed her eyes to give herself a moment to think and compose her words. She did not want to reveal her conclusions to Stanley completely, but she needed to prevent him wasting his time when he could settle down and enjoy life.

'I've given it some thought and will send Smithy a telegram. I will tell him we're staying in the Calgary/Cochrane area, give Mim's address and ask him to let Michael know if he gets in touch. Flitting around in hope, and you rushing around wearing yourself silly – it has to stop. If necessary, we can leave adverts in the city and surrounding towns as we visit them, asking Michael to contact me via Mim or Ted. We can't find him, so it is up to Michael to find us. I am not chasing after him anymore, and I will do my utmost to become independent while I wait for him to find me. I know I would like to stay here, in Cochrane. I have to work out how to do that on a limited budget, but I will do it, Stanley, because the town has captured me here in such a short time,' Kitty said, tapping her heart, conviction and passion in her voice.

'Then I am staying, too.' Stanley said. He bit into his shortbread and waved it in approval.

Kitty leaned back against the sink, facing him. It was time to let go of Stanley, and her heart ached at the thought of him back in England, but she had to stop being selfish.

'No, Stanley. You have put me first enough. Now you must stop being my big brother, the protector, and choose what you want to do – and if that is back in England, then go home. I will be more than fine; I have opened my eyes to where my skills lie, and I will manage with Mim as a friend.' Her words came out in a rush, but she had to remain in control. She focused her gaze on him as he ate the last of his shortbread and wiped his mouth. He laid down his napkin and struggled to his feet. He looked at her, his face serious and grey, and she felt guilty at how exhausted he was – she knew it was her fault.

'I am staying. I have seen more of this country than you, and believe me, it has made me want to stay. The wide-open spaces, the fresh air, and – oh, I don't know – new and exciting opportunities. Kitty, I want to stay, not just because you're here, but because it is what I want to do. And don't get me started on the mountains. I have my eye on a few to climb.' He laughed. 'I am ready to see what sort of life I can build for myself.'

Kitty felt a warmth inside. Life would be much better for her with Stanley at her side, and she had secretly hoped he wanted to remain in Canada. Now they could make plans that would suit them both.

'Well then, we have some serious discussions to have. We can no longer live with you in Ted's place and me here. I must go into Cochrane, as I have letters to post and a telegram to send, so go and rest. I will let Mim know you're back and making use of my bed to catch up on sleep. She won't mind. Then we talk. Agreed?'

Stanley nodded. 'I won't argue. I do need sleep. But you had better hide the shortbread, or there will be none left when you return. I think you have found your calling,' he said, heading into the bedroom.

Later, riding Saahkómaapi slowly into town, Kitty realised she no longer felt so anxious. Her neck and shoulders were relaxed, and she felt unburdened. Having Stanley home was a great relief.

Chapter Thirty-Two

When Kitty returned from the town, she saw Mim and Stanley talking on the porch. Stanley was speaking animatedly. A sleep had done him good.

Ted had also arrived and waved as he hitched Mim's cart to his horse.

'Here she is,' Mim said, waving at Kitty. 'Happy that Stanley is home?'

For some reason, Kitty felt a warmth in her neck and cheeks at the question, as if she had been caught out doing something wrong. She climbed down from Saahkómaapi and smiled.

'I am, because he has just seen me ride a horse for the first time. Stanley, meet Saahkómaapi,' she said, walking the horse over to them.

Stanley was grinning as he patted Saahkómaapi's neck.

'It took me a while to realise it was you on the horse. I thought you were walking into town; it never occurred to me you could ride.'

'She couldn't five days ago,' Mim said. 'She's a capable rider for sure, and Saahkómaapi is in good hands when she takes him out.'

Stanley raised an eyebrow in approval.

'I am proud of you, Kitty Sinopa,' he said and turned to Mim. 'Thank you for looking after her while I was gone. We have brought our troubles to your door, and you have taken us in and helped us in ways I never imagined.'

'They're not your troubles, Stanley,' Kitty whispered. He reached out and touched her hand. His touch sent a pleasurable warmth shimmying through her, taking her by surprise.

'Nor were mine when you helped me,' he said softly.

An air of change moved around them, and Kitty felt a calm she had not experienced with him before. She guessed the pressure of her need to find Michael was no longer a worry to him, and he could relax more.

Mim patted Stanley's back. 'You have shown yourself to be a good man. So, Kitty's told you the name my uncle gave her? He is a tease, but a kind man – he means no harm. I cannot wait for you to meet him, and to hear what he names you,' she said.

'I dread to think,' Stanley said, tapping his prosthesis with a laugh.

Once Kitty had finished wiping down Saahkómaapi and settling him, Ted walked the cart to Mim, who beckoned Kitty over to join them.

'You're back just in time. While you were in town, we discussed Stanley's worry about where to stay, and Ted had an idea,' Mim said and walked to the cart.

Kitty looked at her, then Stanley. 'I enquired while in town, but was only offered land for rent or sale. I wasn't offered properties – there are none available,' she said.

Mim nodded. 'Climb up. I have to meet someone for my own business, but I want you to come along. Ted thinks he might be able to help you, so let's go and talk with him before he moves my cattle into the next pasture.'

Kitty could sense Stanley's discomfort through his silence as they travelled over the rough ground; he had done too much and needed to ease the ache in his hips and back. His stump could only take so much from the prosthesis before it became sore and uncomfortable. She regretted agreeing to go with Mim; they should have stayed behind.

'I know I keep saying we need to talk,' she said, 'but tomorrow we will just sit and do nothing but talk and relax. We can make organised plans, not off-the-cuff ones. We can't stay here, so maybe somewhere in the city will be easier to find. You need to rest. Don't go back with Ted. Take the bed tonight, and I will use the fold-up. I'm sure Mim won't object to an extra night's payment.'

Stanley did not argue. He just sat quietly, looking at the views around them, and Kitty left him to enjoy the peace, appreciating that he had not yet had an opportunity to view Mim's land.

Ted slowed the cart down as they approached a large group of men and cattle mingling on the land abutting the end of Mim's boundary. Mim jumped down from the cart and waved to the group below. One acknowledged her and rode in their direction.

'Boss,' he said and politely touched the tip of his hat.

'My foreman, Vern – Vernon, if you are brave enough to say it out loud.' She said, laughing.

Kitty and Stanley nodded and said hello before Mim moved Vern out of earshot.

While they waited for Mim, Ted explained the cattle and

cowboy life to Stanley. Kitty sat quietly, wondering how she would ever be able to repay Mim and Ted for their kindness.

Ted talked about the move to cattle after the bison numbers declined, and Kitty saw that Stanley was transfixed by his stories.

'I flew planes, which was an experience, but I cannot imagine riding at speed through herds of wild bison. Incredible,' Stanley said. 'Our lives were very different in the area where we lived in Britain, right, Kitty?'

Kitty smiled. 'They certainly were,' she replied.

'My action-packed days are over, thanks to enemy fire, and I have no desire to face any more challenges except skiing. I would like to learn to ski,' Stanley said.

Ted gave a grin. 'We will take you when the snows come. Both of you should learn,' he said.

Kitty said nothing, fearful Stanley would be disappointed if he could not achieve his goal.

When Mim returned, Vern rode off to rejoin his men.

'That's one thing settled. We have another visit, and it will be home to some of those delicious-looking cookies you baked,' Mim said.

She gave Ted a nod as she climbed onto the cart. He smiled and eased the horse around.

As they headed back towards the river, Kitty noticed where they were headed.

'Oh, Stanley, Mim wants to buy this place, but the owner's son is considering selling it to the oil company. She brought me here, and the views around the back are across the Bow River and to the hills. It must have been a lovely home once,' she said as they approached the cabin.

'It looks homely, even in its unloved state,' Stanley replied.

'Want to see inside?' Mim said.

'So long as the roof is safe,' Stanley joked, looking up at the sloping rooftop.

'It leans that way to drive off the rain and melting snow, it isn't falling,' Ted said, laughing as he tied up the horse.

Mim stood with her hands on her hips, surveying the property.

'It needs some basic maintenance, but like mine, it has a borehole and good soil. Inside is all log, too. Log furniture, log walls, everything carved and made by Vern's grandfather and uncle, the old man who died.'

'It belonged to Vern's family?' Kitty asked.

Mim pulled a face, then nodded.

'Vern is fully aware of the situation and has spoken to his cousin, not on my behalf but on his. He explained that he and the others would lose their jobs if the land around us went to the oil company.'

'It has a serious knock-on effect,' Kitty said, 'Vern must be worried. I know you are.'

'I was, Kitty. I was. The good news is that his cousin has agreed to sell it to me, and that's the reason for our meeting,' Mim said.

'That's marvellous news, Mim!' I am thrilled for you,' Kitty exclaimed. 'Vern must be relieved.'

'Congratulations, it has incredible views.' Stanley said. 'The oil companies mustn't be allowed to take all the land. I appreciate that the oil benefits are valuable but this place is far too close to your home, Mim. At least now your cattle and land are safe.'

'They are, and it is a relief,' Mim said. 'I'll show you the back, there's rich, fertile land leading to the river.'

'What are your plans?' Kitty asked.

Mim walked them to the rear of the property, explaining her plans as they went.

'The buildings are staying where they are, surrounded by a large portion of land, so the property sits central, and backs onto the river. I'll fence off the rest to link with mine and expand my stock – maybe sheep, I'm not sure. I had intended to rent the property to settlers, but there's a possibility I have sold it already,' Mim said.

Kitty gasped as she turned to her. 'So Vern met with you to tell you it is sold? Then she looked at Stanley. 'It's obvious that property is valuable here and is selling fast. Maybe we shouldn't rest tomorrow; we must find somewhere to live soon,' she said.

Stanley nodded, and Kitty noticed frown lines across his brow. 'I agree. Mim has been patient enough. We must find somewhere really soon. I tell you what, how about we contact the storage company and get your things delivered? Then you will have everything you need to hand until you decide what to do.' Stanley said, 'Because, I'm sorry, Kitty, an opportunity came my way and I've acted upon it. I've been waiting to tell you, but you have had enough disappointment.'

Kitty's stomach churned. She stared at Stanley, fully aware she probably looked pale and shocked.

'I don't understand. Why did you talk about house hunting and finances with me this morning? When all along you knew you were leaving?' she asked, agitated and shocked. This was the last thing she had expected to hear. A sense of abandonment hit her hard. First it was Michael, and now Stanley. She had not expected him to leave so soon. Stanley went to speak, but Kitty was unsure she wanted to hear his reply; she also knew she could not be selfish.

She looked at his face, which was etched with worry and

tiredness, thanks to the search for Michael, and realised that she needed to release Stanley from the idea that he had to look out for her all the time.

'Don't tell me your plans, you're your own man and do not have to stay on my behalf or explain yourself. If you're heading back to England, be happy, Stanley. I mean it, go and be happy.' She reached out and took his hand. 'Leave, and know I will be fine. I will, I promise.'

Stanley looked down at her hand and gently stroked the back with his thumb while shaking his head.

'I'm leaving Ted's place, but I am not leaving Canada – or you,' he told her.

'Oh,' Kitty muttered. It was the only word she could find to say. Stanley's voice was soft, and his last two words touched her like velvet, soothing and comforting.

'Right, I am happy now that you're sorted with a place to live. That's one of my worries out of the way. Now, where shall I go?' she said, more to herself than the others. She turned away from them, giving herself a moment to think and compose herself.

'You can stay at mine for as long as you need, Kitty,' Mim said, her voice reassuring.

'Or, she could put in some hard work and live with me,' Stanley said, and Kitty heard his teasing tone – she knew it so well and guessed he was holding something back.

'Yes, she could. I can guarantee she's a hard worker,' Mim said, her voice also sounding jovial.

Kitty spun around and stared at them with suspicion.

'The look on your face,' Ted said with a laugh.

Confused and near to tears, Kitty looked at Stanley. He walked over to her, placed his hands on her shoulders and turned her to face the cabin.

'I won't torment you anymore. We're looking at my new home, Kitty.' Stanley said.

'But I don't understand. You haven't seen it before, and have no idea what you're buying,' Kitty said, her confusion increasing. 'Ah, I see. It's a joke, you're all teasing me.'

Stanley turned her to face him. 'I promise, I am not teasing anymore. Mim and I had a long conversation about my worries and finding a home suitable for both of us. Neither of us wants to create a scandal when word goes out that we're not married, do we?' he asked, and Kitty noticed the frown on his face had disappeared.

Kitty shook her head, still trying to process what Stanley had done. His eyes smiled, and he wore a happy grin. Suddenly, he no longer looked drained and older than his years. He had hope and excitement; she could see it in his eyes as he spoke.

Kitty could not have been more shocked. Everything had happened so fast and in their favour that she nipped her arm to ensure she was awake. It was like reading a novel with many happy endings. Michael was the only sad scene, but if things went the way they were supposed to, he would join them, and life would move forward. Although she had thoughts of never seeing Michael again and seeking a divorce, she still felt she had not fought for her marriage, and convinced herself that once he saw her and how determined she was to set things right, their lives would fall into a happier pattern.

She looked at the cabin, eyes wide open like a spoiled child at Christmas. She saw Stanley study her, waiting for a response.

'When Mim told me about the property and her plans, I was drawn in, especially when Mim said you had seen it, and she suspected you would happily live there,' he explained.

'She wasn't wrong,' Kitty said, 'But is this a joke, Stanley.

Have you bought it? I love the place, but for you? It is a bit smaller than Fell Hall. Are you sure?' She was utterly confused, but when she looked at his beaming face, she knew the truth: Stanley had made his first serious investment in Canada.

'Legally, I haven't bought it yet, but on a handshake, yes. Ted spoke with Vern. Mim made an offer at a price Vern suggested and guessed his cousin wouldn't refuse. Her offer to me was one I am not going to turn down. Even though I hadn't seen it, I knew you had, and one day, maybe you and Michael will buy it from me. If he doesn't like it here and you move on, I have lost nothing. You must admit, if we turn this place around and make it our home, temporary or otherwise, we will have a wonderful view and the perfect neighbours.'

Kitty looked over at Mim and Ted, who were looking back at her with encouraging smiles.

'It doesn't seem real. Congratulations, Stanley, you have nearly bought a little piece of Canada. That's incredible – in a week,' Kitty said, walking away and looking at the cabin. She felt a twinge of envy that it was Stanley's, not hers, but was not ungrateful for his offer of a roof over her head.

Chapter Thirty-Three

Dust and cobwebs were Kitty's companions for a week, as she diligently worked through the cabin Stanley jokingly named Fell Wayside.

The cabin was perfect. It connected with the land, unwound the mind, untangled the tension and begged to be a beloved home again. Stanley had made the right choice.

She promised she would help him and live with him, potentially risking her reputation. She told him it was temporary, and, with or without Michael, she would eventually find somewhere, leaving him free to enjoy a peaceful life. Stanley would argue she was to stay for as long as she wanted, but Kitty reminded him he might meet someone and remarry, and the last thing she wanted was to be in the way. But Stanley resisted conversations about the topic, refusing to listen to her talk about leaving.

One morning, just as the sun broke through, they were

cleaning windows when Kitty heard a noise in the distance. She recognised the deep thud of the tribal drums, and guessed they were nearby. The sound grew louder and Stanley looked at her. 'Drums?' he asked.

'They are. I think Togquos is going to pay you a visit,' Kitty replied, pointing along the prairie where a long trail of people moved towards them.

Togquos stopped at the edge of the house, and his young warriors and women and children chanted in their own tongue. The warriors moved around the building, and then the tribe danced. They all wore beautiful, colourful ceremonial robes and headdresses. Kitty and Stanley stood mesmerised.

'What an honour,' Stanley exclaimed when the ceremony had finished, and Togquos said his goodbye, gathered his people and walked back home.

'It was beautiful,' said Kitty. 'It *is* an honour, as I believe they don't always mix with settlers – according to Mim, anyway.'

Stanley smiled at her. 'I think you won him over with your fox-like charm,' he said, nudging her with his elbow.

Togquos joined them again later that day with Mim, still in his ceremonial clothes. Mim was dressed in a heavily beaded and embroidered soft leather dress. Kitty thought it beautiful.

'Did you make it, Mim?' Kitty asked.

'My uncle asked my aunt to give me my mother's. Apparently, this was her first ceremonial dress. My mother was the same size before she had me,' Mim replied. 'He thought you might like to see me wear it for the first time.'

'I do! What a beautiful keepsake. I have my mother's red beret. My uncle gave it to me just before I left. He said it was her favourite and I look like her when I wear it,' Kitty said.

'It will warm your head in the winter,' Mim said and translated to her uncle, who said something in reply.

'He said he looks forward to seeing you wear the clothes of your ancestors.'

Kitty gave a smile. Sadly, he would only see her wearing her beret, but she would wear it with pride.

Togquos said something to Stanley, and Mim did not correct him when he mistakenly believed that Stanley was Kitty's husband. She informed them that, although her uncle wouldn't mind, it was wise to limit who knew the truth to protect themselves from those who might object to their unconventional living arrangements.

Kitty was excited when their luggage arrived from the storage company. She unpacked her few belongings and helped Stanley with his. Upstairs, Kitty's bedroom was the smaller of the two and overlooked the back of the property. Stanley's was to the left and looked towards the Rockies.

'I think the kitchen is quaint, and downstairs is the size of the dining room at Fell Hall,' Kitty said as she finished cleaning the large table and chairs with beeswax, 'but it is cosy. The wooden furniture has had so much love poured into it; it's marvellous. Hand-carved logs from trees felled on the land.'

'The cabin is in better condition outside than I thought,' Stanley replied. 'Much bigger, too, with the extensions over the years. Togquos had the lads climb all over the roof checking for splits, but it is in prime condition. I think the overgrown land makes it look worse than it is, and a couple of Mim's cattle will make short work of that tomorrow.'

'Let them eat the front and sides first. I'm looking forward to seeing what plants are out back. Mim said the woman who lived here had a good collection of herbs, and apparently she was highly knowledgeable about herbal medicine. People came here when there wasn't a doctor available,' Kitty said, watching Stanley pile logs beside the large stone fireplace, while she found homes for the linen.

Stanley's arms were bare and his clothes were grubby, a rare sight. Kitty enjoyed seeing him happy at work in his new home, and she hoped his gamble paid off and he would always be happy living there. She was still processing the fact that the cabin was his, and still carried a smidgen of envy. However, she also liked that he asked her to help organise the inside, saying he would like his new home to have a woman's touch.

Before they left England, Daphne had packed linens, curtains, towels and bedding inside some of his packing crates from Fell Hall. The curtains were clean, and those required were ready to hang. As was Jenny's portrait.

'I'll hang it in my bedroom,' Stanley said. 'It will save explanations about who she was and start the tongues wagging about us if anyone visits.'

'Are you sure, Stanley? It doesn't bother me that dear Jenny is on show. It is my reputation, and I am quite happy to be here alone without other friends if they can't accept my life choices,' Kitty said.

'She will watch over me. The sun won't fade her in my room, it is shaded,' Stanley said, carrying Jenny's picture to his room.

'What about hanging it on the stairway, like you had at Fell Hall? It will be protected from the sun, and Jenny won't be hidden away,' Kitty suggested. Stanley shook his head.

'No, this is a new beginning, and my room will be her new home.' He picked up a hammer and nails.

'I wonder what she would have made of this adventure of yours,' Kitty called out when he had finished hammering in a nail and settled Jenny in place.

Stanley walked back into the main room smiling. 'She would have said I am mad and would not have come with me. She did not have your sense of spirit and drive. Delicate and ladylike was Jenny.'

Kitty gave a laugh which echoed loudly.

'Was that a compliment to me or rubbing my nose into the fact that I am not very ladylike?' she teased.

'She'd have been horrified by this place,' Stanley said, 'but I've lived in worse. This is much better than the billets I first lived in when I started with the RAF. You're here, cleaning and not complaining,' he said, peering into another crate.

'I have no choice,' Kitty said, bluntly stating the truth.

'True, but you're not complaining. If I'm honest, Jenny would not have coped; she was much older than me and our parents matched us – two old families with money, that kind of marriage.'

His statement surprised Kitty.

'Oh, I thought you—'

Stanley cut her off. 'You thought we fell in love, then married like you and Michael.' He shook his head. 'No, we learned to love in our own way, and worked our hobbies and pleasures around one another. I liked cars and planes, while Jenny liked the finer things in life – theatre and opera trips. You and I are pioneers, and for me those days leading a life of luxury has gone,' Stanley said with a wave of his hand around the cabin. 'But I have a feeling I will be happy here.'

'Pioneers. Fools, more like. We are lucky though, we do have an outdoor privy – now there's luxury for you,' Kitty replied and threw a towel his way. 'Go wash and I will feed us.'

'Yes, boss. And you will be pleased to know that I have discussed an addition to Fell Wayside, which will mean our own bathroom, washroom, or whatever you prefer to call it. We can't lean on Mim forever,' Stanley said as he disappeared outside to use the water Kitty had fetched from the river earlier.

The idea of a bathroom closer to the cabin, along with a copper boiler to heat water nearby, excited Kitty. She could cope with the new challenges of living without electricity, but bathing in cold water did not appeal to her. Then she reminded herself not to get too comfortable and settled. This was not her home.

Mim, always the generous friend, had brought them a food parcel that morning, and Kitty and Stanley sat on the newly swept porch steps to eat bread and cheese.

'We have finished a lot of unpacking, which is good, but I have things I probably should have left in England,' Stanley said.

'You could sell it or barter for something,' Kitty said, 'I am making small items to sell when Mim suggests somewhere. I am sure they have markets to sell goods.'

'I admire the way you're coping, Kitty. Michael is a lucky man, and when he eventually tracks you down, he can't deny you are as near to Canadian as an Englishwoman can get, the way you're studying and integrating.'

'I am not holding my breath. I can't live on hope alone,' Kitty said sharply. She rose to her feet and changed the subject. 'If we want to sleep here, we must purchase mattresses tomorrow. We need to burn the old ones.'

'We'll visit Calgary first thing,' Stanley said, then grabbed her hand, 'I am sorry for touching a nerve, Kitty. The last thing I want to do is hurt you.'

Kitty released her hand and walked indoors. Every day she spent with Stanley made her question her marriage more. Whenever he touched her, she felt a tug in her heart. She missed the love of a man. She missed being desired. She might not be ladylike, but she had a woman's desires, and Stanley triggered something. Something she had to ignore.

Chapter Thirty-Four

'Kitty!'

Stanley's voice echoed through the house, reaching Kitty's ears as she sat on the back porch. The tone of his voice suggested his call was about something urgent.

Kitty dropped the sewing project she had been engrossed in, ran to the front and saw him bending and catching his breath.

'Stanley? What's wrong?' she said urgently, apprehensive about what he might say. 'Is it Michael?

Still bent in two, Stanley shook his head and breathed deeply.

'No, it's Mim, she's had a fall from Ipota, and Ted has come to fetch you to look her over.' Stanley pointed towards Mim's home, then back at Ted turning his truck around.

'I'll grab my bag,' Kitty replied, quickly running to get a small valise filled with vials of oils and herbal ointments – a starter kit gift from Togquos after Mim explained that Kitty wanted to learn more about herbal medicine.

On arrival at Mim's, Ted jumped down, helped Kitty to the

ground and waited while Stanley stepped from the cart. 'She's around the back, in the barn,' he said.

Kitty ran around the back of the property and called out to Mim. As she entered the barn, she was surprised to see Mim standing, holding Saahkómaapi's reins.

'Mim, are you okay? Ted said you had fallen from Ipota,' Kitty asked, noticing Ipota was hitched to a post.

Stanley and Ted walked into the barn, and looked at her, then at Mim. Both wore wide grins.

'What is going on? Mim, are you injured or not?' Kitty asked.

'I am afraid you have been a victim of a prank by your friend. I haven't had a fall,' Mim said, her smile wide as she walked Saahkómaapi towards Kitty.

'Stanley asked me a question, and I gave it some thought and agreed. Kitty, your friend has purchased Saahkómaapi for you, and I cannot think of a better owner for him.'

Kitty looked across at Stanley in disbelief. He smiled, a shy smile different from his usual boyish grin. Touched by his generosity, Kitty went to him and kissed his cheek.

'I'll not argue or turn down this thoughtful gift, but you're naughty. Thank you. I adore Saahkómaapi, and he will be well cared for – and useful for both of us.'

Stanley tapped his prosthetic leg. 'Err, have you forgotten? I won't be riding him.'

Mim walked over to the far end of the barn and pointed to a cart. 'I might have the answer to that problem right here,' she said. 'I've restored this small wagon from the back of the barn. I've never used it, and it's going to waste. It only needs a fresh stain and a check-over.'

Kitty and Stanley joined her and walked around the wagon.

Both of them would be able to sit up front, and it had a large open back.

'My uncle has added his finishing touch,' Mim said and ran her hand across the images on the rear of the wagon.

Both Kitty and Stanley looked at the work.

'It's a fox. What exquisite work. What is that next to it?' Stanley asked and rubbed his finger over the images.

Kitty looked at the markings. 'It *is* a fox – I think it is my name!' she exclaimed, peering closely at the artwork.

Mim moved forward. 'It is a fox representing your Canadian name.' Then she touched the image beside the fox. 'This one is for Stanley. In our culture, the eagle is important to us, and my uncle has carved an eagle. You will see it only has one wing. He told me he has named you One Wing to honour your flying days. He said you are like the eagle, filled with courage.'

'I was once, but then I lost it – until I met a nurse who showed me I had to find my courage again,' Stanley replied, looking at Kitty.

Kitty smiled back at him. 'And you did. Togquos got it right.'

'He is concerned he might offend you,' said Mim, 'and has said he will remove it if it upsets you.'

'The loss of my leg is the clipped wing. What a compliment to put such a clever link in a piece of historic artwork. I am not offended. He has carved the truth as he sees it,' Stanley replied.

'He has. You're a brave man, Stanley,' Kitty said, then stood quietly watching Stanley's face twitch with emotion. She recalled when he was told he would never return to the RAF – but although he could no longer fly planes, he did return, and he ensured other pilots had safe flight paths. He had told her stories of when he was in the air, and it was touching that someone as important as Togquos had recognised his bravery in such a way.

Fate had brought them to the right people, the ones who would help them heal from the trauma they had both endured.

'That's so touching, Mim. Please, thank your uncle for me,' Stanley said, his voice wavering, a small tear sitting on his lashes.

Mim nodded; Kitty could see the emotion in her face, too.

'Ted, hitch Saahkómaapi to the wagon.' Mim instructed briskly, and Ted obliged.

'I have worked him hitched three times. He is easy to work with the wagon and happy enough, aren't you, buddy?' Ted said, scratching behind Saahkómaapi's ear, before holding out the reins to Kitty, who still could not believe Saahkómaapi was hers.

Standing beside Stanley, she felt blessed and safe.

'It's a happy day. Thank you so much for Saahkómaapi, Stanley. I'm still lost for words,' she said. 'We'll go into town as independent folk, but this time I am driving.'

Stanley snorted a laugh. 'I said I would have you driving one day, but I didn't expect it to be with a four-legged friend and cart, I can tell you.'

Stanley and Kitty decided to stay in the cabin for the first time. After borrowing the fold-up bed from Mim for Stanley, and Kitty reassuring her that blankets and sheets on the floor would suit them fine for one night, they loaded the wagon and headed back home.

Kitty guided Saahkómaapi while Stanley sat, giving directions through the rocky pathways. Saahkómaapi was a natural, and Kitty felt at ease as she manoeuvred the wagon.

'I think you've done this before, in another life,' Stanley said, and Kitty enjoyed the praise, feeling proud of her achievement at getting them home in one piece.

'Where will he sleep?' she asked, suddenly realising they had nowhere suitable prepared for Saahkómaapi.

'There's the old shed for now, but he will need somewhere secure – a fenced-off pen area.'

The old shed was located at the bottom of the back garden; it was not too close to the river, and the ground was flat enough for a future outdoor area.

'It's going to take some work clearing it out today. Maybe we should go into town in the morning,' Kitty said as she tied Saahkómaapi to a strong fence post.

Inside the shed, they found gardening tools; they needed restoring, but Stanley said he was happy to sit and work on them rather than throw them out. Three high-backed chairs were hauled out for inspection, and Kitty deemed them suitable for the porch. She was happy to repaint them, restuff the seat cushions and sew new seat covers.

'I've found a tethering post for inside the shed,' Stanley said and set to work hammering the post into the ground. Kitty watched him flex his arm muscles and put power into each blow. She had never seen him so enthusiastic and involved in manual labour.

'I think Australia is the other way,' she joked as he worked.

'Saahkómaapi won't be able to pull it up if something spooks him during the night,' Stanley said, standing back admiring his work. 'My arms will ache tomorrow – just as well you're in charge of him and the wagon.'

They worked diligently together, and by the time they had finished, they had washed down the interior of the shed and cleared the floor of debris. They had enough rubbish for a small bonfire.

Kitty had found a large, serviceable metal pan which she thought the previous owners had used to boil water. She took a bucket to the water's edge and, after three trips, decided they had enough to fill the pan. Each time she went to the river, she wondered how often the previous woman of the house had done the same.

Stanley cleared weeds and grass from a large brick surround that they guessed had previously served as a fire pit.

'I think the previous people must have heated water for their bath and washing on that, although I haven't seen a portable bath anywhere, so maybe they washed down in the kitchen like we'll have to for a while. Maybe tomorrow we should look for a privacy screen, or each have a bowl in our room and then empty it out the window,' Kitty suggested. 'It's basic, but workable until you decide what to do about the bathroom.'

'Do you think they washed in the river?' Stanley asked, lighting the fire.

Kitty smiled at the thought.

'Maybe in the summer, but from what I hear about temperatures dropping by many degrees when it snows here, I doubt winter bathing is a regular event,' Kitty said, pretending to shiver.

'Darn, it could have saved me a lot of money,' Stanley said, and they both burst out laughing, making Saahkómaapi snort and his ears stand upright.

'Even Saahkómaapi thought it funny,' Stanley said.

Kitty sat on the floor with her arms wrapped around her knees. She loved the informality of the place and relaxed more each day.

'I hope he will be happy here, and not miss Ipota,' Kitty said, looking at her horse. 'I still can't believe you bought him for me.'

'You deserve him, the pair of you suit one another – and with the surprise gift of the cart, I get chauffeured around, and I can take my time buying a truck. A fancy car will not be much use to us out here in the sticks,' Stanley said.

'I honestly thought we would rent a place in Calgary, and you would be driving some posh car with a name I'd never heard of around the city. I never dreamed you would buy a home in the middle of a cattle ranch, or that we would own a horse and cart, and have to learn to work the land, all in under a month,' said Kitty.

'Oh, I know. What a journey we've had so far, and there's more adventure to come, I feel it in my bones.'

'That will be the weight of the dirt on your skin after clearing the shed,' Kitty said, laughing.

Stanley walked towards her, reached out his hand and brushed it across her hair. 'And you're a walking cobweb,' he said. He moved his hand from her head and brushed it against her cheek.

Kitty held her breath as they looked into one another's eyes, then she turned away.

'Time to wash then,' she said in a matter-of-fact voice, looking at the water in the pan, before walking over to it.

Something was happening between her and Stanley, and it confused her. She had fresh feelings for him; if nurtured, she sensed they could become deep-seated like those she had felt when she first met Michael. Stanley made her feel valued and loved, just as Michael had when they first met, but they had failed one another after marriage. Kitty realised she needed to prevent her emotional feelings, which were likely heightened by the attention she had received, from ruining her friendship with Stanley.

'I'll take some water and wash away the cobwebs, then leave you to have a scrub in private.' She said and carried two jugs of hot water into the house and set them down in the kitchen. Taking a deep breath, she put her mind to gathering towels and fresh clothes from upstairs. As she looked out the window, Stanley was scratching Saahkómaapi's mane. He chatted to the horse as he did so, and Kitty wondered what he told it. Kitty's secret desires needed to be suppressed and never spoken aloud, even to her horse.

Chapter Thirty-Five

Their first evening at home was a success, and neither felt the need to ask Mim for another night's stay. Kitty looked forward to purchasing the mattresses and other items to make their lives more comfortable, but was content that they had managed to wash and eat.

The wood-fired oven was old but serviceable, and she had cleaned it but not used it; instead, they chose to cook outdoors on the fire. Two steaks and fried potatoes had satisfied two hungry workers.

The late evening air was warm, and the trill of cicadas filled the atmosphere, while bats circled above what was now Saahkómaapi's stable, their wings creating soft shushing sounds as they flew. The sound of water rushing over rocks in the river contributed to the soothing melody of nature.

For Kitty, it was a perfect ending to an unexpectedly perfect day. All it lacked was a personal romance, the unexpected kiss, the accidental brush of hands leading to body exploration, and hot passion – things she was missing in her life now that Michael had left her.

'Do you ever wonder what your life would be like if the war had never happened?'

Stanley spoke as he stood looking out across the river at the red sky pinking before the sun set for the night. Getting caught up with the beauty of the evening, Kitty had almost forgotten she wasn't alone, and Stanley's voice startled her. His question altered her thought pattern. What would life have been like without the war?

She would not have trained as a Red Cross nurse, nor would she have met the courageous children of the Kindertransport evacuation programme, which inspired her to join the Red Cross nurse training in Birmingham. In Birmingham, she would never have met Jo, Trixie, Belle, Smithy and, of course, Michael. She would never have travelled to Leeds, then onto Drymen in Scotland, Liverpool, Yorkshire, Shotley Bridge, where she met Stanley, Brancepeth, Durham and now Canada.

'I haven't really, but if it hadn't happened, I would not be here with you. In fact, I wouldn't know you, or Michael, or any of my friends. I didn't have many friends in Parkeston, only a handful of school chums who went their own way in the war; my adult friends are people I met during the war. What about you?' Kitty asked.

While he spoke about the life his father had earmarked for him as an accountant, Kitty looked at him; his skin had caught the sun, and his sandy hair was a lighter shade. She had never taken in how handsome he was. He was approaching thirty, only three years older than her, but back in England he seemed older.

Perhaps it was Jenny's more mature outlook that influenced him. In Canada, he was jovial, and during the afternoon some of his seriousness had disappeared and he had shown a mischievous, boyish side. She could not imagine never meeting him, or embarking on a new adventure with anyone else but Stanley. Michael would have settled into his country, and she would have conformed with whatever he decided, whereas she and Stanley were both new to Canada and had to learn together.

'…and when I sold Jenny's home, I felt nothing but relief.'

Stanley's voice drifting across the porch and into her thoughts reminded Kitty that she was meant to be listening to him, not daydreaming, and looking at him as more than a friend.

'When I think what you had back there, and now this place, I do worry you will miss the luxurious side of your life,' Kitty said.

Stanley turned away, saying nothing. He walked past her and went indoors. He returned with two crystal glasses filled halfway with amber liquid.

'Whisky for the muscle pain. I can assure you I will always have this or brandy in my home. These are the only luxuries I need – this and your cookie biscuits and shortbread.' He handed her a glass. 'Cheers.'

Kitty clinked her glass against his, 'Bottoms up, and here's to us – and whisky with cookies,' she said and took a large gulp. It warmed her throat, and she licked her lips.

Stanley stood looking out at the mountains and raised his glass high.

'To the mountains, a reminder we can't always reach the highest peak, but we can still achieve great things at the lowest point.' He turned to face her. 'To us, and to you, Kitty – the nurse who turned my life around, who fought that dreadful occupational therapist, and whose words of encouragement still whisper in my ear today. To you, my dear friend Kitty.'

She was unsure whether it was the whisky making her cheeks burn or she had blushed at his sentiments, but Kitty knew without having to look in a mirror that her face was blazing red. All the mixed-up feelings about Stanley she had attempted to suppress earlier now swirled around her body.

It was a compliment, Kitty, not an invitation to flirt. Do not do anything foolish. Sip your drink and go to bed. What is wrong with you?

Her gaze fell back to Stanley. *Why now? Why are you tempted by him now?*

'Tomorrow, what will I find in our new town?' Stanley asked as he sat down to face her.

Slightly flustered, Kitty took another sip of her drink to gather herself.

'Our new village. Apparently, it is not a town – there are not enough residents to make it one yet. There's a general store, but I've not seen what else. Do you think we need to go to Calgary for furniture?'

'Might be wise. We'll go early. Let's finish our drinks and get some rest. Tomorrow will be another busy day.'

Climbing the stairs, Kitty thought back to when she climbed the ones at the surgery on her wedding night. She had such high hopes for the future. Michael had chosen to stay in Britain, and their life was to be a long and happy one in England.

It will be a long and happy one in Canada instead. Just sort yourself out, Katherine McCarthy.

As she said the name in her head, McCarthy faded into Pattison – the girl who was naïve enough to think love lasted forever. Had she fallen out of love? Her anxiety about finding Michael had dwindled in the past day or so, but was it because she wanted to set down roots instead of going through days filled with stress? Was she focusing on Stanley to distract her from Michael, from a pain she did not know she carried?

I am so confused! her inner self screamed.

Chapter Thirty-Six

Two days later, Mim arrived with a letter for Stanley. Kitty looked up from raking clear a large section of the side garden and waved.

'Hello! My new vegetable patch,' she called out as Mim tied Ipota to a post next to Saahkómaapi.

'Impressive,' Mim answered.

'Once it is clear, we're fencing off the area near Saahkómaapi's stable and he will be able to roam free instead of being tied up,' Kitty said, laying her rake to one side.

'You and Stanley have put in the hard work. I can see a big difference here,' Mim said, turning one way then another, taking in the changes surrounding the house.

'Come and see inside; we have a clean and tidy kitchen, and the start of what we call our sitting room. The bedrooms are coming together – we managed to get two mattresses home, so I'll bring the fold-up back in the wagon. Thank you.' Kitty ushered Mim forward, eager to show her around.

Mim stepped onto the porch and into the kitchen. She stood back admiring the difference.

'I'll give it to you, Kitty, you know how to put together a cosy home,' Mim said, stroking the curtains leading into the sitting area. 'This is pretty material.'

Kitty handed her a glass of cold mint tea.

'They're from Stanley's old home. His wife had good taste, and they had the money to spend on the finer things.'

'Lucky man,' Mim said, moving on to admire the gleaming cooker. 'Does it work?' she asked.

'It does, and what is frustrating is that I found it has a water heater. Our first night we made a fire and cooked, and I boiled water to wash. When I studied the oven more, I found it. I also found I need to control the heat better for my baking. Talking of which, I have a batch of shortbread for you and Ted.' Kitty lifted down a paper bag filled with baked treats. 'I've found the art to my pastry, too. I have a bucket of river water beside me to cool my hands. They get so hot, and I remember my aunt telling me the secret of good pastry making was cold hands.'

They ventured out onto the back porch.

'This is my favourite place to think,' Kitty said.

'I can see why – it has a better view of the river than mine. I'm pleased you're happy, Kitty. Do you have any news about your husband yet?' Mim asked, her question catching Kitty off guard. She had not expected to have a conversation about Michael with Mim – nor was she sure she wanted to, because it threatened to bring down her mood, but she could not ignore the situation.

'I've not heard from him, and have no idea where he is; there's no news from my friends in England, so he's not been in touch with them yet. In the meantime, I keep busy,' she replied, slightly embarrassed – not to mention irritated – that she did not know where her husband was.

'Where's Stanley?' Mim asked.

'He's working on trimming back an overgrown area near the river, ready to fence it off. He wants to do most things for himself, but some days his stump is sore where he has overdone it, and the heat doesn't help.'

'Then he has the right kind of friend – a nurse – to help him,' Mim said, and rose to her feet. 'I'll go and see him, and give him his letter – it's from England.'

'Probably his solicitor – he was expecting one, but he thought it wouldn't be here for another month or so. He'll be pleased to see you,' Kitty said, pulling on her thick gloves, ready to return to her raking task.

After two hours of work, Kitty was ready to slip into her new swimsuit and bathe in the small natural pool in the river to wash the heat and grime from her body. She stepped into the shallow part of the pool, and the chill of the water sent a pleasant tingle through her legs. Gradually, she immersed herself up to her neck, then pinched her nose and dipped beneath the surface, gasping as she came up again. Rubbing her chilled limbs, she washed away the dirt and grit before climbing out and rubbing herself dry with a towel.

Back in her room, she slipped on a sleeveless cotton dress and left her hair down to dry, then ventured downstairs barefoot. She sat sipping a glass of mint water under the dappled shade of the porch. There was no breeze, and the warm air sat heavy.

'I do all the work and you sit around sipping cocktails,' Stanley teased as he approached the end of the porch. Kitty looked up and smiled at him.

'I've just had my first river bath,' she said with a giggle.

Stanley gave a heavy sigh. 'Lucky you. I could do with one right now, I am as ripe as old cheese.' He touched his thigh, adjusting his prosthesis.

'Can't you remove the leg and slip in on your behind, then ease yourself out with your foot? You don't have to stand up, it can all be done from the edge of the small pool,' Kitty said encouragingly. 'If I hadn't had mine already, I'd dip in with you, but I'll come and stand by if it will help you feel safer.'

It surprised Kitty that Stanley was unsure about swimming. He was gung-ho about everything else.

'It's tempting, but…' he said with caution.

Kitty got off the chair and went to collect her drying swimsuit from the makeshift line.

'We'll go in together, and find a way so that you feel safe and confident enough to do it alone another time.'

'Yes, nurse,' Stanley replied, 'thank you.'

For the second time that day, Kitty had been reminded that she was a friend and nurse to Stanley, and that out there somewhere was a husband.

Chapter Thirty-Seven

Following their bath, Kitty had gone into the cabin to retrieve Stanley's crutches. Now, as she walked back towards the river, she saw someone speaking to Stanley. It was a man dressed in a black suit with a black felt trilby hat, which seemed very out of place at the water's edge. She stopped walking and watched him.

Her stomach churned when she realised she knew who it was from his build and gestures.

Her husband.

'Michael?' she said, as she walked towards them. She smiled, hesitated then went to hug him, but Michael stepped back from her. She frowned at him, then looked at the damp patch on her dress – the reason for his reluctance.

'It's wonderful to see you!' she said, shrugging off his disappointing response, though she knew she also needed to address her own inner reaction.

Seeing her husband standing there did not excite her as she

had expected it would. She had imagined, when they saw one another again, she would run into his arms and he would lift her and swing her around, declaring his love for her, and she would beg forgiveness for her outburst, and they would kiss away the past.

Instead, he stood at arm's length, serious-faced, and her stomach contracted with a sense of dread. She did not want to kiss him, nor did she want to ask for forgiveness. He was not the man she had been searching for; this one was formal, and had a look on his face she had not seen before.

'Hello again, Kitty. I just said to Stanley, you appeared to be enjoying yourselves – together – in the water – I spotted you from the top of the garden,' he said, pointing back to the front of the house.

His voice had a tightness to it, as if he were annoyed. There was no smile, no light in his eyes, and he irked Kitty with his obvious suspicion of her and Stanley. She was not prepared to have him think the worst of them both. Stanley did not deserve this suspicion.

'Water therapy is good for him. We'd just finished exercising,' Kitty replied in a clipped voice.

Her husband had not greeted her with excitement when he first saw her, nor did he call out to her. He had watched, then assumed the worst, before learning the truth.

'Your crutches, Stanley,' she said, laying them down within reach for Stanley to help himself out of the water.

'Let's get Stanley inside and then we can talk,' she said to Michael.

'Still the nurse, I see,' Michael said, his voice bland and not inviting a response.

Kitty tutted, then gave Stanley the support he needed, but

noted that Michael did not get involved. Where was his compassion? He was a doctor, had suffered severe injuries himself, so why would he leave a disabled man to struggle with walking on uneven ground? Was this really her husband, cold and indifferent?

An awkward atmosphere hung in the air, feeling oppressive. Back at the house, Stanley excused himself to go into the sitting room while Kitty rushed to his room for fresh clothes. Michael stood outside, even though Stanley had invited him in.

Kitty handed Stanley his clothes.

'He's not exactly excited to see me,' she said.

'I must admit, he is a tad distant with me, too,' Stanley said. 'Perhaps it was awkward for him, embarrassing – maybe he's angry at us too. After all, seeing his wife splash around with another man is not going to make him happy, is it? Go and speak to him. Repair the past. I'll keep out of the way.'

'Thank you,' Kitty said and went outside.

She beckoned to Michael.

'We'll give Stanley privacy in his own home,' she said and pointed to the front of the property. She did not want to share the back porch with him – not yet, not until things were smoothed over between them.

'How have you been?' she asked softly, walking beside him, aware her feet were bare and her hair unbrushed, still damp from the swim.

'Busy,' Michael replied, batting away a fly.

Kitty expected more enthusiasm. They had been apart for months. He had obviously been looking for her, found out she was in Canada, and yet he appeared uninterested.

'That's good, Michael, but busy with what? Where have you

been? Are you surprised – happy – to see me here in Canada?' Kitty could not pussyfoot around him any longer. Michael appeared to be deliberately making things awkward between them, and she was not prepared to stand begging for forgiveness when he couldn't even find the decency to give her a small smile.

'I'm shocked you're here. I'm not sure why. And this place, what is this, a cosy love nest?' His voice was harsh and accusing.

Kitty gasped, the air wedging itself in the base of her throat. Michael's words were like a sledgehammer against her chest. She steadied her breathing.

'Pardon? A what? It is not, but if it was, you left me, remember? With nothing but a small goodbye fund, I might add. How dare you accuse us of … of what, an affair?' Kitty's voice grew louder as she defended her friend. 'This is Stanley's home. He has been kind enough to put a roof over my head. He drove the length of the province looking for you at every hospital he came across. When he ran out of ideas, he found investor companies because Smithy's friend hinted you were considering an oil investment, and this seemed the obvious place with the new find, and—'

'Stop!' Michael's voice echoed around her, and Kitty stood stunned, shocked into silence.

'There's a roof for you to sleep under back in England,' he said harshly.

Kitty frowned as if to say, *And where might that be?*

'Your uncle's. Or the surgery. I gave you a comfortable home there, but you appear to enjoy living in the middle of nowhere with a crip—'

'Do not say it, don't call him that!' Kitty yelled.

Michael was being deliberately cruel. It was out of character.

'He's done nothing but think of us. He's written to everyone he knows, searched for you in Calgary and beyond, for days without me. The woman on the ranch next door took me – us – in. We had nowhere to stay, no hotel, for the first night. You don't get to come here and vent your suspicions at me.' Kitty was surprised she was not in tears. 'And I had to leave the surgery.'

'Your uncle would have given you a home, or you could have gone to Cornwall, to the inn,' Michael persisted.

'But you had disappeared so I wanted to find you, in the places you might be,' Kitty said, trying to keep her voice civil.

His annoyance and accusations stung, but she also knew she had a role to play in the marital drama; she had asked for a divorce, meaning she was not a victim but the problem.

'We need to talk about the, the…' Kitty stuttered, then took a deep breath. 'About when I suggested a divorce.'

Michael gave a huff in reply and turned away from her.

'I didn't mean it, Michael,' she said.

Michael let out another huff, and Kitty struggled to remain calm. What had gotten into him? Was this some form of punishment?

'I was hurt by you saying you wanted a pure Canadian wife, until Stanley put me right and suggested you meant our children being born out here,' she said, hearing the pleading in her voice.

'Stanley – and children, again,' Michael muttered, but Kitty chose to ignore him. He could not use Stanley as a target for his anger towards her. He needed to understand the situation she found herself in and how Stanley had helped.

'Stanley made me realise I may have misunderstood you. When you left and never came home, or gave me any indication of where you were, I had to give up the roof over my head you spoke of just now.'

'Why? It was a perfectly good house.'

'But it was not ours. You were no longer the village doctor, and it was your contract, not mine. I gave up my job when I found the money you left me to come and find you.'

'You should have stayed in England,' Michael muttered.

Again, Kitty chose to ignore him and continued to explain her situation.

'Stanley took me in to help me gather my thoughts because you had disappeared. All we learned from Smithy was that you might be here, on an investment hunt, and, well, here you are – suited like a city gent, not the village doctor,' Kitty swiped back at him, her anger in full bloom.

'And here you are looking like the wild woman of the prairies, hooked up with the wealthy hero pilot,' Michael responded.

She realised he was spoiling for a fight with her by using sarcasm as a weapon.

'What are we doing? We're going around in circles, Michael, and sparring like wild animals. We are a married couple who have struggled, lost each other, and now we've found each other again. Isn't that something worth celebrating?' Kitty softened her voice. In the past, it worked when Michael's head ached, and his mood darkened. Maybe, he just needed to reset.

'What have you been doing since you left home?' she asked.

'Investing and changing my life,' Michael said, removing his hat and wiping his brow. Kitty relented; it was too warm to stand around beneath the harsh sun. His health would suffer.

'Come and have a drink with me on the back porch – it's cooler. Where are you staying?' she asked, and as she turned her head, she spotted a large black car parked in the shade beside the house – a new, modern vehicle.

'Gracious, is that yours?' she asked, awestruck. It was very much a rich man's car.

'It is. My house is rather special too,' Michael said, and his words stung, and hurt her.

Had she heard him right? 'My house,' not 'our house'.

'A house?' she asked. A slight tremor of hope that he had come to fetch her ran through her body. Then a thought struck her. He could only have known she was in Canada because someone had told him. How long had he known she was in the country? Could he have fetched her to their new home earlier? By leaving her to struggle, was he punishing her? Before the questions burst from her, she asked one, slowly.

'How long have you known I've been here, in Cochrane?'

Michael stared at her, his face passive.

'From when the word came from the Leduc site. A foreman came across with a message for me.'

His answer angered her. Michael had known for weeks that she lived in the area. He owned a property, but had not considered offering Stanley somewhere to stay or asking her to be with him at home again. He had chosen to build his life without her, his wife.

He had not rushed to her, excited that she had flown across the world to be with him. And when he did find her, he accused her of having an affair.

She had struggled to help Stanley create a home and accepted his generous offer to keep her safe while they searched for her husband together, and for what? To be faced with a man she realised she didn't know.

Kitty knew this was the end of her marriage. Even if Michael begged, she could no longer trust him to keep her safe. He had changed, and not for the better.

The war had damaged them far more than she had realised. It had blown a hole through a wartime romance built on hope. Michael had found the post-war excitement he sought without her, and it was time to let go.

Chapter Thirty-Eight

'Sit down, old man,' Stanley said to Michael when they came face to face on the back porch. Michael looked out of place, and Kitty fetched a coat hanger.

'Would you like to hang up your jacket, Michael? It's a lovely suit.'

'I need to speak with Stanley – in private,' Michael muttered.

Kitty felt snubbed – ignored.

'Michael, I think it is me you need to speak to, don't you?' Kitty sniped back.

'I need to speak with Stanley first, so please give us some privacy,' Michael said, his voice firm. Kitty decided that standing and arguing her rights was pointless, so she chose to keep the peace by walking away.

'I'll go and see to Saahkómaapi, leave you two to catch up with one another,' she said, irritated that the man she once loved and had trekked across the world to find had dismissed her before having a civil conversation with her.

When she reached Saahkómaapi, Kitty decided to take him for a ride. The air was fresher, and he was restless.

She and Saahkómaapi ambled through the fields, watching gophers popping their heads from their burrows and scrambling around to find food. Kitty had learned from Mim that they were ground rats or Richardson squirrels and were considered pests, but she enjoyed seeing them scamper across the field as she rode by. She chose to ignore Mim's suggestions about pest eradication.

Eventually, even the little creatures could not amuse her and she closed her eyes to listen to the birds. Her head ached with worry over Michael. How could his personality have changed so much? Did he need medical help and not realise it?

The way he dressed and his boastful ways were out of character and confusing. She turned Saahkómaapi around and rode him back, enjoying the cooling air whipping through her hair and across her face. She pushed the horse faster, braving the speed for the first time, but it was a release of pent-up anger that drove her on. When they returned to the house, Saahkómaapi was ready for a washdown and a feed.

As she worked, Kitty heard the male voices on the porch, but couldn't make out the words. They were not shouting, which was a relief. During her ride, she had realised that by the end of Michael's visit she would have to make a serious decision. Her stomach churned at the thought of living in the city.

Would she go if he asked her? What if she could not stay in Canada without being his wife? Could she legally stay without him? How had she allowed herself to get into such a mess?

Kitty had said goodbye to all she knew in England, and had quickly found a place for her heart to rest awhile. Seeing Michael again came with a serious question. Did she still love him?

His coldness towards her was possibly down to awkwardness

or his injury. Maybe they could try to find what they had before they married and rebuild from there. Kitty let the thoughts ramble, and took a deep breath. It was time to return home and find out what happens next.

Then she heard a woman giggle – it was not Mim. Rushing through the final part of bedding down Saahkómaapi, she said, 'I'm sorry, my friend, but there's another visitor. I promise I will give you the best brush down in the morning – or Stanley will, depending on where I am.'

Her words hit her hard. What if Saahkómaapi had nowhere to live in the city? What if Michael refused to keep him?

She leaned her head against Saahkómaapi's and nuzzled his mane.

'I will fight for you, don't worry,' she whispered, then closed the stable door.

As she approached the porch, the giggling woman came into view. She was dressed in the height of fashion, wearing smart shoes, a contrasting bag and a large hat. She turned to look at Kitty, her red lipstick and slim face instantly reminding her of the character Lizzie French created, Annabelle Farnsworth, a Red Cross nurse who was thought to be a spy but was, in fact, a special agent for Great Britain. Belle, the man-grabbing rich girl, was once an irritant, interfering with Kitty's relationship with Michael during their time in Birmingham. However, as soon as she met the real person, Kitty warmed to the woman, not the actress. The woman who fought with the French Resistance to save Britain, not betray it to the Germans, was a friend. The woman in front of her now did not look friendly. She looked guarded and cold, but maybe she could be thawed out.

Kitty strode forward, taking in the scene before her. Stanley's face could not have been clearer; he was wearing a shocked expression and sat tapping the back of his hand, just as he did when he was her patient. It was a movement that calmed him after a frustrating, painful physio session. What was wrong with him now?

'Michael,' Kitty said, thinking the correct thing to do was to address her husband first.

Michael looked her way and a flicker of something showed in his face. A look of disgust? Displeasure? Kitty shrugged it off. She had just ridden through dusty fields on a horse; she was not exactly temptress material.

'I'm sorry,' she said, turning to the woman when it was obvious Michael was not going to explain who she was, 'we've not been introduced.'

Kitty held out a hand, but the woman only looked her up and down. Kitty guessed she looked like something that had been dragged across the prairie, but she was not going to be snubbed by a stranger.

She moved her hand closer. 'It's clean, and, as I said, we've not been introduced. Are you a friend of Stanley's or Michael's?' she asked politely. Still the woman looked at her with disdain.

Kitty withdrew her hand. 'I assume she's not a friend of yours, Stanley?' Kitty said sharply, looking at him.

Stanley shook his head. 'If you'll excuse me, I am going to rest on my bed,' he said and threw Kitty an apologetic glance. She frowned back at him.

'Stanley?'

Stanley gave a slight shake of his head as he clipped his prosthetic tight, rose to his feet and limped away. Something was wrong. Stanley was hunched and limping; he looked worn out and had a defeated air.

Kitty swivelled around to face Michael. 'What is going on,

and who is this … this *rude* individual?' she snapped, staring at the woman, then back at Michael. This had gone too far; he was not behaving like a man finally back in his wife's company. There was no spark of happiness, nothing but a blank stare back.

At last Michael spoke.

'Her name is Alexandrea, and we're close friends. She was a voluntary visitor when I was in the hospital over here when I had my neuro treatment during the war. She helped me find my way again.'

Kitty listened, but she was unsure if she was hearing his words correctly.

'So, why does your *close friend* choose to be so rude to your *wife*?' she asked with heavy sarcasm, as she moved to a seat and made herself comfortable. She began to feel in control of the situation, but was still wary of what was about to unfold.

'Because she wants to be you and is nervous,' Michael said, his voice softening, He gave Alexandrea a smile, then looked directly at Kitty.

Kitty jumped back to her feet, her anger plain in her face. It was all obvious to her now. Michael had been having an affair. He had bought a house for his mistress, and more, judging by the car and their clothes. While Stanley had been searching for him, and Kitty had fretted over ruining their marriage, Michael was swanning around with another woman on his arm. It was all too much to hear.

'She wants to be barefoot, ragged from working the land to keep a roof over her head, and ride a horse because she has no money for a car? She wants to live in a foreign country, grabbing whatever comes her way, in the hope her husband, the man she loved, comes to find her, because she has run out of ideas as to where in the country he might be holed up? Or if he was even still alive? She wants to be that woman?' Kitty gasped for breath as the words flowed out of her, venting everything she had to challenge her husband. She was no fool; she knew what he meant. The woman wanted to be his wife!

Michael stood wide-eyed, obviously stunned by Kitty's outburst. He had never witnessed her in such an angry state – but then Kitty had never been angry like this before.

The woman went to his side.

'He means the divorce you offered him is accepted.' The woman spoke with a slight accent, and Kitty guessed she was French-Canadian. But Canadian, nonetheless. The woman Michael wanted to bear his pure-bred children. Not that Alexandrea came across as the maternal type.

Kitty gave a slow nod, then another.

'And *now* it makes sense. You were his pen pal? The friend who wrote from the Canadian hospital, who I always assumed was a man named Alex?' she said.

Michael fidgeted with his hat. The woman gave a slim-lipped smile.

'Alexandrea – Alex to Michael,' she said crisply.

Kitty gave a slight smile of understanding.

It was done: the finale of her marriage drama was over and she was not the guilty party. Michael had created the situation in the hope that she would accept that she had ruined everything, paving the way for him to have what he wanted in Canada.

'Then why marry me, Michael? Why wreck our lives during a time when we should have been rebuilding them? All through our two years, you communicated with your "friend". I never asked to see the letters, assuming it was just male chit-chat. Plus, it was private to you. I trusted you, but you and your pen were having an affair with some volunteer tart!' Kitty shouted, past caring how she presented herself; he deserved her anger.

'The divorce. What will I gain from it?' she said abruptly and noticed Michael glance at Alexandrea.

'I mean, as his wife, surely I am entitled to something. I mean, Michael, you left me with around ten pounds, which was my own money anyway.' Michael shrugged and opened his mouth, but Kitty was not going to let him speak.

'So, how will you ensure I am comfortable?' she asked. 'I can tell you now, I am not going to sign or agree on a divorce unless I am compensated in some way, so I can enjoy a – what did you call it – a "rather special" house.'

She felt strong and brave as she punched out each word. She stood her ground. This was a battle, not about love but of survival.

'You know he still made love to me during the snowstorm in England at the beginning of the year?' she spat at Alexandrea. Then she raised her eyebrows quickly at Michael, signalling 'Don't mess with me.'

It was time to make her point. He had played both women. He had probably not intended to, and when he had head pains, he sometimes became confused, so perhaps it was true that he had found comfort in her arms. But was that all she had been – a comfort blanket until the time came when he could see clearly? When he knew he could no longer be her husband, he pushed her into creating a pathway out of their lives. He had not given her credit for being a dutiful wife and concerned about his whereabouts. He had moved on, thinking she would do the same.

Somewhere inside, buried beneath a heap of pain and sadness, Kitty had to find a way to retrieve forgiveness.

They needed to be friends again, to protect their past, and remember when they were one another's lifeblood during the war. It was something that should not be thrown away for the sake of happiness, it was a life lesson that no matter what had happened between them, there was still a door open for friendship. Orphans had very little to cling to when their parents died. She knew Michael's painful memories of loss, because they were much the same as hers. Friends had been the core of their support during the war; without some of them, they would never have survived the horrors. They had leaned heavily on one another. Hatred fuelled war, and she did not want to hate Michael.

'We need to talk without anger, Michael. I'm sorry I sounded bitter, but it's the shock. I had expected angel trumpets and rainbows when I saw you again. I moved here to find you and to heal our relationship. I've discovered a different side of myself since moving here, and I've found that I can survive whatever is thrown my way. All I want is for you to be happy. If that is not with me, then have the divorce, and I wish you and Alexandrea a good life.'

She turned to face Alexandrea, 'Michael is yours. I can't compete with new love. I have no idea what my future holds for me now, but please let me remain his friend.' She felt the gentle tickle of a tear rolling down her cheek. This was a momentous time in her life, a battle neither would win, but one which, if resolved amicably, would allow her to rethink her future.

'Thank you, Kitty. I think friendship between us all is the way forward.'

Alexandrea surprised Kitty with her soft voice and thanks. Kitty looked at Michael.

He stood looking at her, his eyes damp. His face wore the

same look as when she lifted her first patient, unaided and under fire, across the sandy beach at Normandy: a look of admiration.

'I need you to forgive me, Kitty. You don't deserve the unhappiness I have caused you. I never expected to feel something for Alexandrea when we met again. I truly didn't. I expected to want to rush back to England and be with you, but…' Michael's words failed him.

Kitty watched without resentment as Alexandrea touched his arm.

'But you realised we were crutches for one another,' Kitty replied. 'Yes, we loved one another during the war, but afterwards, when you craved excitement and I wanted the life of a homemaker, neither of us could cope. You have been the brave one by facing the truth. I have wallowed in self-pity, and dragged poor Stanley into our mess.'

A silence fell between the three of them. Alexandrea still held onto Michael's arm, but he removed it, smiled at her and stepped forward towards Kitty.

'I still need you to forgive me. Can you do that, Kitty?' Michael said, holding his arms out.

'I can,' she said.

Kitty went to him and allowed her husband to hold her for one last time.

They were the survivors of a war that had drained every soul around the world; it could not be allowed to destroy a friendship – life was too precious for resentment and anger to destroy a second chance. Kitty needed to let go, and embrace her new future – to find happiness once again.

Chapter Thirty-Nine

'Feeling better?'

Stanley's voice drifted across Kitty's bedroom. She moved in the bed and winced as the sunlight glared through a gap in the curtains.

Her mouth felt like sandpaper, and her head pounded and felt heavy as she tried to sit up in bed.

Stanley stood in the doorway fully dressed, grinning like a schoolboy.

'Brandy?' Kitty asked.

'You want more?' Stanley joked and stepped into her room.

Kitty lay back on her pillow and thought back to the previous night. After Michael and Alexandrea left, she went indoors, poured a generous brandy and sat on the porch crying. Stanley joined her and brought with him the brandy bottle and a glass for himself. He consoled her and reassured her she was going to get through the pain, then they sipped and chatted until the early morning.

'We overdid it, didn't we?' Kitty said, groaning as she moved.

'One of us did. One of us enjoyed a couple of drinks and helped the other up the stairs,' Stanley said, his voice sounding tired but teasing.

Kitty rose upright in the bed. 'How on earth did you manage that?' she asked.

'You were very obliging when I asked you to crawl,' Stanley said, looking very amused.

Kitty shook with laughter. 'What an ending to the day.'

'How do you feel about Michael? I know the drunken side of you is accepting and forgiving, but how do you really feel?' he asked.

'Devastated that my marriage was a sham.'

'It was a mistake, but neither of you knew what was going to happen. You held onto the past until Michael found a mighty confusing way of leaving, but nevertheless he left and gave you both space to think,' Stanley said kindly.

'She – Alex – seems okay. Glamorous. I wonder what his house is like,' she said. 'Can you believe he did that – bought a house? And that car, it's a bit on the posh side, but I bet you're jealous.' Kitty looked at Stanley.

'No. I want a truck. I want something that suits my new life,' Stanley replied, 'And well done, old girl.'

Kitty looked at him, puzzled. 'What for?'

'For taking it on the chin, and giving him your blessing. That can't have been easy.'

Kitty eased her legs over the side of the bed, took a moment to allow the head spinning to pass, then set her feet down on the floor and walked to the window. She opened the curtains, flung open the window and inhaled the sweet air.

'It was easier than I expected,' she said. 'Thanks to his affair, it's all over between us. It hurts to be betrayed, but I am relieved it's over.' Kitty gave a soft sigh and rubbed her temples to ease her headache. 'We realise now what love we had has died – had already fizzled out. I pursued him because I felt I needed to make it work. We live in a time where women are graded by their level of wifely duty, and I tried my best.'

'You did your best, and never forget that,' Stanley replied firmly.

Kitty let his words settle. Praise and comfort in one sentence.

'By the way, I have asked him for some form of funding to help me, as I never expected to be in this situation. I'll soon be out of your hair,' Kitty said. She was glad Stanley couldn't see the sadness in her face. It was moments like this, when they moved into each day, comfortable in each other's presence, that she enjoyed the most. Not having that gave Kitty a fresh sense of impending loss.

'Coffee?' Stanley asked.

Kitty turned from the window and shook her head, then winced. Stanley laughed and Kitty picked up a pillow and threw it in his direction.

'I'm going for a swim, then I'll have some. Poor Saahkómaapi will need attention today.'

Stanley threw the pillow back at her.

'He's had it. I've turned him out into Mim's pen and explained the situation to her. I didn't know what the right thing to do was, but I felt you might need someone else – a woman – to talk to, so she's coming over shortly. I'm going to hers to help Ted saw wood, then I will be back for the afternoon,' Stanley said and went downstairs.

Kitty listened to his uneven steps, and a wave of sorrow came over her. There was so much to miss about Stanley at the start of a new day, but she would have to get used to it when she found her own place.

She shook herself free from the melancholic thoughts and changed to go swimming. She pulled on her new bathing suit, which was in the same shade of red as her beret. It gave her a sense of closeness to her mother. When she saw it in the store window, Kitty recalled a day at the beach the summer before her parents died. Her mother had worn a red swimsuit and a straw hat with a red ribbon. Kitty's guess was that red must have been her mother's favourite colour. Without hesitation, Kitty bought the bathing suit and declared it to be her new favourite colour too.

Armed with her towel, and hiding her tired eyes behind large sunglasses, she took a slow and steady walk to the river, enjoying the warmth on her skin and the freshness of the air. When she reached the river's edge, she stood a while watching it drift past, mesmerised by the sparkling ripples. Kitty imagined it was washing away her fears and her past, and that eventually there would be a moment when there were only crystal-clear, refreshing moments remaining in her life. In the privacy of the pool area, she jumped in and switched off the world.

After her soul-soothing swim, Kitty went back to the house, changed into a loose dress, drank coffee and then began baking. It was hot work, but she persevered; they had to eat, no matter the weather. Slowly, the headache eased, and by the time Mim arrived, a refreshed Kitty was singing softly to herself, kneading dough.

'Stanley said you might look trampled and unkempt. Hungover was the other word he used.' Mim laughed, and Kitty joined her. 'But here you are singing and looking as pretty as they come,' Mim said as she stepped inside the kitchen. She pulled out a large piece of beef and laid it in the sink.

'For salting,' she said. Kitty gave her a blank look in return.

Mim studied Kitty's face and then looked at the meat. 'I take it you have never salted meat before.'

'I've never preserved anything before. My aunt used to pickle and preserve fruit and vegetables, but I can't recall her salting meat.'

Mim rolled up her sleeves. 'Well, there's no time like the present, and I will soon have you bottling fruit and vegetables for winter. You'll have a pantry full, that's for sure.' She set Kitty to work.

When Stanley returned home, all the chores were done, and Kitty had new skills under her belt.

'It's good to see you coping well, Kitty. I like seeing you happy again – and hangover-free,' he said as he rinsed his hands and face in the sink. Kitty threw him a towel.

'I am both hangover-free and happier because I have an outcome. Anything else I have to deal with will be a doddle,' she said.

A few days later, Mim took Kitty on a foraging walk through the forest. Mim's hair was plaited and feathers woven into it. Her ankle-length, sleeveless dress was made from soft hide and had a fringed hem. It was decorated across the neckline with polished glass beads, and painted symbols adorned the back. On her wrists, she wore a woven bracelet with animal teeth dangling from it, and on her feet were moccasins. She walked with confidence and was light-footed as they moved amongst the trees.

'I notice you're more traditional in your ways and clothes since I have been here, and you met with your uncle again,' Kitty said as they collected pine needles to crush and make a poultice, and other medicinal aids.

'I feel close to them now, and my aunt accepts me back too. Like I am teaching you, she is doing the same with me. They will soon return to the chief and main tribe to celebrate Ookaan, the sun and summer season. I will miss my daily visits,' Mim said as they were greeted by the children when they walked towards them.

Kitty watched Mim interact with everyone, looking so at home and relaxed. It never mattered how many times they visited, Kitty was always in awe of the close-knit community. Today, she was to have her hair braided by one of the young girls, a promise made on the last visit, and Mim was making a ceremonial headdress. Kitty treasured these days, and she was secretly pleased Michael had never shared this side of her life. It was her discovery and way of learning to live off the land, rather than him leading the way and her following dutifully as his wife. Fate had given them both a second chance at finding happiness in peace.

On the return walk home, Mim was quiet. Too quiet. Something had upset her, but Kitty felt it was not the time or place to intrude on her friend's thoughts. She walked a little way apart from her, admiring the scenery and recalling the names of the berries and bushes they brushed past.

'They want me to go back to the reservation with them,' Mim suddenly said, 'and for the first time, I feel I belong, and want to be amongst them. Our people have lived and travelled for food on this land for thousands of years, and my mother took away my birthright to remain part of a wider family. Yes, I would never have met Dan had we stayed, but he was taken from me, so he was never meant to be my life for ever.' Mim barely drew breath as she spoke. Her voice was softer, more girl-like than that of the feisty, independent woman Kitty first met and had grown to love. Their friendship was new and fresh, but it felt as if they had been kindred spirits for a lifetime. Kitty felt honoured that Mim had trusted her enough to share her troubles.

'You do look as if you belong back with your people, Mim,' said Kitty. 'It must be hard for you. Maybe go and try it for a month, then stay longer if it works out. After that, organise the cattle business into your life with your family. I'm sure Ted will run things for you and Vern; he'll help. Stanley and I can definitely do our bit in some way. Do not turn away what's in your heart until you know if it is not right for you.'

'Like you and Michael. There is a change in the air for us both, Sinopa,' Mim said wistfully, almost whispering as she looked skyward through the sun-dappled pine trees. Kitty doubted she realised she had used her native tongue when saying Kitty's gifted name.

'We are strong women. Both of us have adapted and overcome. I hope you can decide what is best for you, and find happiness again,' Kitty said and waited for her friend to compose herself. Her vulnerability was on full show, and she needed patience and time.

Kitty sat beside the river, watching its flow and listening to its song, while Mim sat quietly chanting a few feet away. Kitty relaxed and sat back, then began to reflect on things from her past. She recalled eating her first doughnut and enjoying a coffee from Jo's Donut Dolly van, when the American crew had a

British driver. She remembered treating the injured Canadian lumberjacks in Scotland. Never in her wildest dreams did she think she would drink fresh coffee, learn to make her own doughnuts and see lumberjacks work tirelessly in Canada. She recalled the day Michael gave her a jade ring and had a Scotsman play the pipes just for her. She remembered when Stanley arranged picnics and parties for her birthdays, and how she held him after Jenny died, and he whispered his thanks.

She had been through tough times and deserved better days. Once Mim was ready to head home, Kitty would write to Michael, requesting him to formally organise the divorce and to make payments to Stanley for her travel and board, as well as a payment she could use to rent a property when one became available in Cochrane. She was not foolish in her thoughts. Kitty knew it would not be an easy life, nor a wealthy one, but Mim had taught her how to value riches in another way. Life was about becoming rich – not in money, but in the spirit of friendship. Kitty planned to earn enough from her baking to stay in Canada; it was time to settle, and this was the place she wanted to set down her roots.

Chapter Forty

'Michael wants to see me,' Kitty said to Stanley, one day at the end of July, as they hoed a large area where they intended to plant winter vegetables. The soil looked rich and fertile. They had already worked a plot for potatoes.

'Do you think it is the settlement agreement this time?' Stanley asked. He leaned on his garden fork, stretching himself upright. 'He must be paying over the odds for his solicitor to work so fast on this divorce.'

'I think it might be. He promised me a substantial sum for me to purchase my home rather than renting one. I think the letter from my uncle shook him up a bit and reminded him of the promise he made to my aunt and uncle when we first got engaged.'

Kitty's uncle had written a harsh letter of disappointment in response to her letter home regarding Michael. It had arrived quickly, with a large "URGENT" written across the front. It came at a timely moment, when Kitty and Michael were discussing how much he was prepared to pay towards a rental property and for how long.

Kitty had signed one set of divorce papers and returned them to Michael, following an invitation to visit his home. Both she and Stanley had put on what they referred to as their Sunday best and ventured to the edge of Calgary to an estate of brand-new houses. Large affairs with driveways for modern, shining cars loomed towards them as they drove Stanley's new truck along the streets, searching for Michael's home, which he said was the largest on the estate and set back on its land. When they turned a corner, they saw a sprawling building with enormous windows. Kitty quipped that she was lucky she didn't have to clean them. Stanley, however, was not impressed with the modern architecture, and said he preferred the rustic rawness of his house or the graceful ageing of Fell Hall. He also refused to go inside, insisting Kitty needed to be alone with Michael to discuss private business.

Slightly uncomfortable, knowing Stanley sat outside waiting in the heat, Kitty kept her visit brief. During it, she signed more papers to dissolve her marriage to Michael, refused a cocktail from Alexandrea and agreed to take the grand tour. Alexandrea showed off her new electrical hoover and made Kitty think it was time she bought a new broom, as the head on hers was wearing thin. The showing off of newfangled domestic items did nothing to make Kitty feel envious. Not even the sparkling new electric oven. She had mastered the art of a wood-fired one and had no desire to own something cold and glistening in a kitchen with no personality.

Nothing in Michael's home made her think of him; it was stark, ornament-free, and the walls were filled with modern artwork. Kitty knew it was no use offering anything from their home in England; it would not have a place in Alexandrea's décor. She gave them a set of napkins with a maple leaf that she had embroidered. Michael accepted them with good grace, and Alexandrea placed them in a cabinet drawer.

While she listened to Alexandrea boast about the parties she hosted for her neighbours and where she purchased dainty pastries, Kitty noted that neither Michael nor Alexandrea had approached Stanley and invited him inside.

Slightly annoyed, but keeping her opinion of their rudeness to herself, she said her goodbyes.

A few days later Kitty was thinking about Michael's first visit.

'What did he say to you the day he found us? I've never asked you, but when you refused to step inside his house and he did not rush to show it off to you, I am guessing there was something said between you, and it has upset you,' Kitty said. 'I wanted to ask before, but it never seemed the right time.'

Stanley stabbed his fork into the soil and turned it over. 'It was nothing. He got off his chest what he wanted to say, and we've chosen to keep our distance from one another. I do not want to get involved with him and his new ventures.'

'Ah, I see. He wanted you to invest in something, but was annoyed when you refused,' Kitty said and returned to weeding the plot.

'Something like that,' Stanley said, closing down the conversation and pointing to Ted walking their way. 'It looks like the post has arrived.'

A letter with Jo's scrawling handwriting and another from Meryn had arrived from England, along with one from Michael's solicitor. Stanley walked away with Ted, asking his advice on when to plant for the Cochrane weather, and Kitty was grateful for his discretion as she tore open the solicitor's envelope.

The divorce agreement was official. Also inside was a notification of a final figure, which Michael would not pay out if she contested it. He considered that the money was enough for Kitty to purchase a home of her own. She stared at the figure and realised how wealthy Michael had become. She would not refuse the money; it was generous and more than she would have received had they still lived in England. She lay on her back and looked at the sky. A few clouds headed towards the mountains, but the sun still bled across the land. Allowing herself to breathe and release the past, Kitty rose to her feet, walked to a shady spot and tore open Jo's letter.

Dear Kitty,

How are things? Have you found him? Do you need me? How's Stanley?

He's a good man. Heart of gold to put up with you. Does he get a medal after you and Michael are reunited?

Things are good here. Gina says hi.

I have no intention of leaving America and have applied for my permits to become a citizen.

The same will happen for you one day. I am convinced Canada will capture your heart, and I think it is a country which will suit you.

Chin up, old girl. Hello to Stanley.

Your friend,
Jo x

Kitty smiled to herself. Jo was never a letter writer, but her humour was always welcome, and Kitty was grateful she had made the effort to write. She opened Meryn's, hoping the news was good and life was treating her fairly.

Dearest Kitty,

We hope you are well - that's me, Kedrick, Pots and Wenna.

Everything is going well, both health-wise and business-wise. The weather is unpredictable, but tourists are slowly returning, and no one minds the weather; they are grateful to be returning to a life without the war hanging over them.

My upsetting news is that Bobby has returned to America. He couldn't settle in Cornwall because he needed to see his family again, and I understood. The war brought him here, and they will want to celebrate that he survived, and he needs to hug his mother again. I suggested he return to them and see how he feels about us when we are not always together, then make up his mind. I am willing to go and live there with Kedrick, but it will be up to Bobby, and I will honour his decision. It will break my heart, and sadly, something tells me we will not see each other again. I will continue writing to him for Kedrick's sake, and to remind Bobby of his duty to his son back in England.

I am resigned to the thought that I may never be a wife and may be unlucky in love, but I am happy enough to be a mother. Kedrick is my world, and I am always grateful to those who supported me and helped raise him.

Your news about a horse and visiting an Siksika reservation is quite different to what I was expecting, but then you have always led a fascinating life. I'm pleased Stanley has a new home, but I do find it difficult to imagine him working the land after having a gardener for most of his life.

Keep me updated on you and Michael if you find him. I still cannot believe that he left you. Thank goodness you have Stanley for company or I would worry more about you than I already do. I have enclosed a photograph of us all. Bobby took it before he left, so there's a copy in America and now Canada.

Please send us one of you on the prairie, and Stanley gardening!

Take care, my dearest friend.

Much Love from Meryn x

Kitty walked back to the house and laid the letters down on the table. She sat down and, rather than immediately writing replies, read through the payment agreement from Michael and thought about what to do next – how to go about finding somewhere nearby that was similar to Stanley's home. The five thousand dollars Michael had arranged to be placed into a bank account in her name would undoubtedly help her find something decent, but it would have to be somewhere between Cochrane and Calgary. She wanted something ready to live in immediately, and within easy travelling distance of Stanley and Mim, on foot or by cart. She still wanted to help Stanley on his land, and doing up a place for herself would take all of her energy.

Outside in the yard, she heard Stanley say goodbye to Ted, and placed the kettle on the stove. She cut large slices of fresh bread, buttered them and laid cold beef with pickles beside them on a plate. Stanley had a stomach with a routine switch, and Kitty knew by the clock in the kitchen that she had four minutes before he walked in to eat. She covered everything with a cloth, then took a tin from the pantry with a fresh-baked apple pie inside and cut two wedges.

'Ah, I'm starving after that work. You're a mind-reader,' said Stanley when he walked in. He washed his hands, pulled out a chair, poured two cups of tea from the pot and looked across the table at her.

'Did he do the decent thing?' he asked.

Kitty nodded and pushed the envelope his way. She watched as he read it and then looked up at her. He gave a low whistle.

'I take it you're satisfied?' he said, smiling at her as he folded the letter away.

'I am. More than satisfied, and surprised he can afford to give away such a large sum. And it is more than I imagined.' Kitty replied. 'Now all I have to do is find somewhere to spend it on.'

Chapter Forty-One

August crept in with a heat Kitty had never experienced before. Mim and Ted both said it was the hottest they'd known for years, and Stanley spent as much time as he could cooling off in the river inlet.

The morning of her birthday, Kitty decided to swim before tending to Saahkómaapi and clear her head of the disastrous house hunt she had endured the previous day. The cool water felt delicious against her skin, making it tingle – a sensation she had not felt since she last made love with Michael. A swell of sadness exploded inside as she realised she would never feel like that again. Gentle strokes of her breasts, tender lip bites, neck kissing and many other orgasmic pleasures would never come her way again. She was moving towards her thirties faster than she would like; she was settling into a new lifestyle and recovering from a divorce; there was no room in her life for dancing and meeting another man.

Kitty had accepted the harsh reality that she would probably never give birth to a child. Adopt maybe, but carrying her own child and continuing her bloodline would not happen. Time was not kind, nor was it on her side. Kitty allowed the tingle of the water ripple over her again, then she dipped below the surface and held her breath before jumping up. Drops of the sweet-tasting river water trickled across her lips, and she licked them dry.

It was a day to enjoy, not to contemplate a life that had not yet happened.

Once she was back at the house, she pulled on a cotton blouse and a pair of baggy floral dungarees, wound her hair into a loose bun and pushed her feet into a pair of moccasins Mim had given her. She left Stanley a note to say she had gone for a ride towards Mim's far boundary. The views of the Rockies were breathtaking from that point, and there was an area where she could slip into the pine forest for the ride home.

Releasing the cattle in the land below were the men Mim hired, and Kitty saw Vern weaving amongst them. She waved, and he rode over to speak with her. He looked so handsome on his horse, and Kitty wondered if he was married or dedicated to being a single cowboy.

'Any luck finding a place to live?' Vern asked as he jumped down from his horse and helped her down from Saahkómaapi. They stood on the raised ledge and looked below at the activity from both cattle and cowboys.

'No joy. I will have to look further afield,' Kitty replied with a sigh. Vern took off his hat and dusted it against his thigh before placing it back on his head.

'I'll keep my ears open for you, and if you ever need a rancher, I know the trustworthy and the cheaters, so come to me first. I recruited all of Mim's. Good men.'

'Tell me what you do in a year. It fascinates me – we have nothing like this in England – cowboys, I mean. I wish to learn something about the life of a cowboy. Do you have time to spare?' Kitty asked, smiling up at him.

'For you, always, but not right now. How about I come by yours early evening?' Vern replied, returning the smile.

Kitty thought about his suggestion, and an idea came to her. 'That's a great idea. I'll ask Mim and Ted to join us – eat with us,' she said, and remounted Saahkómaapi. 'I'll head to Mim now. I look forward to seeing you later.'

Vern waved her away, and Kitty rode to Mim's, then back to Stanley.

'Stanley, I hope you don't mind, but I've invited Mim, Ted and Vern over to eat with us this evening. I have plenty of food prepared,' she said as she poured herself a coffee.

'I think it is a grand idea to celebrate your birthday. I was going to suggest a picnic, but an evening with friends will be better. Now, I have a place to show you and it's within walking distance. I need to stretch my good leg, so are you up for viewing it?' Stanley replied.

Kitty looked at him, puzzled. 'I thought I had seen them all,' she said.

'This one has just become available. Ted told me about it and arranged for you to see it; Mim knows all about it, so I've suggested we stop by to find out more,' Stanley said.

'Then what are we waiting for?' Kitty said, laughing, and guiding him by the shoulders towards the door, followed him outside.

As they walked towards Mim's, Kitty noticed Stanley was walked much more slowly than normal.

'Are you having problems with your leg?' She asked.

Stanley stopped walking. 'I think I will have to invest in a new prosthetic leg. This one is worn and not suitable for the uneven ground. Ted said there is a specialist doctor I can speak to, so I will make an appointment soon. I worry I won't be able to work the land so well if I ignore the problem.'

'Then why on earth are you pushing yourself so hard? I'll fetch Saahkómaapi for when we return home, then come back and get you. I take it the stump isn't blistered too badly?' Kitty replied. Stanley shook his head.

Mim greeted them at the front of her home as she watered the herbs and flowers on her porch.

'I've made you a cold drink inside,' she said.

'And for that we're extremely grateful,' Kitty replied, bowing and laughing as she wiped her brow with her handkerchief.

'Come in, rest,' Mim said and beckoned them.

Sipping her drink, Kitty looked around at Mim's home and thought back to the ones on the reservation; they were so very different. Mim had lived within hide walls, bricks and mortar, and pinewood logs. Stanley had only ever lived in a large mansion. She wasn't sure about Ted.

Then she thought about the homes she had enjoyed. A small terraced house, a room in a nurse's home or two, a closet room in a castle, a hut in a POW camp, a cottage, a Cornish inn, a moderate-sized English country house, a large stately mansion, and now a pine log cabin. Each place held a piece of her heart, and she hoped she could put a larger piece into her new home.

'So, where is this place for sale that Stanley mentioned? Do you know the price?' Kitty asked Mim.

'It's local; the price is negotiable with the owner, so I can't say. Do you want to go and see it?' Mim asked.

'I do, and I hope it is suitable, because, to be honest, I am getting a bit downhearted, aren't I, Stanley?' Kitty said and turned to Stanley, who smiled at her.

'"Unbearable" is the word I would use,' he said and grinned.

Mim laughed, 'While you two are still friends, I think we'd better go.'

Chapter Forty-Two

Ted pulled Mim's cart round, and they climbed in, but as he began moving, Stanley shifted in his seat and gave a deep sigh. It was obvious to Kitty he was uncomfortable.

'Ted, sorry to trouble you, old man, but would you mind if we fetched my crutches? I can't walk properly with this darn stump today. Even sitting is beginning to irritate.'

'We'll stay home. Make arrangements for another day, Stanley. It's not fair on you,' Kitty said, concerned Stanley would push himself for her sake and cause himself more damage.

'My crutches will help me,' Stanley said, 'and you don't want to lose out on seeing the property.'

When they arrived at his house, he climbed down with Ted supporting him, and they went inside. Mim watched them.

'Stanley is a good man and will do anything for you,' she said. 'I wish I had a friend like him at my side. Vern is my closest male friend, and Ted is family.'

'Stanley has always looked out for me. He sees me as his little sister,' Kitty said.

Mim threw back her head and laughed. 'I think you will find he sees you as more than that, and probably wishes for more than that too.'

Shocked by her statement, Kitty shook her head. 'I think you see something that is not there, Mim.'

'Maybe – but … a conversation for another day. Why is fetching a set of crutches taking so long? Let's go and flush them out,' Mim said and jumped down, securing fly and cart, and strode towards the house.

Kitty rushed to her and pointed to Saahkómaapi. 'He's content, and look, Stanley carved his name on a plaque above the stable.'

'He's got a good owner, and you have a good friend. Now, where are those boys?' Mim said with a giggle.

Inside the house, Ted and Stanley were looking at papers spread across the table.

'What's distracted you?' Kitty asked, joining them.

'Oh, it's plans for a washroom – but I've altered them. It's going to be a side extension to the property rather than a stand-alone building,' Stanley said.

'That's exciting. It will be wonderful when it is finished,' Kitty said and stepped to one side to allow Mim to look at the plans.

'I wish I had thought of that,' Mim said, tapping the plans.

'It will be easier than building where you first thought,' Stanley replied.

Kitty looked at the plans again. They were for Mim's property.

'Oh, I thought you were looking at the plans for your house,' she said to Stanley.

Stanley eased his back straight and grinned. 'I am.'

Kitty frowned, then smiled. 'I see, you're using the same plans. Will you run the extension from there?' she said, pointing to a long wall situated between the front of the property and the kitchen window. 'There's room for a doorway and a decent-sized extension.'

Stanley shrugged. 'It will be up to the new owner; I am prepared to share the plans when I sell,' he said, and looked her in the face with a serious stare. 'You're standing inside the property that is now up for sale, Kitty. Mim is moving back to her family, and I have agreed to purchase her place. There are no stairs, which I need nowadays, and it is a viable business. A good investment,' Stanley said, his voice so serious that Kitty realised how much thought he had put into the purchase. She also knew he had no fears about her offering to buy the house.

'Stanley, how much would you be willing to sell Fell Wayside for?' she asked, knowing full well he had already worked out the figure, wanting her to buy it.

'I am selling for four thousand dollars. The price will include the building of the washroom, and I will pay for any legal costs. There's only a small amount of work done so far, and you helped with most of that, so I think it's a fair price and one you can afford. If you're serious about it, then we need to do it formally,' Stanley said.

Mim interjected before Kitty could say anything.

'Ted will take me home, and we will return for our meal to celebrate your birthday and to find out whether you have made a decision.'

A dazed Kitty saw her to the door. 'I've invited Vern to join us this evening. I never realised you had sold to Stanley, so if Vern doesn't know, we had better be discreet,' she said.

Mim smiled. 'It was Vern who suggested I return to be with my family, and to sell to Stanley, and his idea worked. I look forward to hearing your news later.' She beckoned to Ted to take her home.

Kitty walked over to the table and looked at the plans laid out there, then over at where the bathroom would be, and nodded to herself, before turning around to Stanley, who was sitting prosthetic-free on the comfortable sofa.

'Yes, Stanley. I agree to buy this place from you. I love it, and will have the most wonderful neighbour. It makes sense. We can care for one another, but still have our independence.'

Stanley gave a slight cough and held out his hand.

'It's agreed. We'll get the ball rolling tomorrow, but for now, I will rest until our guests arrive.'

Kitty leaned down and kissed his cheek. As he moved his head, their lips brushed briefly, and they both pulled back, laughing awkwardly.

'Happy birthday, Kitty,' Stanley said.

'Thank you. I have just treated myself to a birthday gift, a new house!' Kitty said, spinning around the room. She felt light-hearted, secure and ready to start life afresh in Cochrane.

The evening party began when Mim arrived with Vern and Ted. Stanley played host and fussed over Kitty. She watched Mim and Vern chat on the porch and sensed this was a secret new romance for Mim. Vern was keen, Kitty could tell by his attentive manner.

Kitty turned her attention to Stanley and watched him plate up his share of the buffet she had laid out. His sun-bleached hair enhanced his tanned skin. His arms were more muscular than when they arrived, and his smile a great deal wider. Every day, she noticed something more about him, and each time she took a moment to appreciate him as a friend, Kitty began to doubt her feelings. They were growing towards a love she would never have for a sibling; it was almost a need, a deep desire. Living in the same home as him in the past and present always brought her calm, or gave some other sense to her life. He took risks for her as an individual; he always paid attention to her and was thoughtful towards her needs. Kitty's understanding of the love she had for Stanley altered. It was not the love of sibling and sibling; it was that of a woman falling for a man.

'Daydreaming about owning this place?' Stanley's voice cut into her thoughts, and Kitty gave a slight shrug. Stanley laid down his plate and went to her. 'I know you well enough to see you're worried or upset about something. Tell me. You do know you don't have to buy the house, you can live with me until one you really want comes along.'

Kitty went to turn away from him, worried she would betray her feelings for him, but he grabbed her hand and pulled her close.

'Michael was a fool, but don't allow him to sit inside your head for ever. You have plenty of time to make a new life, meet a good man and start a family. You, my darling girl, are quite a catch, and any man would be extremely lucky to marry you.'

Enjoying the vibration of his voice against her cheek, Kitty remained still. Stanley's arms around her strengthened her feelings. She was in love with Stanley, and soon she would struggle to hide the fact.

'I keep thinking this is not real life. It is a dream, a long holiday,' she whispered.

Stanley still held her close.

'It started out as a nightmare,' he said, 'then felt like an adventure, but we've made a start on a different lifestyle that suits us both. You belong here; it is almost as if an old soul has given you a new lease of life. I love seeing you cope – and your handling of Michael was admirable.'

Laughter came from the porch, and Kitty and Stanley moved away from one another.

'I had better go to our guests. Thank you, Stanley,' Kitty said, picking up a plate of fruit.

'For what?' he asked, returning to his own plate.

'For the hug. I needed it,' Kitty said.

'I will always be there to hug you, Kitty. That's a promise. Ask me any time,' Stanley said and gave her a cheeky wink.

Chapter Forty-Three

Outside with their friends, Kitty thought about the days when she would be alone, when they were all busy and living apart. She watched and listened as they praised her baking and devoured the treats she had made for her birthday.

'I think I would like to open a bakery,' she suddenly announced, and watched as Stanley hesitated before taking a bit from a maple syrup pastry. 'Or at least find somewhere to sell my goods.'

Vern was the first to speak. 'My men will be first in the queue. Your muffins went down well last week.'

Mim nodded her agreement. 'You have a talent, and it should not go to waste. I think there would be enough trade to keep you busy.'

Ted tapped his plate. 'If you bake what I have just eaten, I can get regular orders from the guys in Calgary.'

Stanley also gave a nod. 'I agree with them, don't waste your talent. It's a good idea. You once said you were told your mother liked to bake, so this is her gift to you. Run with it, and see.'

'It is something for me to think about now I have a home,' Kitty replied.

After a successful evening and Vern sharing his stories about his days as a cowboy, which Kitty found fascinating, their friends returned home. Stanley helped her clear away the dishes, and they both relaxed with a cocoa before bedtime. It all seemed natural and comfortable to Kitty, like a marriage between two compatible partners. Putting her feet up on a small stool she had rescued from the wilderness in the garden, she gave a contented sigh.

'What a day!' she said.

'One you will never forget,' Stanley replied.

'For sure.' Kitty used Mim's favourite expression.

'I enjoyed surprising you by buying Mim's place,' Stanley told her.

'That was definitely a surprise. But I am going to miss you, miss this,' Kitty said shyly.

Stanley sipped his cocoa. His silence unnerved Kitty.

'But I will be fine on my own, not scared,' she said quickly to reassure him she had no intention of being a burden to him.

Stanley struggled to his feet. Kitty watched as he walked towards her, leaned down and removed the stool from beneath her feet, and gestured to her to stand up. Kitty did as he asked.

'I am scared, Kitty,' he said, lifting one of her hands and holding it.

'I've never known you to be scared. You will run the business well, if that's what you're worried about,' Kitty said reassuringly, squeezing his hand.

'I am frightened of losing you as a friend,' Stanley said, his voice low and sad.

'You won't ever lose me as a friend, Stanley,' Kitty said urgently, shocked that he would think that way.

'Not even if I did this…'

Stanley leaned forward, and his lips were on hers before Kitty could blink with surprise. He held her tight and close, and she felt the passion and warmth, and did not hold back in her response. She kissed him with equal passion, sharing with him what her words could not. His kiss was bold, but not frenzied; it was a statement. She felt his love as it surged through her body, and from the way he held her tighter, he felt hers. There was no turning back from this moment, no retracting and remaining friends; this was a declaration, a joining together of two hearts. She and Stanley loved one another.

Eventually, they pulled apart and stood looking at each other. She knew Stanley was studying her for any sign of regret, and she smiled at him.

'And the surprises continue,' she said. 'How long have you felt this way?'

Stanley looked down at his feet, then back up to her face.

'Ever since you fought my corner with that dreadful occupational health man who tried to belittle me, but you would have none of it. As my nurse you set him straight and I returned home,' he said, almost apologetically.

Kitty was shocked. She gasped.

'But you were married to Jenny.'

Stanley bowed his head. 'I was, and as I explained before, we had to grow our love, which, when I met you, I realised was not true, deep and solid love. It was companionship love with the odd romantic effort by me thrown into the mix.'

'What made you test the waters tonight?' Kitty asked.

Stanley smiled. 'It was when you said you would miss this, us. I wondered if you felt the same about me. I've felt something from you for a while, but I put it down to you needing the love of a friend during the dreadful things you were going through. So I thought it was now or never. Or else both of us would hide a love that should be aired and celebrated after so many years.'

Kitty leaned forward and kissed him again, then stood back.

'Now what do we do?' she asked.

Chapter Forty-Four

The following morning, the warmth of the sun flowed through the window and filled the room. Kitty stretched out in her bed, then remembered: Stanley was lying beside her. Everything had happened so fast that she could not believe it wasn't a dream. In one month, she had divorced Michael and laid her heart bare to Stanley.

Stanley's declaration of love was like something out of a romance novel. For him to speak so openly took courage.

Their lovemaking the previous evening began with a hint of awkwardness. However, as the moments unfolded, the world around them faded into insignificance. It left only the deep connection they shared – a far cry from the sibling-like love they had always claimed to have – a connection that led to a tentative exploration of one another's bodies. Entwined in rumpled sheets, they had whispered declarations of love, each word laced with sincerity and commitment to make their new life together succeed.

'Good morning,' Stanley said, and leaned over and kissed her forehead. 'I am going to get out of this bed before we repeat last night, and half the day is gone. We need to talk, my love.'

Kitty shivered with pleasure.

'We certainly do, but I am disappointed you don't want to stay and play,' Kitty teased and ran her hand across his chest.

'Oh, I do, believe me, I do, but I have an appointment with Mim and her solicitor in an hour, which is why we need to talk before I go.' He tapped her nose playfully. 'There's always later.'

After they had washed, dressed and eaten, Kitty and Stanley sat at the table, Stanley with paper and pens in front of him.

'Obviously I don't want you to buy the house from me now, because we won't be living apart, but I know how much you like this place, though it is no longer practical for me. So I've had an idea.'

He spent a moment drawing diagrams and then pushed them in front of her.

'What do you think?' he asked.

Kitty studied the drawings.

'You want to move this over to attach to Mim's – your place?' she asked.

'It would make a wonderful family home, and we could have a big bedroom downstairs, away from the main rooms of the house. You could have a large kitchen to take care of your new bakery business,' Stanley said, his voice filled with boyish excitement.

'A family home?' Kitty questioned.

'Yes. You want children, I want children, we want a family, and well, after last night, I think we should consider starting soon,' Stanley said, laughing.

'Not out of wedlock, I don't,' Kitty replied bluntly. A shiver of concern ran through her. Stanley was getting carried away. She was serious about her love for him, but she would only have children after getting married.

Stanley rose from his seat and stood in front of her. 'Would you risk marriage again?'

'Only if I am asked, and then it depends on who is doing the asking,' Kitty said, smiling.

Stanley shook his head at her in amusement.

'I can't go down on one knee, but I can ask you to marry me. Kitty Pattison, will you be my wife?'

Kitty looked him in the eye and smiled.

'Yes, Stanley Walker-Fell. Yes, I will marry you,' she replied and put her arms around his neck, kissing him with a passion that showed her love for him. It no longer felt awkward or strange.

'You know Michael won't believe this is fresh and new to us, don't you?' Stanley said with concern.

'So what if he doesn't? It won't hurt us. He chose his path, and we're following ours, and we waited until I was divorced, whereas he didn't, and I think he will be too busy with his own life to worry about us. Mim and Ted know we've been nothing but friends, but I'm guessing they've seen what we both feel for one another before we did,' she answered.

'It's been hard trying to tell myself it wasn't right to love you so much,' Stanley said, 'and I had to sit back because you loved Michael.'

Kitty pulled a face.

'I am not sure I truly loved Michael. I realised sometime back that we got married for the wrong reasons. It opened my eyes when I knew I had fallen in love with you – romantic love, not sisterly, though I kept trying to tell myself that's what it was.

What we have between us is true love and is nobody's business but our own.'

'I agree,' said Stanley. 'I will sign to buy Mim's place, and we can merge the land and properties; a rebuild isn't difficult with this type of house. In a few years, I think electricity will be available, but we'll manage as we are for now.'

'I like how we manage now. I will miss my oven, though, I am sure that plays a part in the results you enjoy. I wonder if I can keep this kitchen as a business-only one. Divide the house, maybe the master bedroom in there'—she pointed to the sitting area—'and keep the two bedrooms upstairs; that way, Mim's place can be for general living areas. A study for you and your business, maybe,' Kitty said.

Stanley looked at her, his eyes wide and smiling. 'We're really doing this. I can't believe my luck! We are going to have an incredible life here, Kitty. It will be tough at times, but we are made of strong stuff. Come with me today, and we can break the news to Mim.'

'You're not walking there, so yes, I will come and drive you. I am amazed by what has happened since May. I'll go and change my gardening clothes.' Kitty rushed upstairs to her room, where she pulled open a drawer and lifted out Michael's grandmother's sweetheart pin and the jade engagement ring he gave her. Kitty decided to return them to him; they were his family heirlooms, and she no longer had any use for them. She looked in the mirror and observed how much happier she looked. Then she thought about the letter she needed to send to her uncle. His reaction would be one she wished she could see rather than read about, much later, but there would be nothing he could say or do to spoil her happiness with Stanley.

As they drove Saahkómaapi down the pathway, Stanley

talked about his ideas for the land and their future. Kitty felt a surge of happiness; a weight had been lifted off her shoulders, and she had never felt more alive or excited about their next adventure.

A while later, Kitty and Stanley sat in front of Mim and explained their situation and their plans for the two homes. Her face was attentive as she listened, and then she gave a light laugh.

'The idea about the homes is new to me, and it's a good idea, but you two falling in love is no surprise. I can tell that you have loved one another for a long time, but only now have had the time to realise it and the freedom to act on it, too.'

'We have to find out about the legal side of marrying over here, and then we can set a date,' Kitty said.

'Will you invite Michael?' Mim asked, and Kitty was taken aback.

'No. This is a fresh start for me – I would be uncomfortable.'

'He's already warned me off, so I would only invite him if Kitty wanted him there,' Stanley said.

Kitty looked at him, 'Is that what he did when he wanted to talk to you privately? When he decided to come and say hello and introduce his mistress?'

Stanley raised his eyebrows and nodded. 'Yes, he had quite a few choice words for me, which is why I had no desire to enter his house when you visited them.'

Kitty hitched her back straight. 'Then he won't be welcome in any area of my life from now on. He is not the Michael I remember, and it's a shame.'

Mim put her hand out in front of Kitty. 'Do not let him ruin this special day. Remember him as the war hero, and release the other feelings you have towards him. It is a heavy load to carry.'

Mim turned to Stanley. 'Let us go and sign papers, make this house sale official.'

Kitty put her hand on Mim's arm.

'Before you do, are you certain you want to give up the place where you feel close to Dan?' she asked.

'Like you, I have to release the past, Kitty. Dan is in my heart. In a place just for him. I have opened another space and wait to receive the blessings of a future. I am ready to return to my family. My heart is full, knowing that you and Stanley realised your love and will live here. Time moves us on for a reason.' Mim stroked a stray hair from Kitty's forehead. 'Be happy, little Sinopa.'

Chapter Forty-Five

Kitty had asked Ted to deliver a letter to Michael, and received one in return agreeing to meet with her at The Rockyview Hotel. She told Stanley about the meeting and explained about handing over the heirlooms. The items were material things with happy memories attached, but Kitty knew that, if she kept them, she would always be reminded of the unpleasant times, and memories like that were not what she wanted in her life anymore.

When they arrived at the hotel, a large group of cowboys was standing on the stoop, laughing and chatting. Each one touched the brim of his large hat in a polite gesture of greeting. Kitty suddenly felt nervous and out of place. She was dressed neatly and had no reason to feel self-conscious, but the sensation still crept inside her. Michael arrived looking smart and businesslike, but more relaxed than the last time they had met.

Kitty had chosen not to sit before he arrived, and she walked towards him. They stood awkwardly in front of one another before she held out her hand.

'How are you?' she asked.

Michael smiled. 'Feeling slightly odd that we're shaking hands in a hotel.'

'Shall we sit?' Kitty asked.

'I'd rather not, shall we walk?' Michael said, and Kitty wondered if he was avoiding the gossip that might arise.

'I'll give you these first,' Kitty said, handing over the ring and sweetheart pin. 'It's only right you have them back. They belong in your family.'

'Thank you. I did wonder if you would keep them, but I hoped you would return them. I would not have asked you for them.'

'I know.'

Michael tucked the boxes safely in his pocket and then held the door open for her to step outside. They strolled the main street, chatting about his oil investments and business opportunities.

'Do you not miss being a doctor?' Kitty asked.

'I did at first, but then I noticed my nightmares had subsided, and there was a change in my moods. The stress was not helping me, so I chose a different career with less responsibility, and I have no regrets,' Michael replied.

'Are you and Alexandrea getting married?' Kitty asked, 'You seem very happy together.'

Michael stopped walking and looked at her. 'We get married next week. A quiet affair.'

Relief washed over Kitty. Michael had not given up their marriage on a whim; he really did love Alexandrea.

'I am very happy for you both, and I hope you have a

wonderful day and life together. I mean it, Michael. We both deserve happiness,' she said. She took a moment to consider telling him about Stanley, but decided to wait until further into their conversation. Anxiety she had not expected to experience had returned. Conflict with Michael was now the last thing she wanted. She wanted to walk away as friends, with a clean slate.

They stopped by the railway and watched the endless line of cattle and lumber wagons roll past.

'What was your journey over like?' Michael asked, 'Did you travel by train?'

'We flew in, then took the train. It was tiring, but I enjoyed seeing different parts of Canada.'

'Do you think you will remain here?' Michael asked and turned to face her again, indicating they should continue walking.

'In Cochrane? Yes. In fact, Stanley has just purchased the ranch next to the house. He is the owner of a cattle ranch now,' Kitty replied, waiting for the moment when she would tell him about her impending marriage to Stanley.

Michael stopped walking. 'So he's staying?'

Kitty nodded. 'We both are. We are looking for contractors to move the house and attach it to the cabin, creating a large family home.' She spoke slowly and clearly, her instinct telling her now was the right time to let him know the route she was taking with Stanley.

'We? So I was right. You and Stanley were having an affair,' Michael said harshly.

Kitty raised both hands in front of her, preventing him from walking away.

'Stop right there. We didn't have an affair. Our marriage was ruined by only one of us doing that.' Michael, she noted, had the good grace to blush.

'It came out of the blue, taking us both by surprise. Our relationship as a couple has only just happened. On my birthday, we both opened up about our feelings for each other, and it wasn't what we had thought. We thought of ourselves as siblings, but it appears we have fallen in love – been in love for some time,' she said in a rush. 'Like you and Alexandrea.'

Michael shrugged.

'It doesn't matter to me what you do. I wish you good luck. I don't think you'll cope as a rancher's wife, but who knows,' he said.

'I will,' Kitty retorted. She wasn't going to let Michael dampen her dream with negative comments. 'It's the happiest I've been for years. Once you and I divorced, I realised we married for the wrong reasons,' Kitty said.

'Yeah, we did. I don't think we knew how to let go as we'd needed one another for survival so often, we were almost like a good habit,' Michael said, giving a light laugh. Kitty joined him.

'A good habit, that's one way of describing us. I don't like how you warned Stanley off, though. He never deserved that – he really didn't. It was unfair and unkind. I will leave it up to you to decide whether to do the right thing,' Kitty said.

'I'll have a word. Is there anything you need on the prairies?' Michael said, and Kitty was surprised by his offer.

'That's kind of you. What I would like is for the oil companies to stop badgering for the land around us. It won't be for sale, so if you have any influence in that area, I would be grateful,' Kitty said.

'Consider it done. It is my area of expertise, and I know

where there is more fertile land for us to explore – where we should get a good strike,' Michael said, smiling.

As they walked, Kitty could sense the barrier of unease lift, and she relaxed.

As they said their goodbyes, they hugged each other. Watching him drive away, she knew for certain that her heart belonged to Stanley. Michael was her past, but having cleared the air, they would remain friends. She thought it ironic that the roles of the two men in her life had reversed, and, because of that, she could start anew in Canada with a sense of relaxation and ease.

Chapter Forty-Six

The contractors worked quickly once the plans were signed off and agreed, and Kitty, along with Mim and Ted, packed everything into the cabin and barns at the end of August.

Stanley supervised the move amidst the chaos surrounding them. Each day brought new challenges or victories, but the September nights were calm and soothing. It was during these precious moments spent side by side that they began to open up about their feelings for each other. They decided to wait until they were married to share the same bed again, but they allowed themselves the joy of holding one another and absorbing the love between them before bedtime, deepening their bond beyond the friendship they had once shared.

During this time, they learned to set aside the past and embrace the present. Their experiences since leaving Great Britain had been a whirlwind of emotions, the most consuming of which was the hidden love they felt for one another. Once this love was acknowledged, it became explosive, catching them both by surprise. The quiet moments they shared were perfect for reflection and connection.

Whenever she lay in Stanley's arms, Kitty felt safe and content, as if the world had stopped so that they could enjoy the stillness.

One evening, they were discussing their wishes for a quiet, intimate wedding in the grounds of their home.

'I suspect inviting Togquos along will counteract the quiet. He is bound to surprise us with a wedding tradition involving drums,' Stanley said.

Kitty gave a soft sigh. 'I hope so. To have a blessing from the Siksika would make me feel accepted, and it will be a good omen for our life together on Canadian soil. I love the drums, and how different their songs are – the sounds and melodies have a raw, natural flow. I feel the vibrations in my chest, touching my heart. It is so expressive, like nothing I have heard before.'

'Are you nervous about tomorrow?' Stanley asked, stroking Kitty's neck as she rested her head on his chest. His touch sent thrilling sensations throughout her body. It was difficult not to respond more intimately.

'Michael's visit? Not really. I'm not sure why he is coming, probably something to do with the oil companies. He's married and enjoying life with his glamorous wife. I'm more nervous about this place being ready for our big day,' Kitty replied. 'I want everything cleared for the ceremony. Jumping rocks and timber is not my idea of walking down the aisle – or grass path in our case, but I trust the contractor and Vern's team to have it wedding day ready.'

Stanley shifted in the bed and sat upright. 'We can still marry in church if that's what you prefer. I am sure one will oblige.'

Kitty sat up beside him. 'No, being a divorcee is frowned

upon. Besides, I want to be outdoors in the air. I want something different, more connected to who I am now – who *we* are. You said you were happy to have a simple affair on our own land. Have you changed your mind?'

'Not at all. We have a special licence, and I have new clothes. I am ready,' Stanley said.

'And my dress is nearly finished,' Kitty said.

'You have so many talents – I never realised,' Stanley replied.

'I've never had the time to find out what I can do other than nurse and rescue people and tend to orphans,' Kitty said. 'I would not change a thing, but I am glad I have the opportunity to find out more about myself.'

'I look forward to seeing what you have created,' Stanley said. 'I do worry that you haven't experienced the white wedding dress, though. Your outfit for your wedding to Michael was a suit, if I recall. Navy wool, I think you described it – nothing like the material you bought in Calgary, I'm sure.'

'I felt so frumpy in my suit, but we had no money or coupons to buy me a dress, so I made do. This time it will be much different.'

Kitty had purchased a bolt of pale lavender cotton and a roll of broderie anglaise lace when she and Mim went in search of a wedding gown. Stanley only knew the colour was not going to be virginal white. Kitty felt that would be wrong, since she had been married before, and she and Stanley had already shared intimate moments.

She had looked at dresses in stores, but nothing inspired her, and all she kept thinking about was the image of an Edwardian woman in a simple, loose, white cotton gown, known as a lawn dress. Kitty had seen it in a historical magazine she had purchased on the journey across Canada. The style of the dress was ideal for a hot day and would make a lovely wedding outfit. The more they shopped, the more the image kept flashing in her mind. It was a dress she could reuse if she adjusted the hemline and dyed it for a more practical outfit.

After explaining her vision to Mim, they visited a fabric store and came across the perfect solution. Each day, Kitty sat and worked at her dress in the smallest room in the cabin. It was not the ideal place, but with the house nearing completion, it was the only place available that was free from prying eyes.

'I will feel more of a bride in the one I am making. It is quite feminine for me. Vern said he has a special gift for me, but I won't be able to have it until the wedding morning. I dread to think,' Kitty said, laughing.

'Ah, apparently I am getting one too. It will be interesting to see what we receive,' Stanley replied. 'We have such generous friends.'

In the morning, they watched as the last of their house merged with the cabin, and the pipework and drainage for the bathroom were plunged into the ground. Once the ground clearing started, Kitty set about cleaning and organising their new home. Her priority for that day was the bathroom. She had four days to finish it before her wedding day.

Outside, she heard Stanley talking, and she guessed Michael had arrived. She peered through the window and saw them shake hands. Michael looked out of place, and Stanley looked hot and tired. She stepped outside.

'Hello, Michael. What do you think?' she asked, smiling, not really bothered about what he thought.

'I've just said to Stanley, he has made a smart move. With a large house on all the land he now owns, the property price will have risen. Because of that, I've had a word with the oil companies, explaining you are close friends of mine and are not to be hassled into selling. I have signed papers for you which state they will leave you alone,' Michael said, nodding approvingly as he looked around.

'That's good to know, and thank you,' Kitty replied, and Stanley repeated her words.

Kitty looked at Michael. 'We wondered if you would like to join us on our wedding day. I know it will feel a little odd, but we should seal our friendship and be civil with one another.'

Michael looked to her, then to Stanley. 'I wish you both every happiness, but please don't think me rude as I will decline. I don't think Alexandrea would accept the invitation, and she certainly would be uncomfortable if I came alone. Thank you, though. It was thoughtful.'

Kitty felt relief. She and Stanley had only invited Michael to attend out of politeness and appreciation of the effort he had put into helping them. Just the thought of Alexandrea looking down her nose at everything had made Kitty hesitate at first, but because she suspected – and hoped – that Michael's wife might decline, Kitty had decided to ask.

'That's understandable. If you change your mind, feel free to join us,' Stanley said, and Kitty nodded her agreement.

When Michael left, Kitty heaved a sigh of relief. The tension in her neck eased, and she turned to Stanley and kissed him.

'I am so lucky to have you in my life,' she said, and laughed as Stanley agreed and left her to organise the final clean-up.

For the rest of the day, Kitty cleaned and unpacked. Stanley had a box of personal items which she left alone, along with the portrait of Jenny, wrapped carefully in a blanket. She wondered where the picture would hang after they were married. To keep it safe, she took it upstairs and into what had been Stanley's bedroom. She looked around the room and wondered how many years it would be before a child slept there.

Aware that age was not on their side, she and Stanley had already discussed adoption after a year of trying for their own. Unwrapping the new bed in their new bedroom, Kitty set about making it, and replacing the curtains. She smiled as she smoothed down the sheets. Only Stanley would be sleeping there until after their wedding, and she could not wait to share it with him when they were officially married.

Satisfied that she had done enough for one day, she went to her wedding dress and sat finishing the bodice and adding the delicate lace around the three-quarter-length sleeves. The design of the dress would not restrict her movements. She did not want to feel hot and uncomfortable; it had an elegance to it, but also a country charm. She had debated wearing a hat, but opted to have her hair plaited like her mum, and threaded with flowers, feathers and ribbons like the Siksika. She wanted a natural theme to complement the magnificent natural surroundings she now called home.

Chapter Forty-Seven

The sun cast long golden streaks over the prairie grasses, which swayed gently in the breeze, rustling musically, and Kitty took a moment to listen.

Birds called, and she heard Saahkómaapi's sighs beside her. She was not riding him to the ceremony; she was leading him, decorated in his lavender ribbons, instead of her carrying a bouquet. He was an essential part of Kitty's daily life, and she wanted to express to Mim how much he meant to her.

In the distance, Stanley looked like a small boy, standing in front of the Rocky Mountains. She could not see his face, just his outline; she had a short walk ahead of her before she could catch a glimpse of his smile.

In the middle of a clearing, a small wooden arch stood wrapped in ribbons and lavender sprigs, matching the colours of her dress. Kitty stood barefoot in the grass, her comfortable wedding gown rustling softly around her legs. Her hair, worn loose after changing her mind about the plait, cascaded over her shoulders – no veil, no floral crown – just her, feeling radiant and free.

'I don't want to disturb you, but I have your gift.'

Vern stood to one side, looking smart in his black shirt, with what appeared to be an attached red shawl with a fringed hem, black Stetson and red-black etched boots. He was holding out a pair of golden brown suede boots.

'For your feet over the rough ground. Every cowgirl should own a pair,' he said, wearing a wide grin. 'They have your new initials on them.'

Kitty took them from him and looked at the engraving. *K W-F.* She slipped her feet into them; they were a perfect fit, and sat neatly against her calves. She let her dress fall back into place and poked the toe of one of the boots out from beneath the hemline to see the effect.

'I love them! What a perfect gift. Thank you, Vern,' she said and kissed his cheek.

'Kissing a man in front of your groom, that's not wise,' Mim said as she approached them, and burst out laughing. She kissed Kitty on the cheek, then pulled a small item from her pocket. 'I know you didn't want anything in your hair, but I made it small so it will sit gently on the side of your head. It has the blessing of the sun baked into the beads.'

She handed Kitty the small hair decoration. Kitty traced her finger along the shape. The shades of soft lilacs and pristine white were highlighted with small black marks; a tiny strip of fur served as a tail. It was a dainty fox.

'I will wear it and treasure it always. Thank you, Mim. It is beautiful,' Kitty said, holding back tears of gratitude for such thoughtful gifts.

'We will leave you to compose yourself, and go to check on

Stanley,' Mim said. 'He was nervous when Ted and Vern saw him this morning. He wants everything to be perfect for you. He followed the picture you showed me, and it looks lovely down there. Enjoy every moment, little Sinopa.'

Stanley had insisted on creating her dream from a magazine, which she had earmarked in places for inspiration, and he refused to let her see the result. She couldn't wait to see what he had achieved. Kitty watched Mim and Vern walk away.

She waited until she saw them talking to Stanley, then took her first steps, walking slowly towards them. The scent of sweetgrass drifted through the air as she crushed it beneath her, and a hush seemed to fall around her; Kitty felt as if nature itself was holding its breath, honouring the importance of the moment. She shook off the memory of standing outside the registry office in Durham during a rainstorm; this was different, a different man, a fresh new romance and a picture-perfect setting.

Stanley waited beneath the arch, standing tall in smart earth-toned trousers and a crisp white shirt. She smiled at his new Stetson, guessing it was the gift from Vern; he also wore a leather beaded waistcoat, and Kitty had no doubt it was a gift from Mim. He had never looked so comfortable and at ease.

His eyes shimmered with emotion as he caught his first glimpse of her, the softest smile curving his lips. Kitty's body shimmied with pleasure.

Behind him was a simple flower arrangement in a large ornate vase. His mother's family heirloom. Baskets of fragrant herbs were scattered among their guests, who sat on hay bales covered with soft lilac quilts.

Everything felt intimate and deeply connected to the land.

As Kitty reached Stanley and they took each other's hands,

the steady rhythm of native drums began to rise, pulsing like the heartbeat of the earth itself.

'You're beautiful. You take my breath away, Kitty. How can one man be so lucky?' Stanley said, wearing a wide smile.

'And you're a handsome cowboy, perfect for this cowgirl,' Kitty said, showing off her boots, and creating a ripple of laughter among the guests.

Gradually, the drums played out their last beat, and the song that followed was delivered in a low, powerful voice, a blessing carried on the wind. Togquos sang proudly as he honoured their union, and Kitty felt a tightness in her throat. She wished her uncle could be part of the day, but Togquos was a good representative of a father figure, and it gave her comfort.

They said their words of commitment to one another with firm, clear voices, and when they were declared husband and wife, Kitty and Stanley kissed – slow, tender and certain. The guests rose. Togquos, his wife and sons, women Kitty had befriended, Stanley's cowboys who were not working, Ted and his new girlfriend Wawetseka – who lived up to her name, which meant 'pretty woman' – Mim and Vern, all stood clapping, laughing and crying out with joy. Then the drums began again, more joyful now, and Kitty and Stanley took their first steps as husband and wife, surrounded by their new friends and the timeless land that promised them a lifetime of happiness.

'Well, that was easier than I thought,' Stanley said as they moved across the ground.

'Did you think marrying me would be difficult?' Kitty asked in mock annoyance.

'Never!' Stanley declared and kissed her firmly, expressing to Kitty how much he loved her. 'Let's eat. There are steaks with our names on them over there. I am starving.'

Kitty oversaw the carrying of their wedding cake from the house to the laden food tables. Two large tiers of fruit cake, where the fruit had soaked in brandy and maple syrup for a week, were simple yet flavoursome. Kitty had opted not to use icing, so as not to overpower the sweetness of the fruit. Togquos was her biggest fan and visited the table for several slices throughout the evening, demanding with a laugh that she make him one each time he visited. Mim suggested that he would be Kitty's most enthusiastic customer once she had established her bakery.

Their guests ate enthusiastically, and each one praised Kitty for her catering skills. Stanley's driving team placed orders for the following day, and Kitty laughed them away.

When the sky darkened into deep sapphire, stars pricked through like silver baubles. A large fire was lit, and the celebration continued into the night – dancing, songs and laughter, enjoyed by everyone, beneath the open prairie sky. Their wedding day had been perfect, their evening memorable, and their night held promises of a bright future.

A figure at the end of the pathway caught Kitty's eye, and she beckoned to them to join the party. Another person joined them, and Kitty's heart melted with happiness. Her friend Jo had brought her uncle – and they'd made it just in time to bring yet more joy to her day.

Chapter Forty-Eight

Kitty turned to Stanley. 'Go, I'll catch up,' he said and let her hand drop. She ran down the grassy pathway and straight into her uncle's arms. She then turned to Jo. 'Thank you for bringing him all this way, Jo!' Kitty grabbed her friend and held her tight.

'I just received instructions from Trixie and Smithy to attend and details about fetching your uncle. I applied for leave, it was granted, and here we are. Someone paid for our tickets – luxury all the way,' Jo said.

Kitty's uncle nodded in agreement.

'I'm guessing your new husband had something to do with it. I hesitated at first, I will be honest, but then Doreen reminded me this is a once-in-a-lifetime event – me travelling to Canada, not you getting married again,' Kitty's uncle said cheekily. 'I must say you have scrubbed up well for the day. Pretty as a picture.'

'I love the cowgirl boots!' Jo said, as Kitty hitched her dress to show them off.

'I made the dress, and the cake. Come and have food and meet our friends.'

Her uncle stroked her cheek. 'Your mother's gifts have passed on to you. I am so proud of you, Kitty.'

It thrilled Kitty to know she had inherited her creative side from her mother.

'Frank, Jo, what a wonderful surprise!' Stanley said when he arrived at Kitty's side.

'Thanks to you,' Frank said, shaking his hand. 'I'm mighty grateful, son – and sorry we were delayed, but we're here now. Congratulations.'

Stanley looked at them, puzzled. 'Thanks to me?'

'For the luxury travel tickets. Only someone like you has that kind of money,' Kitty's uncle said.

Stanley shook his head. 'I had no idea,' he said, genuinely.

Kitty and Stanley looked at one another. 'Surely not,' she said.

'Who else?' Stanley said. 'Because I promise you, Kitty, I thought about it, but decided it would be too much to ask of your uncle, to travel so far. Besides, I would have contacted them directly.'

Kitty turned to her uncle and Jo. 'We think it might be Michael. He's still in touch with Smithy.'

'A doctor's salary would never cover the costs,' Jo said.

'And why would he pay for me?' Frank asked.

'Michael is oil-rich now,' Stanley said. 'He's worth a fortune. I think it is his apology to you both, and he knows how close you are to Kitty.'

They took a walk to the wedding area and introduced everyone. Kitty and her uncle enjoyed a dance to a tune on a fiddle played by Vern, and the night slipped into the early hours. Kitty was exhausted, so she knew her uncle would be weary from travelling and the time zone changes. Mim and Jo helped set up the spare beds, and eventually Stanley and Kitty climbed into their own.

'What a day! And to think Michael gave us such a gift. What a wonderful thing to do,' Kitty said as they snuggled close.

'I know, very generous of him. They have two days here, and then Jo is taking Frank into America to fly home from there. He is going VIP, but doesn't know it yet,' Stanley said. 'By the way, I love you, Mrs Walker-Fell.'

'And I you, my love. Always,' Kitty said.

Bleary-eyed and overwhelmed by the previous day, Kitty walked barefoot through the gardens to the river and sat with her feet dangling in the cool water, going over the highlights of the wedding in her head. Her uncle's arrival with Jo was a huge one, but it was the simple one of seeing Stanley look at her with so much love when she walked towards him that she treasured the most.

'Good morning, Mrs Walker-Fell.'

Vern greeted her with a wave and a smile.

'Morning, Vern. Thank you all for yesterday, and for clearing the grounds this morning. Are you busy with the cattle today?'

Confirming he was keeping everything running smoothly until he and Stanley could regroup and discuss new ventures, Vern looked at her feet. 'No boots today?'

Kitty shook her head. 'I am wearing them later, but one of my favourite things to do is to walk barefoot and sit by the river every morning.'

'The land has captured you with its treasures, and you will

never leave now,' Vern replied. 'Talking about treasures, there's a blueberry bush begging to be picked. It's behind the stable. Your guests might enjoy them.'

'I'm sure they will. I can't believe uncle and Jo are here. It is such a surprise.'

'Stanley is a good man for arranging it for you,' Vern said.

Kitty looked at him, 'Stanley is good, but we think it is my ex-husband, Michael, who paid for them to come. We thought it would be a tough journey for my uncle, so neither of us asked him to attend. How wrong we were to think my uncle wouldn't travel well – another surprise.'

'So, the man you divorced paid for it as a surprise, and wasn't at the wedding himself? Shame he didn't come along, to see them and enjoy the feast. It was a good wedding.' Vern smiled, touched his hat and walked away.

Kitty went over to the blueberries and filled a basket, then headed back home.

The sound of laughter and the rush of water greeted her as she entered the house. It was enormous and alive, just as she and Stanley had imagined. She heard dishes clatter on the countertops in the kitchen, and her new husband's voice, cheerful as he stood in the bathroom door and spoke to their surprise visitors. He was demonstrating the power of the pump as it flushed the water away. Kitty smiled to herself. Stanley was so proud of his design and extension.

'Good morning!' Kitty called out. Her guests were seated round their large kitchen table. 'Fresh blueberry and strawberry pancakes for breakfast?'

Everyone turned to look at her. Kitty had chosen to wear her wedding dress again, as it made sense to enjoy it on such a special occasion.

Stanley went to her and kissed her cheek. 'There you are, my beautiful wife,' he said, then he whispered, 'I missed your morning cuddle.'

'I couldn't sleep, so I went berry picking before the animals enjoy them first,' Kitty said, 'And you were sleeping well, I didn't want to disturb you.' She kissed him back and walked over to the table. 'Isn't it wonderful to see our new house so alive and with such special guests?'

Kitty went to her uncle first and kissed him, then to Jo and did the same. For a change, Jo did not object.

'It is, and the bathroom is a luxury,' Stanley said. 'It's a good job you didn't arrive last week – we only had that portion of the house.' He went on to explain what they had done and what the future held, while Kitty mixed the batter and prepared the fruit. A wave of contentment washed through her, and she smiled. It was the most thoughtful gift Michael could have given her.

'I must go and thank him – I will send a message via Vern, just in case Alexandrea isn't aware of what he has done. It seems rather generous – not that I am complaining, but he has already given me a divorce settlement. I'm going to use it to set up a bakery business, as I already have a roof over my head thanks to my husband.' Kitty said as she served pancakes piled high on a plate.

'Tuck in, and try the maple syrup. It is local and perfect with the tart berries.'

Chapter Forty-Nine

After breakfast, they took a tourist day out to Banff, a quaint village nestled beneath the mountains. Kitty and Stanley had planned their visit as a honeymoon treat, but they did not mind sharing it with Frank and Jo. Armed with his camera, Frank took endless pictures. They ate ice-cream and sat admiring the views surrounding them.

'Your dad had an adventurous spirit, Kitty. He would have found a way of climbing the Rockies. He would have enjoyed rafting down the river beside your house. It was ironic that water took his life, because he swam every day, rain, shine, or snow, from a young age. My brother was braver than me,' Frank said, his voice wistful and sad.

'Kitty goes to the river every morning to see the sunrise and dip into the water, then she returns home to bake. It sounds like both her parents gave her the adventurous and creative spirit I love so much,' Stanley said.

'And you're brave. You flew on a plane to get here. We know how daunting that can be. You are the best uncle I could ever ask for. Thank you for sharing my parents with me. I can't remember much about them now. I can't wait until the autumn – or fall, as they say here – when I can wear mum's red beret again,' Kitty said.

'I'm still getting my head around the fact that you learned to ride a horse in a day! Mim is in awe of you for that achievement. I like her – and her no-nonsense approach, too,' Jo said. 'Kitty Walker-Fell, cowgirl extraordinaire.'

Kitty laughed. 'She's a good teacher and the no-nonsense approach scared me into doing it right.'

On the way home, Frank slept and Kitty smiled at him. She had one more day to share her new life in Canada with him. And she wanted him to make peace with Michael. Her uncle was concerned that Michael, living close to her and Stanley, might stir up trouble or upset them both. Although Kitty had reassured him that she was sure Michael's act of kindness meant he had no intention of upsetting her, he was not convinced.

When they arrived back at Fell Wayside, Michael's car was parked on the edge of the property, and Vern was standing, talking to him.

'Wake my uncle up, Jo. Let him compose himself as we drive down,' Kitty said, turning around and looking at her dishevelled uncle. When he woke, she explained about Michael, and her uncle hastily swept back his hair. Once they parked, he adjusted his shirt and tie. He was old-school, and his tie and hat were never left to one side when he was out and about.

'Michael, how good to see you,' Stanley said and offered his hand for him to shake.

Kitty smiled. 'Yes, it is good to see you, and there are two people in the car who want to say hello. And we all want to say thank you.'

Michael frowned. 'Thank me?' he asked. Kitty knew him well enough to spot the slight twitch of a smile in the corners of his mouth.

'Yes, you. What you did was a wonderful thing. I had hesitated about getting my uncle here, and never thought of asking Jo to chaperone him, then it was too late.' Kitty said. 'They arrived during the party.'

'Young man.' Kitty's uncle's voice had a friendly tone, and she was relieved to hear it.

'Frank. Good to see you, sir,' Michael said formally. The two men shook hands, and Jo held hers out to Michael.

'It's good to see you again, Michael. Is your wife here?' she asked, her gaze fixed on the car. Kitty knew she didn't care either way. Jo was car mad and would love to be behind the wheel of Michael's.

'Sadly not. Her mother took ill, and Alex went to Toronto yesterday morning to be with her. I thought I would take the opportunity to come and see you, Frank, and you, of course, Jo,' he said, smiling at her, 'but I do want a chat with Frank – alone if possible.'

Kitty watched as Michael and her uncle sat on the porch talking. Her uncle's head bobbed up and down as Michael spoke to him.

'Oh to be a fly on that wall,' Jo said, and Stanley laughed.

Kitty stood quietly as Michael handed her uncle a package.

'Now I want to know what's going on,' she said.

When the two men had shaken hands, and walked back to

join them at the car, Michael produced another package from the trunk.

'This one is for you and Stanley. A wedding gift. As I have told Frank, don't open them until after my other gift to you this evening.' He smiled at their puzzled faces.

'I have invited myself to your home, and with the help of Vern, I would like to share something with you. Please be at your wedding arch at eight o'clock, ready for sunset.'

Kitty looked at him and put her hands on her hips.

'What are you up to, Michael McCarthy?' she asked.

'That would be telling, Mrs Walker-Fell. Let's just say I've made mistakes and am trying to show you I am sorry and still a friend to you both,' Michael said.

Hearing him say her new married name was strange, but not awkward. Michael said it in a bantering way, and it sounded natural.

For three hours, they speculated about what Michael was up to, and nothing sensible came out of their thoughts. They still chatted and tried to guess as they walked with lamps towards the arch.

Kitty gasped and Jo clapped when they arrived.

A row of chairs sat facing the arch, which now had a large white sheet stretched across it, and what looked like a camera on legs facing it.

'A cine camera!' Stanley declared, and everyone laughed as Frank moved the lamps closer to provide better light for taking a photograph.

Suddenly Michael appeared from behind two trees and a

bush at one side of the garden area. He was casually dressed in a loose-fitting blue shirt, a pair of denim trousers and boots. He also wore a Stetson.

Kitty and Stanley looked at one another.

'Good evening,' Michael said, and looked up at the sky. 'The sun will set shortly, and I will begin my show. Vern is keeping watch on the generator for me.'

'What are you up to, Michael?' Kitty asked.

'I'm about to show you something I watched, and wanted to share it with you all. I think you will find it interesting.'

'Is it an investment plot?' Stanley asked.

'It is a plot which was invested in, yes,' Michael replied.

'Well, this should be interesting,' Jo muttered, and everyone laughed.

Michael started the cine camera, and soon a black and white image shone out at them.

'It's me!' Kitty said pointing to the figure moving on the screen.

She jumped and walked to the screen for a closer look. 'Yes, it's me. Where did you get this ... this magic?' Kitty asked Michael, who stood grinning at her.

'We're looking at our wedding. There's me waiting for you, but this is from sideways on,' Stanley said, looking at the gap that Michael had walked out of. 'Were you there, filming our day?'

Kitty looked on in amazement. Her ex-husband had secretly filmed her wedding and flown her uncle and best friend to join her on her big day. This was the Michael she once knew. She recalled the Scotsman playing bagpipes, a surprise Michael had arranged when he returned from a mission and they had been apart for months. Michael had a way of saying sorry with grand gestures. The wedding surprise was just that – his apology for the affair. He had witnessed their wedding and not shown his face out of respect.

Michael nodded. 'I had the idea, and Vern helped. I wanted you both to know I regret my behaviour, and I am no good with words. I love Kitty in a way that I now know is that of a true friend. A woman I could turn to in my hour of need. I am fond of you, Stanley. Also a friend I turned to when I needed help. This is my apology. I would very much like to remain your friend.'

Stanley walked over to him, and Kitty watched as they went to shake hands, but Stanley pulled Michael into an awkward hug. She heard her uncle give a light cough. He was not a man for expressing his feelings, although the letter he wrote her when she first arrived was filled with an outpouring of love and encouragement. Doreen had softened him.

Jo went to Kitty and put her arm around her, and Kitty leaned her head on her friend's shoulder.

'It's going to be okay. You don't have to give up on Michael. Just be his friend without the awkward bits,' Jo said.

Kitty smiled to herself. Like Frank, Jo was not emotionally expressive, but her words made sense.

Michael spoke again, and Kitty watched his face as it softened and lost the worried frown. She knew he was on edge; his surprise was a risk.

'In your boxes are cine cameras of your own. Film your lives and send them to one another,' he said to Frank and Kitty. 'I have only this copy, but it is a gift to you both. The projector is yours, too,' he said to Kitty.

Kitty stood staring in wonder. 'Uncle Frank, I can send you our life out here if you get a projector of your own.'

'No need. One is on its way to your home, Frank. It is too

bulky for you to carry back. I know you all think I am throwing my money around to try to win favour among you all again. That's partly true,' Michael laughed, 'but you were all there for me without question when I was injured, and nigh on comatose. Marrying Kitty was the only way I thought I could repay her. After writing to Alex and opening up to her, I knew I had made a mistake. I was fond of Kitty, but I was ruining her life by feeling trapped and letting my moods get in the way of her happiness. I did what I do best when I can't face the truth: I ran away. But, in true style, Kitty and Stanley flew here to find me. We have gone down different paths now, and all I want is for you to be happy, Kitty. Forgive me?'

Kitty went to him and kissed his cheek. 'You're forgiven, so never ask again.'

Stanley shook Michael's hand. 'I am grateful to you for making her happy again, truly.'

Michael gave a nod. 'I think you have exceeded that task.'

They sat back and watched the film through. Stanley's face when he saw her walking towards him, Togquos sitting with a plate piled high with Kitty's cookies, Mim and Vern snatching a moment to kiss, and Kitty's face when she saw her uncle. Michael captured her running in her pretty gown and showing off her cowboy boots, and Jo standing back to admire her and the boots. Michael had captured every emotion of their wedding perfectly and when the movie ended, Kitty burst into tears.

'What a wonderful day it was, and I will never forget tonight. I think Michael has eaten enough humble pie to last him a lifetime. Talking of pie, I have apple or blueberry tart in the house, and Stanley has bought us a bottle of champagne. I think it is a great combination to finish off the party,' Kitty said.

'I have one more announcement to make,' Michael said. 'I am

leaving. Much like my new wife has left me – I think she will forgive me eventually. She loves my money.' Michael gave an awkward laugh and Kitty gasped. She heard the others around her do the same.

'My investments have opened doors I could never have imagined. After what I did to Kitty, explaining I wanted an adventure then running away, I knew I had to share my next idea for adventure with Alex before I went on it this time. She is not happy and has moved in with her mother. She will move home when she is ready.'

'Michael, what have you done?' Kitty shouted. 'You loved her, and gave up on us for her, for what? What is more important than Alex and all you walked away from?'

'Everest,' Michael said bluntly.

Stanley looked at Kitty and then at Michael.

'Everest? I assume you mean climbing the darn thing. Have you gone mad? You're newlywed, and want to put your life at risk?'

Kitty touched Stanley's arm.

'Adventure. He wants adventure, and until he's had it, he will never settle.' She looked over at Michael. She smiled at him, understanding him better than she ever had.

'I'm having mine, when it was Michael who wanted to have one. I understand, and I know no amount of nagging from friends and family will stop you.'

Kitty went to Michael and stroked his cheek. She remembered his expression from past rescue missions. It would glow; Michael of old thrived on the burst of energy. Now he stood before her, grey tinges in his skin, a dull light barely glowing in his eyes. Eyes that pleaded for help. Michael had come to her for permission to enter the burning building. He could never shake the memories of war until he had found the same rush of adrenaline again during peacetime.

'Go, but come back and tell us about the thrill of Everest, or whatever other adventure you find. That is the only thing we ask of you, Michael McCarthy.'

Epilogue

October 1949

'Ready?' Mim whispered to Kitty.

Kitty nodded. She looked around her bedroom, a bright and cheerful room, with a clear view of the mountains and their prairie meadows beyond. The orange and amber glow of the trees surrounding the boundary always took her breath away. The window was open, and the autumnal air drifted in. She heard Stanley's laugh, faint in the distance. He had worked hard on creating an extension for what they called the McCarthy Cinema.

Alexandrea sent word in May that Michael had failed to return from his Everest attempt. A week later, they received the news that the rescue teams had found him and the others from the expedition beneath a rock fall. Alex told Kitty that she had asked for Michael to remain buried there, and ensured a private service was held in Cochrane to honour his life. Alex asked Kitty to attend and talk about his wartime experiences. They were united in their grief and it moved Kitty that Alex had found it in her heart to understand and forgive Michael, too.

After the memorial, Alexandrea showed Kitty a letter from a survivor of the tragic event. It appeared Michael had put himself in danger to save the young man. He had died doing what he had always done best as a doctor during the Blitz and on Juno beach. He died a hero, not a man trapped in a life led by one investment after another. He had died living life as the true Michael McCarthy.

Kitty's mood was low for a few days, and Stanley could not have supported her more during her sadness. His reassurances that he knew she loved him, deeply loved him, helped her mourn Michael.

One morning, Kitty decided to bake more than they could eat or sell, which helped take her mind off the tragedy. Knowing she needed to shake off the sadness, she invited their crew to celebrate Michael's life. She asked Stanley to film it and, true to character, he said he was more than happy to capture the memory.

And now, as the afternoon glow of the sky turned from rust to pale orange, Kitty lay on their bed waiting to deliver their first child. A baby probably conceived on the evening she officially opened her small bakery at the end of the long driveway, closer to the roadside. Her business had grown faster than anyone anticipated, and soon Ted drove a van sign-painted 'Kitty Bakes' to the oil fields and beyond.

'Then push, my girl. Push.' Mim's soft voice was reassuring and as gentle as a mother to a child of her own.

The soft mew of her son, Frank Stanley Michael Walker-Fell, clung to Kitty's heart as she watched his father hold him. Her husband whispered to little Frank about the characters of the men he was named after.

'Tell him about yourself, too,' Kitty encouraged as she lay back listening.

'Me? I am the luckiest man alive,' Stanley said and handed their child back to her. 'And totally in love with the bravest, kindest and most hardworking woman I know.'

'Your daddy is the hero. He took on a mission and saw it through until the end, and *I* am totally in love with *him*,' Kitty whispered to Frank.

For weeks, they adjusted to life as parents, and Kitty watched Stanley grow as a devoted father every day. He did not sit back and let her do it all; he took on the daunting task of nappy changes and consoled his son through the crying spells. In England, they would likely have had help at home, but in Cochrane, they were comfortable with their challenges and overcame them together.

1950

Life for Kitty and Stanley settled into two steady businesses, and watching over their son. Togquos adored Frank, whom he named Sipiskomaapi – Night Boy.

Frank Junior was a night owl; he napped during the day and lay contented beneath the stars, or wrapped well, cooing at the flames in the fireplace at night. If he became fretful, Kitty would place his feet on the ground outside, cold or not, and whisper soothing words to calm him; it worked every time. She carried him papoose style, as taught by Mim, and he learned the heartbeat of the forest in every season. He rode with her on Saahkómaapi, and ate the food from their own soil and livestock.

Ted and Vern were his best friends; they would carry him to show him new and exciting things, and Stanley would sit and read to him his own stories of animals in the wild.

Life for her child was as close to nature as they could make it and both she and Stanley agreed that city life was not for them. Although they knew that family and friends back in Great Britain struggled to rebuild their war-torn lives, neither of them felt guilty about remaining in their adopted country.

Frank had already learned to love the outdoors, often sitting in awe of the birds flying above him. During warm weather, he would sit in her arms in the river, splashing and chatting with her. His time of innocence was so brief that she wanted him to absorb everything and love his country as much as she and Stanley did.

As she watched Frank explore the flavours of a piece of grass, Kitty contemplated the future of her child. It saddened her to think Michael would never achieve what she had – a Canadian-born child. One who would inherit a large ranch and cattle farm, along with two bakeries – and potentially more in the future – making him a wealthy young man. However, she wanted more for him than just a focus on money; she didn't want him to become bored with what she and Stanley had built. She wanted him to learn the ways of the land, the art of survival and the importance of serving his community. Her son's namesake, her uncle Frank, had received a cine film of his great-nephew crawling and swimming, and returned one of scenes of Harwich, and of Frank walking the promenade, and Doreen enjoying an ice-cream by the old lighthouse. There were also images of her parents' and brother's grave. Frank had done his utmost to write about his childhood, and life with her father, and about how her parents met.

She put them in a memory box marked 'Our Lives in England'. She sent photographs to Meryn, Wenna and Pots, and token native gifts to Trixie and Smithy. All in turn sent memories of her and Stanley in England for Frank to learn about as he grew up.

Stanley had achieved his dream and learned to ski. It was not elegant, but it was a brave and skilful attempt, also captured on film. Kitty had never been so proud, and she noticed it had bolstered his confidence. Kitty sent the film to Jo, who had purchased her own camera set-up.

Jo crossed the border on several occasions to bring Frank gifts. She adored him and promised to take him to New York when he was older. She also promised Kitty and Stanley to care for him should anything happen to them. Kitty spoke about her concerns and her friend reassured her that, although she was sure it would never happen, she would ensure Frank was taken care of in the best possible way.

1953

Vern had informed them of the impending visit by Princess Elizabeth and her prince, Philip, to Cochrane Station. The princess was carrying out royal duties on behalf of her ailing father, King George. It was a time-restricted stopover, lasting only ten minutes, before the Royal couple headed to Calgary.

An excited Kitty was determined to secure a prime spot in the crowd and catch a glimpse of Great Britain's future Queen. As the couple drew close, Kitty admired the fur worn by the princess, but was thankful for the blankets around her shoulders, covering her thick winter coat. In the severe minus thirty-degree weather, everyone was wrapped warmly, including Frank, who sat on Stanley's shoulders waving a flag enthusiastically.

'Isn't she beautiful?' Kitty said, turning to Stanley.

'She is, but not half as much as my wife. O queen of my ranch, I could never adore another woman as much as I adore you,' he replied, dropping a kiss on her cold nose.

'Then we had better hope for another son as I would hate for you to have to choose between a queen and a princess in the spring,' Kitty said, smiling and then nodding at his emotionally overwhelmed yet smiling face.

Stanley let out a loud whoop, and the Royals and crowd looked over at him in perfect unison. Kitty gave a giggle.

'Yes, I think we have completed our mission, Squadron Leader Stanley Walker-Fell. Over and out.'

Acknowledgments

Writing book four has been a challenging yet rewarding journey, marked by both incredible highs and sad lows.

My thanks, as always, go to my publisher, Charlotte Ledger, the One More Chapter team, and HarperCollins UK, CA and US.

Huge thanks to my author buddies who cheer me on, especially Deborah Carr and Christie Barlow, who keep in touch every day.

Special thanks to all authors who have touched my life in some way throughout the writing process.

Huge thanks to my son and daughter-in-law for moving to Cochrane, Alberta. What an inspiring visit I had to your wonderful town when I needed to know where Kitty was headed next.

To Team Glynis – keep going!

Last, but by no means least, to my close friends. Thank you for understanding when I'm unable to make a coffee date due to looming deadlines.

To my family, my love always. X

To my husband, thanks for 46 years and for still standing in my corner. Love from the real me. X

Credits: Glenbow.org

A journey into war, but not one she'll take alone…

Orphan Kitty Pattison is young, naïve and ready to do her bit for the war effort when she volunteers with the Red Cross and pledges to help those most in need. It's one of the most nerve-wracking moments of her life, but then she meets fellow volunteers Joan Norfolk and Trixie Dunn, and a bond of friendship is forged in the fire of life on the wards during the Blitz.

Days are spent nursing injured soldiers back to life and nights are spent anticipating bombs falling from the sky and then trawling through the wreckage to save who she can, but the light and laughter she finds with Jo and Trix see Kitty through the darkest hours.

AVAILABLE NOW IN PAPERBACK, EBOOK AND AUDIO!

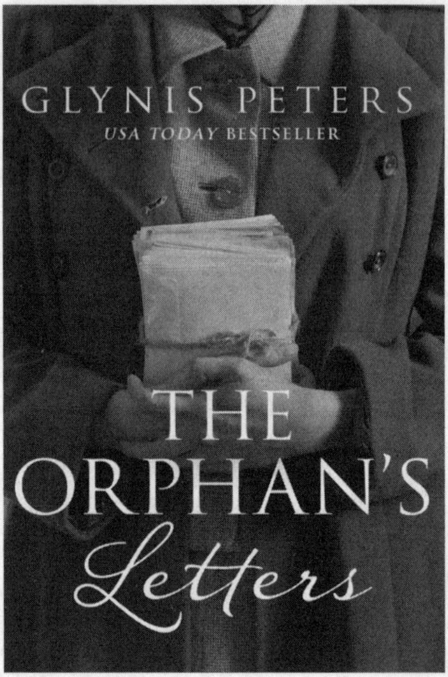

Absence makes the heart grow fonder, but does nothing to heal the pain of spending every minute waiting to hear the worst…

As the Second World War rages on, nurse Kitty Pattison's life takes a nomadic turn as her work with the Red Cross sees her traversing the country, moving from post to post.

With her best friends Jo and Trixie also scattered across the UK, and her soldier sweetheart Michael off on the continent undertaking medical missions he can't discuss, the war takes its toll and long days are followed by sleepless nights interrupted only by nightmares of what she's seen on the wards.

AVAILABLE NOW IN PAPERBACK, EBOOK AND AUDIO!

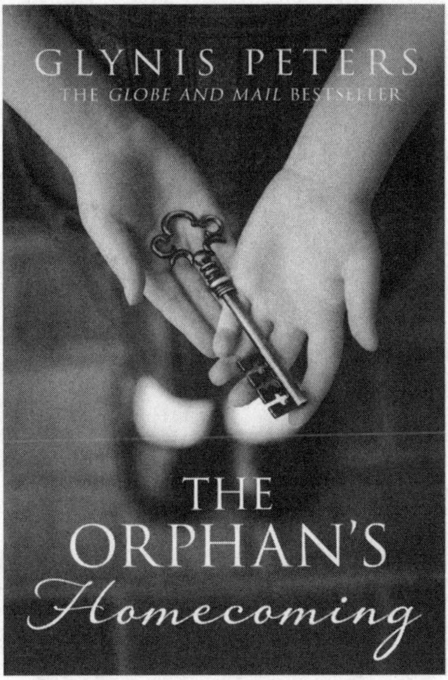

Could the shifting winds of change finally carry Kitty home?

After five long years of endless warfare, Red Cross nurse Kitty Pattison has seen her share of heartbreak and loss. And now, with her beloved fiancé Dr Michael McCarthy recuperating from a head injury across the ocean in Canada, and her dear friends Trixie and Jo scattered to the four corners of the war effort, it's harder than ever to battle through the heavy-hearted moments that mark the passing days.

But as she tends to the lost and wounded, Kitty finds a resilience of spirit within herself she never thought imaginable. Because with everything the war has taken from her, it has also given her a conviction that it can never destroy the things that really matter in life – love, friendship, and hope.

AVAILABLE NOW IN PAPERBACK, EBOOK AND AUDIO!

YOUR NUMBER ONE STOP

ONE MORE CHAPTER

FOR PAGETURNING BOOKS

The author and One More Chapter would like to thank everyone who contributed to the publication of this story...

Analytics
Imogen Wolstencroft

Audio
Fionnuala Barrett
Ciara Briggs

Contracts
Laura Amos
Inigo Vyvyan

Design
Lucy Bennett
Fiona Greenway
Liane Payne
Dean Russell

Digital Sales
Laura Daley
Lydia Grainge
Hannah Lismore

eCommerce
Laura Carpenter
Madeline ODonovan
Charlotte Stevens
Christina Storey
Jo Surman
Rachel Ward

Editorial
Rosie Best
Kara Daniel
Catherine Jackson
Charlotte Ledger
Laura McCallen
Jennie Rothwell
Tony Russell
Sofia Salazar Studer
Helen Williams

Harper360
Emily Gerbner
Ariana Juarez
Jean Marie Kelly
emma sullivan
Sophia Wilhelm

International Sales
Peter Borcsok
Ruth Burrow
Bethan Moore
Colleen Simpson

Inventory
Sarah Callaghan
Kirsty Norman

Marketing & Publicity
Chloe Cummings
Grace Edwards
Katie Sadler

Operations
Melissa Okusanya
Hannah Stamp

Production
Denis Manson
Simon Moore
Francesca Tuzzeo

Rights
Ashton Mucha
Alisah Saghir
Zoe Shine
Aisling Smyth
Lucy Vanderbilt

Trade Marketing
Ben Hurd
Eleanor Slater

The HarperCollins Distribution Team

The HarperCollins Finance & Royalties Team

The HarperCollins Legal Team

The HarperCollins Technology Team

UK Sales
Isabel Coburn
Jay Cochrane
Sabina Lewis
Holly Martin
Harriet Williams
Leah Woods

And every other essential link in the chain from delivery drivers to booksellers to librarians and beyond!